the enthusiast

the enthusiast

a novel

charlie haas

NEW YORK • LONDON • TORONTO • SYDNEY • NEW DELHI • AUCKLAND

HARPER PERENNIAL

This book is a work of fiction. References to real people, events, establishments, organizations, or locales are intended only to provide a sense of authenticity, and are used fictitiously. All other characters, and all incidents and dialogue, are drawn from the author's imagination and are not to be construed as real.

HarperCollins books may be purchased for educational, business, or sales promotional use. For information please write: Special Markets Department, HarperCollins Publishers, 10 East 53rd Street, New York, NY 10022.

FIRST EDITION

Designed by Laura Kaeppel

Library of Congress Cataloging-in-Publication Data

Haas, Charlie.
The enthusiast : a novel / Charlie Haas. — 1st Harper Perennial ed.
p. cm.
ISBN 978-0-06-171182-4
1. Periodical editors—Fiction. I. Title.
PS3558.A173E67 2009
813'.540—dc22 2009001221

09 10 11 12 13 OV/RRD 10 9 8 7 6 5 4 3 2 1

For B.K.

part one

empty orchestra

1

I was bicycling home from my last day of high school when I saw a bright yellow stripe go tearing across the sky. It slowed down, made a sweeping turn, and raced back the other way, fifty feet above the six black buildings in the middle of town.

I pedaled faster up the hill toward the buildings. They were vacant, but they'd recently been the home of Controlled Dynamics, an aerospace-defense company that did a lot of classified work. For a second I wondered if the flying stripe was a secret project, forgotten in the shutdown, that had broken out of the buildings and was searching, duckling-like, for its engineer dad. As I got closer I saw that it was made of fabric and shaped like a parachute with its sides cut off, the ends dipping down as the middle strained upward: a really big kite.

When I crested the hill I could see the guy flying it. He was sitting on a low three-wheeled cart that was being towed by the fifteen-foot kite, working the heavy strings with his hands and steering the cart with his feet, easily doing thirty. It was late afternoon and seventy-five degrees, the sky a vibrating turquoise. Our town, Rancho Cahuenga, was in the desert east of L.A., with constant irrigation to keep the lawns from dying in peace.

When the guy saw me he pulled the kite straight overhead, stopping the cart. He looked twenty-five, with a surfer's build and haircut.

"How you doing?" he said, reeling the kite in and letting it fall on the grass. "I'm Don."

"I'm Henry," I said. "I've never seen one of those."

"Kite buggy. Want to try it?"

"Okay." I'd never been that good at sports, but how bad could I be at a sport no one had heard of? "Thanks."

He stood up off the cart and led me to the parking lot. "You live around here?"

I nodded.

"This is a great spot. Is it always empty?"

"Yeah," I said. "It's out of business." Controlled Dynamics had shut down six weeks earlier, putting half the adults in town, including my father, out of work.

"Exquisite," Don said. "This was *created* for buggy." He gestured around the windy parking lot, empty except for some guys loading desks into a truck marked OFFICE LIQUIDATORS.

Don had another kite in his van, the same shape but smaller. He got it out and handed me its lines. "Try flying this one first," he said, and left me in the parking lot while he went back to riding the buggy with the bigger kite.

I had to run only a few feet before the breeze lifted the kite. In half an hour I was swinging my arms to work the lines, crouching and swiveling to keep the kite up when the wind shifted.

Then I learned to do it standing still, and the kite and I had an understanding. When Don saw me picking places in the sky, putting the kite in them and making it stay, he rode over to me. I sat on the buggy as he took the small kite from me and gave me the lines of the big one, which was hovering overhead. "Just drop it a little toward where you want to go," he said.

I did, and for a second I thought the wind would pull my arms off. Then the buggy moved out. The low-centered gravity and tight steering were like a race car's, my outstretched legs were inches off the ground, and the shock of speed was doubled by the quiet, with only a faint hum of wind in the kite lines. I sped wide-eyed past Dad's old office, finally exercising my California birthright to go fast on something crazy.

There were five seconds of exhilaration, followed by fear, as I shot down the rise toward an asphalt curb. Don had said to brake by steering upwind and doing a 180, but it took me a circle and a half to stop, while all of Rancho Cahuenga—school, the mall, the dentist's, the ravine we used to bounce down on our bikes, Linda Stuber's house where, fully clothed, we ground against each other on her parents' bed, and the freeway out of town—smeared past me. The tour took six seconds. When it ended I was laughing, gasping, and hoping Don liked the site of my dad's termination enough to stay, because I wanted to go again, not just once but till far-off further notice.

Our family moved to Rancho Cahuenga just before I was born, when my brother Barney was two. Dad was a deputy program manager for completions at Controlled Dynamics, trying to keep forty scientists on schedule, while Mom put in palm trees for a living and Barney was a genius who'd tested off all the charts there were.

Mom seemed to be taking a wait-and-see attitude toward adulthood, but Dad had signed on eagerly. He was modestly overweight and spent his weekdays in suit pants, a faintly shiny short-sleeve business shirt, a tie and tie clip, but no jacket. It was the executive uniform at Controlled Dynamics, and when he went out to lunch with his colleagues they looked like a roving band of assistant principals. Mom dressed for work like an iffy hitchhiker, in shorts, sandals, and a Mexican dishtowel shirt. She had muscles and a brown-bag tan from carrying eight-foot palm trees off the truck in her arms, and kept her hair in a short flip she could wash every night.

Barney was thin and four inches taller than I was, his long face a perfect setting for his stare of concentration. He wore gray T-shirts and olive-drab shorts every day. When he turned twelve the pants got long, but that was all the self-consciousness puberty got out of him.

I spent a lot of my childhood staring at Barney's stare, which looked around our bland landscape and saw number series and decaying waves of motion. At its fiercest, the stare bounced off the air an inch in front of him and went back inside his head, where there were weightless particles, one-dimensional bottles, and all the other things that people like Barney can prove are real and people unlike Barney hurt themselves just trying to think about.

My favorite room in the house was Barney's, filled with a science kid's essentials—microscope, centrifuge, periodic table pinup, and a record collection of hectic Yes and Genesis. I spent hours in there, nailing his science fair easels together and listening with rapt incomprehension as he explained his experiments. When I was eleven I started to see the burden he carried.

The town was built on science and a lot was expected of him—not just for his future, but for everyone's. At thirteen he walked around sometimes with the gravest of grownup faces, like a NASA spokesman taking questions when radio contact with the mission is lost.

The hundred-acre housing developments surrounding Controlled Dynamics went up fast, but you could tell the planning was enlightened because half the streets curved for no reason and there were lots of traffic-calming cul-de-sacs, making the local road map look like a drawing of beans on a vine. Biking to school, I'd see construction crews fanning out over the lumpy dirt plots of a new phase. A week later there'd be fresh wood framing on the concrete slabs, and then Tyvek, rebar, PVC pipe, and new families moving in before the next holiday themed the mall.

One Saturday I rode my bike onto Rheostat Way and out into the sameness, under a sun that made the new houses age faster than Cadillacs. There were two house models, the Ponderosa (tan shingle, tanner stucco) and the Klondike (the Ponderosa reversed, with an extra half-bath), alternating for miles, with an occasional frying toddler on a Big Wheel for color. I thought when I grew up I'd have to see nothing but interesting cities, maybe two or three a day, to even things up.

After a mile I turned my bike toward home and increased my speed to Mach Schwinn, a kid's escape velocity, the houses a flipbook about nothing happening. With a leaning turn, I shot into our cul-de-sac and up our driveway, where I jammed on the brakes and peeled rubber. I hadn't planned it, but there it was: my own smudge, an eighteen-inch variation in the landscape.

I rode out and did it a few more times, the lines getting longer as I gained technique. The last time I rode up, Dad came charging out of the house. Panicking, I hit the brakes harder than before, making my best mark yet and almost swerving into him as he asked what the hell I was doing.

"I was just—"

"You were defacing the house," he said. "This is part of the house. The house isn't something you play with." When I got yelled at, it was always by Dad, or—only a handful of times, but the worst handful I could imagine—by Barney. Mom tended to avoid these scenes. Her own parents had been yellers, and religious ones at that.

It was Barney who rescued me, coming out of the house and saying, "Dad, are you worried about the driveway? I think it's okay. That rubber's only a few microns. It'll wash away when it rains."

Dad stopped yelling. He nodded as if he were weighing the argument, but in Rancho Cahuenga, Barney's brilliance was like being thirteen and having the Bomb.

"Don't do that again," Dad said to me. "And hose it down, now." He went back inside.

"That's not really what he's mad about," Barney said. "They lost the aileron contract."

"He told you that?"

"That's not likely, Henry. He doesn't talk about things that go wrong. I heard it at school. My point is that you can't rely on everything he says. Like that music? That's not the real samba."

Dad played light Brazilian on the living room stereo whenever he was home. The low-normal Baroque of "Summer Samba" was embossed on our brains.

"The real samba's about life in the slums," Barney said. "There are guys in Rio de Janeiro that stand on top of moving trains. They call it train surfing. Sometimes they get killed, but they don't think their lives are worth anything anyway. That's the kind of thing the songs are about. The government puts the singers in jail."

"Have you heard it?"

"Do you think the record store here would have that?" His comforting always had an element of pop quiz. "They only sell the most popular crap in the world. That's what keeps it popular." He pointed at the rubber lines and said, "I think they look good, actually. At least it's different from the other driveways. Were you trying to see something? Like how long a mark you could make?"

"I guess."

"Then it was an experiment. Your materials were the bike and the driveway."

"Can you do an experiment if you're not trying to?"

"Sure. That's how they got penicillin."

"Actually, I don't even know why I was doing it."

"That's even better," Barney said. "Your materials were the bike, the driveway, and you."

When I was thirteen and Barney was fifteen he won his second regional science fair. A month later the phone rang after dinner. Dad called us all to the kitchen and handed the receiver to Barney with a grin.

"Yes. Thank you," Barney said calmly into the phone. "Okay. Yes." When he hung up he said, "I'm going to the nationals. It's in greater Chicago in three weeks."

Mom and Dad hugged him, but then he said, "I want to take Henry. Just the two of us." They talked it over and gave us permission the next day, not even seeming hurt.

Travel without parents was new, but Barney aced it, whisking us by plane and shuttle to a six-story business hotel in Highland Park. We were surrounded by science kids, and because there were only geeks around, there were no geeks. Barney relaxed, the stare easing into a near-smile, as he talked mesons and photometers into the night.

When he spoke to me about those things at home I could only nod. Now he'd found other people like him, whose voices mumbling, "Cool proof," wove with his. At first I was afraid he wouldn't want to talk to me at all, but instead he was nicer than usual, introducing me to everyone and saying I'd been a huge help on his projects, as if I'd sweated over the postulates with him instead of just washing his slides.

We made friends with a Korean American girl from Indiana whose polypeptide experiment came in first, followed by Barney's fluid dynamics problem, and a curly-haired guy from the Bronx High School of Science who described everything he liked as "choice." The four of us ran laughing down cinderblock hotel stairwells, ate shrimp cocktails and ice cream from silver bowls, shook hands with smiling men in suits, and committed egghead vandalism. We didn't have minibar keys, but Barney picked the lock on ours in thirty seconds, and instead of drinking the liquor, the way normal high school kids would have done, we invented the antigravity minibar, gluing the snacks and bottles in upside down to make the next business traveler rethink his assumptions.

The second night, after the awards dinner, I woke up at 2:00 A.M. and found Barney out on the balcony in his gym shorts. I joined him at the railing and he said, "You see what happens when we get out of that town?"

The *we* killed me. I'd never been as close to him as I was then, watching the blobs of light bounce on the surface of the swimming pool and feeling like an ex-kid, a tetherball cut loose and flying.

One night near the end of my senior year Dad came home late, didn't put on samba, and sank into a living room chair, pale and sweaty. Mom and I stood looking at him for a few minutes before he said, "We're going under."

"Oh shit, sweetie," Mom said. "I'm sorry."

"They were trying to keep it going another quarter," Dad said. "Trowbridge had a conference call with everyone from his place in Vail."

I said, "So, but your job—"

"I don't have a job anymore," Dad said. "No one does."

For the next two months the *L.A. Times* doled out revelations of Controlled Dynamics's contract-padding and trick accounting, climaxing with the news that the company's management had drained the employee pension fund. When the CEO told a reporter that the employees were his family, and that he'd pursue every conceivable avenue to see that his family was made whole, we knew we were screwed.

Dad sent out three hundred résumés. He had some projects lined up around the house but he forgot to get finishing nails on his first trip to Lumber City and never went back. On most days he opened the garage door, put a web chair at the top of the driveway, and sat looking out at the street with the not-now eyes of a guy riding public transit. A lot of his fellow ex-executives did the same at their houses. You could take a twenty-minute detour to avoid passing Controlled Dynamics, and many people did, but there was no way to miss all those sad puppet theaters of the unemployed.

Barney was at Cal Poly on scholarship, and Dad and I were

getting along better. We had a lot in common. He was a middle manager and I was a middle teenager, not an athlete but not one of those guys who get beaten up all the time, either, and bright but not nearly as bright as Barney. My biggest talent at school was writing book reports that sounded like the books. Dad and I let other people amaze us—Barney, Dad's scientists, and Mom, who'd never believed in Controlled Dynamics anyway. One night a few months after the layoffs, when Dad was pushing his dinner around on his plate like a kid, she said, "Look on the bright side. It's not your whole life, okay? It's just the work part."

"That *controls* the other parts," Dad said.

"No, it doesn't. We should be having fun," she said, pointing to the living room, where "One Note Samba" was on the stereo. "We should go to Brazil. To Carnaval."

"What am I celebrating?" Dad said. "Going broke?"

"Carnaval is *held* for broke people. It cheers them up. Celebrate being out of that job."

"You're right," Dad said, pulling farther back in his chair as if the bright side were a confession being beaten out of him. He waited for a long enough pause, got up, and went out to the garage. A few minutes later I went out there and pulled a web chair up next to his.

"Is there anything?" I said.

"A salad bar," he said. "I'm waiting to hear back."

"The one on Cathode? Fresh Connection?"

He shook his head. "In Altadena. In a mall."

Seventy minutes away, and not even freestanding. Right then I wanted to join the Communists. That would have been just like me, signing up right before they went bust, but I wanted some heartless comrades to help me kill the directors of Controlled Dynamics, burn their second homes and salt the earth.

I waited for a lull and then got up, the same technique Dad had used to get out of the kitchen. Given the pension situation, it might be my only inheritance.

The day after my first kite buggy ride, Don came back and brought a friend. They rode their buggies for hours and let me take a few turns. By noon there were thirty spectators. I called my best friends, Cliff and Andy. We watched all afternoon, clapping when they swung their kites across the sky to change direction. Three days later we drove to Torrance to buy kites and buggies, denting the college money we'd saved from our fast-food jobs. Mom and Dad had figured out that I could go to state college in the fall if I worked part time there, but I was free for the summer. The layoffs were killing the Valleycrest Mall, and all the local burger work had gone to forty-eight-year-old physicists.

One day Don and his friend left for a dry lake they'd heard about in New Mexico. Cliff and Andy and I set up a slalom in the parking lot and buggied every day, our lines singing over the premises that had stolen our fathers' balls.

Dad, in his web chair, asked what part of the parking lot we were riding in. When I told him, he nodded, transit-faced, and said, "Those were the new rows. That was when we put people on for the B-1. Dave Gotbaum used to park there till he got Ted's job." I stopped telling him about it.

We got a few more guys into buggying, and the security guard who'd stayed on for the mop-up waved at us from a window sometimes. One day in August Andy saw him and said, "It's weird that they've never tried to stop us. You'd think they'd be scared we'll break our legs and sue them."

"There's no money left to sue them for," I said.

"That guy is doing it anyway," Cliff said.

"What guy?" I said.

"This lawyer in L.A. He's suing them for everyone that lost their pension."

"Why?" Andy said.

"It's public-interest law," Cliff said. "It's the thing where they crusade for the little guy."

I found out the lawyer's name that night, made myself wait until 9:06 the next morning, and called him. "Mr. Troup?" I said. "My name is Henry Bay. I'm a student? I live in Rancho Cahuenga? And I heard that you're suing Controlled Dynamics."

"Well," he said, "our firm has filed a suit on behalf of some former employees against some former officers of that company." He sounded about sixty, his voice eastern and precise.

"My father's a former employee," I said.

"We'll be making claim forms available down the road."

"Okay. Thank you. Um, the reason I'm calling? I'm going to be going to college there in the fall. In the L.A. area."

"Yes?"

"Yes. At Cal State Los Nietos. In the pre-law program." I'd checked it on the paperwork fifteen minutes earlier. "I was wondering if you had any openings in your office for someone to help out part time. Just running errands or anything."

"I see. Well, there's nothing like that right now, but why don't you give me a call in a few months, around November? There might be something along those lines then."

"Okay. Sir? I really believe in what you're doing. They really messed things up here."

"I'm sorry. Tell me your name again?"

"Henry. Henry Bay."

"The fiduciaries at that company were cowboys, Henry. It was the Wild West and they thought they could make their own law, if you will. Fortunately, there are mechanisms in place for bringing the cowboys of this world to terms."

"Yes. Thank you. Thanks very much."

"Surely," he said, and hung up.

I was too excited to sit still. I went outside and walked, getting out of breath so I could breathe in more of my first purpose ever. We'd all been acting like this was how it was, you got in your web chair and shut up, when all this time there were mechanisms. And I could help. I could make coffee. "Very strong and very black, Henry," I could hear Troup say. "We have eighteen hours to put these papers before Judge Harridan so our friends from Controlled Dynamics can learn a little something about fulfilling one's obligations."

"It's already brewing, sir. I've learned a few things myself these past few weeks."

His snowy eyebrows would flicker and he'd hand me an inch of paper. "Then tell me what you make of this finding, Henry. Your expert opinion." But with a twinkle. I'd pour us each a cup and start reading, helping Dad in a way not even Barney could.

A few days later Barney came home on a break from summer session. He'd gone college-style, a button-down shirt and corduroy sport coat with jeans and sneakers. As we walked to AM/PM for charcoal, he said, "Dad's a wreck, huh? Is he looking for work?"

"He's waiting to hear from a salad bar."

"Those jerks," Barney said, nodding toward the Controlled Dynamics buildings. "They got talented people in there and had them work on crap. Not just talented people. Dad. He believed in it."

"There's a guy who's suing them," I said. "I might get to

help." I told him about Troup, the cowboys, and my decision to take pre-law.

"Jesus," Barney said. "Henry, that's great."

"We have to see what happens," I said. "Dad says he doubts if we'll get anything."

"I hope you nail these people," Barney said. "I hope you ream them out completely. That's great that you can do something like that."

My face flushed and I turned away, pretending to study the clouds over Capacitor Parkway.

A week later, by the speed run, Andy said, "Did you guys know there's a magazine?" He took it out of his daypack: *Kite Buggy*, with a cover photo of a guy riding ten feet off the ground. The big cover line was STEPPIN' OUT FOR SOME AIR WITH FREDDY PASCO. The smaller ones were PARA-KITE TORTURE TEST! and DO *YOU* NEED CUSTOM STRUTS?

In retrospect, the halftones and color registration were criminal acts, the paper was Bumwad Brite, and of course there was a magazine; there's a magazine as soon as five people find a new way to hurt themselves. At the time, though, I knew none of that.

I read it in bed that night. There's a once-only Eden for you, your first copy of a magazine about your first enthusiasm. You need a strategy (page by page? flip through and go back?), but you'll read that first one twice anyway. There were motor-drive photos of Freddy Pasco in action, a story about a buggy breaking sixty miles an hour at the Bonneville Salt Flats, and ads for better wheels than the buggies came with, better bearings than the wheels came with, and bushings machined in someone's garage, using the same space-age metals that Controlled Dynamics had relied on for precise Pentagon-bilking applications.

The next day I typed a letter on loose-leaf paper and mailed it to *Kite Buggy*'s parent company, Dobey Publications of Clayton, Illinois.

Dear Sirs,

I think you have a great magazine. However, I believe you should know that the two-point turn that was suggested in your last issue ("All the Right Moves," June) could result in the rider being pulled off the back of the buggy at high speed, with extreme impact to the head. I think this was a shortcoming in what was an otherwise excellent story.

Here in Rancho Cahuenga, we have what we feel is an outstanding facility that we put together at the former headquarters of a large concern. It features hills, a speed run, and a slalom. As many as 8 riders have used it at a given time.

Yours,
Henry Bay
Rancho Cahuenga, California

A few days later I got a scrawled note on the letterhead of the Clayton Quality Fast Printing Company:

Dear Henry,

Thanks for the heads-up on the 2-pointer. We'll be printing your letter in a future "Buggy Tracks" column.

Sounds like you have a great setup out there. Want to do a story on it? Photos?

Go buggy,
Jim Rensselaer

As a Future Litigator of America, I recognized the breezy thanks and the offered assignment as the sops they were, but I was over there buggying every day anyway. I borrowed Dad's camera, shot two rolls, wrote a page of copy, and sent it all off. A few weeks later, as I packed for college, an envelope arrived with two copies of the new *Kite Buggy* and a note from Rensselaer: *Henry—Good stuff. Thanks, Jim.*

There were four photos on the cover, two of them mine. The headlines slashed across them were ANDY WEISS RIPS IT AT RANCHO and CLIFF STARNER: "I'M TAKIN' IT TO THE EDGE!" The story on Cliff said he lived in Florida, where buggy dealers were putting people on waiting lists. "Sarasota this year was intense," he was quoted as saying. "Chicks, kites, and waves. Damn." A shot of me illustrated an item on Alabama: BIRMINGHAM IS BUGGY-BURGEONING! A photo of Andy accompanied my piece on Rancho Cahuenga, which had been amped to the point of hallucination. "The primo buggy park is drawing mega-crowds," it said. "City fathers are coming from all over the U.S. to check it out."

I was annoyed by all the lying, but no one else was. Andy bought five copies and Cliff kept saying the "chicks and waves" thing in a "whoa, dude" accent till we begged him to stop.

The night before I left for college, I put my kite and buggy away in the garage and stood there for a while looking at them. I wished I could take something with me—the kite, a leaf rake, a web chair with my despondent dad in it. Finally I turned the lights off and went inside, and in the morning I left for Cal State Los Nietos to save my family.

2

Walking through the college library with an introductory law book in my hand, I saw a broad-shouldered blond guy sitting at a table shaking his head with melancholy awe at the book he was reading. He looked up, saw me, and said, "Have you *read* this?" as if we already knew each other and he was sure I'd want to be alerted to the book's contents right away. He held it up: *The World Rushed In*, by J. S. Holliday. I shook my head.

"The gold rush," he said, and read aloud, running his spread fingers under the words as if sight-reading music: "'What a dilemma they faced. They had to justify their staying in California far longer than expected, leaving wife and family with insufficient funds; had to argue that another season in the mines would surely produce success. At the same time, they had to explain why no one else should come to California.'" He closed it and sighed. "What have you got there?"

I held up *Property Disputes and Contests*. "The sequel?"

He nodded and stood. "Gerald Hauser. History major. From Peta*lu*ma," he said, getting the most from the klaxon place name.

He was tall, with reddish skin and expectant blue eyes. In the age of Seattle flannel he dressed like a guy just back from World War II, in saddle shoes, pressed gabardine pants, and a spread-collar shirt cut like a sail.

"I could eat," he said. "I've been sloshing that gravel all day in my lucky pan that I brought from St. Louis. Would you like to join me?"

We went outside. Cal State Los Nietos, just east of east L.A., looked disappointingly like my high school, the same low brown classroom buildings and smog-tolerant ice plant, with high-rise dorms thrown in. For a few years I'd been picturing a college version of myself, a lanky guy leaning in a doorway, shrugging hair out of my eyes and looking wry, but Los Nietos wanted me to be the same non-lanky study hall doodler I'd always been.

Gerald talked all the way across the darkening campus, about the gold rush, Increase Mather, Albert Ayler, and the debased public architecture we were passing. When he got going his hand gestures and self-astonished voice made him look like a trader on the commodities floor. The names he cited, like his clothes, were from worlds I knew nothing about. I heard Barney saying, "You see what happens when we get out of that town?"

"Look at this," Gerald said, stopping to point at the glass-and-concrete student union, his hand an upturned bowl that asked, "What *happened* here?"

"This is a car dealership," he said. "They're not the buyer's friend in there, either. This is not the home of the no-dicker sticker." His expression had that sad wonder in it again, as if he were standing on a cliff and watching the age of craft and proportion sail away for good. He dropped the hand onto my shoulder and did a car salesman's too-close voice. "Henry, let me ask you something, Henry. Henry, is there a number in your mind that would cause you to walk out of here with a college education today?"

"There is a number," I said, "but it's irrational."

"You people are all the same," he said.

He lived in the same dorm I did, but coming into his room from the fluorescent corridor was like falling for a prank. He'd nailed graying redwood planks over the white walls and replaced the plastic furniture with a bedroll, a scarred card table, an old wooden swivel chair, lamps with scorched shades, a propane camp stove, and an ice pail. It was a cabin in there. He wouldn't see his security deposit again in this world.

"I can't stay too long," I said. "I have a job at Doctor Taco."

"What do you do over there?"

"I'm a fry chef. I've got hot fat spattering on my arms all the time."

"Ah." He took a bowl of stew from the ice pail, put some in a saucepan, and lit the stove.

"The worst part is cleaning the fryer hoods," I said. "You have to put the filters in a garbage can full of acid. They give you gloves, but they're not long enough, so you get acid down your arms." I rolled up a sleeve and showed him the red stripes.

"That sounds good," he said. "Is there travel? You have conventions?" He took beat-up blue enamel plates and tin forks out of an old oak cabinet. "Where are you in from?"

"Rancho Cahuenga."

He shook his head. "Controlled Dynamics. My, my."

"You know about that?"

He paused, turning the answer into a story. "I come to town, I have to connect for propane," he said, pointing to the camp stove. "I have to find my man. It turns out he's by the railroad tracks. Have you been down there?" I shook my head. "That's the *end* of town. Your cars on blocks, your discarded appliances, your three-legged dogs with open sores. My man sells propane, live bait, and Mad Dog 20/20. That's what's by the tracks. In fact, they're tearing the depot down right now." He pointed to the wood on his walls. "I acted swiftly. Sheetrock is a great invention, but it smells like a bank branch."

He turned the flame down and stirred the stew. "Now, the train station—at one time, that was where you had your tintype picture taken. Family portrait every five or ten years, you in your only suit, your wife in the bonnet, standing under the name of your town. You know what they're putting there now? An automated ticket kiosk. Stainless steel. You pose in front of that, it's out of the picture." He gave me a plate of stew. It was tomatoes and a trace of meat, thickened with corn meal.

"But in their day?" he said. "The railroads screwed *everyone*. The farmers, the miners, the Indians, the government. When we say 'the golden spike,' we're making use of our language for once. So, Controlled Dynamics . . . yeah, I followed that. That's modern-day." He waved the modern day away. "But the railroad men were lions. These guys now are small-scale replicas. With hearts like cafeteria veal." He measured the thinness with his fingers. "But they did try to carry that fucking torch."

Gerald could talk to anyone. One day he came to pick me up at Doctor Taco when I had twenty minutes left on my shift. "I know I'm early, big boy," he called to me from the counter. "I'm gonna have some of this food I keep hearing about."

My co-worker offered to take Gerald's order. Gerald read his name tag, said, "Ramon, I'm Gerald," and shook his hand. "Henry and I are taking some young ladies to a foreign movie this evening. He could use a little something foreign. What's the best thing to eat here?"

"I don't know," Ramon said. "I guess the Enchi-Rito." Gerald nodded. Ramon got one from under the heat lamp and sold it to him.

Gerald tasted it, watched the great age sail away again, and said, "Ramon, do you eat these?"

"No, I don't eat that. I bring a sandwich."

"Right. Do you mind if I do a little work on this? I've got some groceries out in the car."

Ramon shrugged. It was 4:40 and we were slow. Gerald dashed outside, came back with a brown bag and started pulling out vegetables. "We're gonna doctor this taco," he said. "Its own freezer truck won't recognize it." He looked around at the deep fryers and the grill. "Is there a stove?"

"Stove, no," Ramon said.

"See, a restaurant with no stove," Gerald said. "They'll put these kinds of obstacles in a man's way time and again." Ramon nodded. "That's a great tattoo, by the way," Gerald said.

"Thank you."

"We'll do this on the open grill here," Gerald said, cutting up onions and bell peppers. Ramon reached for the grilling oil, but Gerald stopped him. "Yeah, we're not gonna be using that today," he said. "That was made by scientists. The international zaibatsus give the scientists a few million carloads of animal debris and they make that. Years later it turns up in breast milk, and hearings are held. Here we go." He took a bottle of olive oil from his groceries and poured some on the grill. "You know about Sam Giancana?" Ramon shook his head. "He worked at the Mafia," Gerald said.

"Mafia, yeah," Ramon said.

"He was called Momo by those who knew him. He worked closely with President Kennedy." The vegetables hit the grill sizzling. "Momo had himself a house in Chicago. Little kitchen in the basement. He was fixing himself some sausage and peppers one night. Peppers just like these sweethearts here. A man with all that wealth and respect, he could have called up any place in town and had it sent over, but he knows it's better when you cook it yourself." He split the Enchi-Rito open and dumped its filling onto the vegetables. "That's when they came in and killed him. A twenty-two-caliber weapon was used."

"Shit."

"I know. A man can't even eat his supper." He opened four cellophane spice envelopes and shook them over the food on the grill. Oregano and cumin steamed up the room.

"They finished him in the finished basement," I said.

Gerald smiled and said, "That's right, big boy." Ramon looked at me blankly. I never knew what to say to Ramon. Gerald scooped the stuff on the grill into the Enchi-Rito wrapper.

Ramon said, "Did they eat it? The guys that killed him?"

"That's what I want to know!" Gerald yelled, throwing up his hands. He and Ramon laughed. "It wasn't reported! It's going to be missing from the record forever!" He handed the Enchi-Rito to Ramon, who took a bite.

"Damn," Ramon said. "That's great." I finished changing the fryer oil and threw away that day's paper hat. For weeks afterward, Ramon asked me when Gerald was coming in again.

• • •

Some people wondered what a history degree was good for, but I knew Gerald's success after college was guaranteed, that he'd have no trouble with the future because he knew it to be a weak fifth Xerox of the past. He told me that the people who really made money in the gold rush were the ones who sold the miners their pickaxes and sturdy pants. He would find the next gold rush, talk his way in, and know exactly where to stand.

He educated me more than college did, dragging me to museums and nightclubs in L.A. One evening, walking to his car to go hear jazz, I complained to him about pre-law. It wasn't the numbing subject matter that bothered me but the pity my fellow majors expressed when they heard my plans to go into public interest. Raised in a renaissance of land flips and LBOs, they knew which law schools fed into the business-moll firms of New York and Houston, and exactly how much the associates made there. They couldn't understand why I'd want to be on the losing side. I thought Gerald would be with me on this, but he sat on a bench by the library, closed his eyes, and said, "I see a K-car."

The K was an economy model that Chrysler had introduced to stave off insolvency. "I dig the brother Lee Iacocca," Gerald said. "He's not a railroad man. He means it. But I can hear that little four-banger. I can see a small office building in one of our nation's tertiary markets. Primary and secondary areas, the rent is prohibitive. I see metal desks and acoustical ceiling tile, and in spite of that tile I can hear the dental equipment in the next office. I see a Silex with half an inch of coffee always getting burned in it. The ground coffee comes on a truck from the office-supply place." He opened his eyes and looked placidly at me.

"You don't think it's a good thing to do?" I said.

He shrugged. "I'm just telling you what I see."

"I should get going," I said. We didn't go to the jazz club and I didn't speak to him for two weeks. I missed him, but I owed it to Dad.

Our estrangement ended on November first, when I called Dan Troup, the lawyer who was suing Controlled Dynamics. He said there was an opening for an intern two days a week, and that I could come in the following Tuesday and give it a try. That afternoon I caught up with Gerald at the dorm's front doors and said, "Hey."

He gestured up at the building's façade, twelve stories of gray slab with slotlike windows and flattened concrete drip marks. In a Slavic accent he said, "One day they come and said my farm is collectivize. Three years I wait the permission to come Moscow. Now I live in all-modern worker building." He opened the door. "Pliz." Relieved, I followed him upstairs and told him about my appointment with Troup, and we figured out the three buses I would take to get there.

I got up at five on Tuesday and put on my suit. On the first bus, I read a newspaper someone had left behind. A mail bomb had been sent to a laboratory that developed satellite tracking systems, killing a research assistant and costing an engineer half her hearing and most of her left arm. A communiqué sent to *The Washington Post* took responsibility for the bomb, which it said was a blow against "the tracking, banding, and tagging of the most endangered species of all, the free-ranging human individual." The communiqué's signer, "Freebird," had claimed credit for three other attacks, all in the past year. The parts of the bombs that were recovered were handmade and untraceable. The name Freebird was believed to be taken from the old Lynyrd Skynyrd song that jokers were always requesting at rock concerts, regardless of who was playing. The problem for the jokers was that while the bomber was at large, yelling "Freebird!" at a concert would cause people nearby to wheel around and ask, "Song or the guy?" If you said the guy, it could lead to a fistfight, but of course so could the song.

The last bus went up Sepulveda Boulevard, a tertiary line through a primary city: movie theaters converted to Apostolic churches, marble banks turned Army Navys, and bowling alleys that were still bowling alleys. I thought the neighborhood would stay like that all the way to Troup's office, which would have the Silex and ceiling tile Gerald had predicted, and that Troup would be the flinty avenger I'd been picturing since our first phone call. He'd wear Haband and drive an Aries K, but the fiduciary cowboys who screwed deputy program managers and their fry-chef children would be sorry they'd ever heard of him.

I saw myself, the lanky one, sitting next to him in court and handing him smoking-gun depositions. The cowboys would be almost openly snickering at him when the trial started, but by the time he got to his summation those smirks would be coming in staticky, and when he wound up with "Because these are *lives* we're talking about, ladies and gentlemen," they'd be gone. He'd bite his lip, look up at the slow-grinding ceiling fan, then turn back to the jury. "I'm done."

But the bus continued to Century City, where the buildings were shiny and tall. Troup's firm had half of a fifteenth story, and the waiting room was as big as our first floor at home. Swallowed by a bottomless suede sofa under gleaming Chagall posters, I tried to read *The Financial Times* and *Golf Digest* while my graduation Weejuns bounced nervously on the three-inch carpet.

After twenty minutes Troup came out. Instead of the white-haired scrapper I'd expected, he was forty and smooth, in a blue dress shirt with white cuffs and collar and an expensive haircut that draped over one ear, Edwardian hip. He spoke in the same deliberate way he had on the phone, though, so that "Would you like some water?" sounded as if he'd roughed out the offer by himself for a few days and then finalized it with his partners that morning.

We went into his office, which had two brass nautical clocks and a view of the fancy shopping center next door. He leaned against his desk, the antique-dining-table type, folded his arms, and looked somewhere over my shoulder as he spoke.

"The Controlled Dynamics situation continues to unfold in an interesting way," he said. "The other side filed a request to deny access to certain of the documents. We've filed a request to deny their request. We hope to have a ruling on that within sixty days."

"That sounds good," I said. "So the trial could be . . ."

"Could be some time off, yes. You have discovery, motions. . . . The lead counsel for the other side is a fellow named Ken Radnitz. Kenny was with a firm here in the building at one time. It's interesting. He and his wife are fencers. You know, with those suits with the heart on them. I think they've won some of the competitions. Not many people I know are involved with that. It's a little off the beaten area. How are you enjoying pre-law?"

"Good. It's good."

"Okay. Let's try you out on some proofreading."

I spent the rest of the day in a room with a stack of documents and two hundred books of statutes, getting up only to go to the bathroom and to buy a chili dog from a catering truck outside. On the bus ride back to school I wondered how Troup could fight for the little guy from an office like that, or think fencing was interesting, but I decided I was overreacting. The clocks and the haircut could be ploys to lull the cowboys into thinking he was like them, when really he'd never be like them. It was possible.

The next day his secretary called to say I could keep coming in on Tuesdays and Thursdays at a hundred dollars a week. It wasn't enough money to give up frying, I had to drop a class, and the eyestrain from the proofreading gave me myopia. The addition of glasses made me look less lanky than ever.

My third week there, Troup leaned his head into the room and said he was going to a settlement conference with some opposing lawyers on a product defect case and that I should come with him to take notes. As we walked across the shopping center to the other lawyers' hotel, he said the case involved a boat part made by a company in Minneapolis, and that it was possible to hurt yourself because of the defect but, between Troup and me, you'd have to work at it.

We met the two other lawyers in a conference room with fruit, coffee, and a bowl of wrapped candies. The three of them talked for a while about judges and lawyers they knew and then took out copies of the settlement. They changed a thirty-day waiting period to forty-five, made discount vouchers available in Guam, and added a phrase to cool out the attorney general of Maine. It took twelve minutes, after which they stood up and gossiped a while longer. Troup, gesturing widely with his left hand as he recommended restaurants, swept a handful of the wrapped candies into his coat pocket with his right.

Walking back, I said I was surprised that the opposing lawyers had flown in just for that. "Henry," Troup said, "they live in *Minnesota*. The whole key to this work is compassion for people." I smiled with him, which made me feel complicit in the candy grab. As we got on the footbridge from the shopping center to the office buildings, I saw some high-school kids hanging around a fountain, the boys playing hacky sack and the girls talking in shrieks. In Rancho Cahuenga or Los Nietos my three months of college would have made me feel like their uncle, but now I wanted to go join them. Troup saw me slow down on the footbridge and said the shopping center was considered premier.

In March I got a phone call in the dorm lounge, an unfamiliar voice with office clatter in the background. "Yeah, Henry Bay? Jim Rensselaer at *Kite Buggy*. I called your house and they gave me this number."

"Oh," I said. "Hi."

"You got that issue with—I'll call him back—you got the issue with your stuff in it, right?"

"Yeah," I said. "That wasn't my stuff, though. You put in people saying things they never said. They were in places they've never been in."

"Yeah. No, we blurred the geography a little. We wanted to spread it around." I was trying to be stiff with him, but he didn't seem to get it. "Yeah, that looks like shit, Devon. Henry? You get spring break there, right? You have plans for it?"

"I'm not sure yet," I said. Troup was going to Telluride and I'd put in for double shifts at Doctor Taco.

"How'd you like to cover a major buggy event?"

"I don't know."

"It's at a dry lake in Nevada. It's going to be great. I'd go myself but it's right before we close the issue."

"I don't have a car."

"That's okay," he said. "Can you borrow one?" I didn't answer. "Look, I'll tell you what. You go there, take some notes, take some pictures, and then come here and we'll work on it together. You can meet everyone. You'd just drive up to Las Vegas and fly here. Wait, hold on a second." He put the phone down, came back after a minute, and said, "That's a regular college you go to, right? Not like a weird Bible college or anything? No offense. It's just whether you can get a student fare."

"It's a state college," I said. "State university."

"Perfect. So you can come here. We'll pay you."

"I don't know."

"Henry, be a guy. It's a perfect spring break. Don't tell me you're going to Florida. You know what that is? It's a bunch of girls in bikinis. This is Clayton, Illinois. We've got girls in jumpers." A woman in the background cheerfully said, "Fuck you," and there was laughing.

"Are they corduroy?" I said.

"Corduroy, muslin. It's a wide-open town. Henry? We'll put you in a hotel. You can look over my shoulder if I start screwing around with your prose stylings, okay?"

I had a fatal weakness for people who spoke smartass and could get me speaking it too—Barney, Gerald, and now this guy. Weighing Doctor Taco's fryer hood against a kite buggy event and an office where they blithely told the boss to fuck himself, I chose the trip.

Gerald was going home for spring break and wouldn't need his car. I dropped him at the airport and drove into the desert, a sun-wrecked eternity of sand, scrub, and the occasional yucca. On the highway along the Mojave Preserve the air was so dry I didn't seem to be sweating, but when I walked into an air-conditioned Denny's I was soaked in thirty seconds.

In the afternoon I crossed into Nevada, got off the freeway at a town consisting of two casinos and an outlet mall, and followed Rensselaer's directions to the dry lake. There was no road, but steel poles every fifty feet marked the way across rose-tinted dirt that had cracked into a hypnotic pattern of polygons.

After twenty minutes I started worrying that I was in the wrong place, till I saw a kite in the sky, then two and then seven, and cars and vans parked by a big plastic shade tent. Kite buggies were crossing the lakebed in all directions, their lines buzzing softly in the hot wind.

I parked on the fringe. There were a hundred people, mostly men, with bodies ranging from young and athletic to sixty and shot, T-shirts that said things like BUGGY TILL YOU FRY, and the goatees and handlebars that come standard with speed sports. There were no spectators and no media but me, with a borrowed camera and a Los Nietos Geckos spiral notebook.

I knew I should interview people, that someone was probably nailing the essence of the sport just out of my earshot, but I was already getting curious looks for being there without a buggy and doing something that looked like work. I smiled in response, ducking my head to emphasize my harmlessness, and eavesdropped on the lulling hum of enthusiast talk.

"What are those tires off of?"

"Roof-tarring machine. We tried wheelbarrow tires, but that was pushing it."

"Let me tighten that. What this country needs is a Phillips-head dime."

A guy getting ready to race his buggy on an improvised oval course said, "If I'm turning behind someone, should I have my kite high or low?" and the guy he asked said, "If you die, can I have your stuff?"

After the race a guy did a few figure eights on two wheels, came to a stop, and then sat there with one wheel off the ground, deftly working his kite lines to stand still in the shifting wind. No one in Rancho Cahuenga would even have tried that. When he dropped the wheel and let the kite fall, I ran over and held it for him while he wound up his lines.

"Thanks, man," he said, and flipped up his sunglasses. He had a wide smile, grooving black eyes, and a windbreaker imprinted with the logos of a kite maker, a buggy designer, ChapStick, and Desenex. "Freddy Pasco."

"I know," I said. "I'm Henry Bay. I'm from *Kite Buggy*."

"Oh great. Yeah, you guys did that thing on me. Jim, right? The guy I talked to? How's he doing?"

"He's good." I pointed to where he'd been two-wheeling. "That was great just now."

"Thanks. Yeah, this is some funny wind today." I scribbled *fun wind tdy* in my notebook. "If it's steady tomorrow I'm going to try and get some air. So what do you guys think, is this going to catch on? I'd love if I could do it full time. I'm top-ranked now and I'm selling toner."

"Yeah," I said. "It's starting to spread out now, geographically. Jim was saying."

At sunset everyone drove to the casino hotels or made camp in the desert, barbecuing under plastic canopies rigged to their vans. I dined on the Vienna sausages and Gatorade I'd brought, unrolled Gerald's sleeping bag, and made camp fifty yards away from everyone else, in accordance with the journalistic ethics I was making up in the course of the trip.

At sunset the next day I drove to the Las Vegas airport. I started to write up my notes on the plane, but the lights went off and I woke up in St. Louis four hours later with the fake flu of airplane sleep. I took a bus across the Mississippi into southern Illinois, got to Clayton at midday, and stepped out into a world that felt like I'd been born missing it.

Unlike Rancho Cahuenga, Clayton had taken its time being built, and was fading gradually now instead of crashing all at once. A Clayton street was twenty different colors of weathered paint, a make-good for all the treadmill walks I'd taken past the Klondikes and Ponderosas back home. The air off the river had twice the ply of what I'd grown up breathing. Kids bicycled slowly past frame houses on soft asphalt that dipped where the trolley tracks had been. Business was slow downtown, and the talk under the awnings kept pace with it.

The Hotel Clayton was four floors of blanched brick, with a lobby full of pedestal ashtrays and lodge meeting plaques. I showered and changed in a room with old duck-hunting paintings on the wall and set out for the Dobey offices, in a squat three-story building on the edge of downtown.

Up a dim flight of stairs there was a waiting room with a worn orange couch and blown-up magazine covers on the walls: *Kite Buggy, Tropical Fish Owner, Crochet Life,* and *Nine-Hole Golfer.* I told the receptionist I was there to see Rensselaer, and she pointed at the doorway to a bigger room.

There were six people in there, all under thirty, working at metal desks. They were acting aggravated—shaking their heads over pages of copy, recoiling in horror from page proofs, and jerking off air cocks to denote the intelligence of distant phone callers—but you could tell that the aggravation was their happiness, that the whole scene was an elaboration on the cheerful "Fuck you" I'd heard on the phone.

"Henry?" A long-haired guy, thin except for a spongy waistline, had his hand over the mouthpiece of his phone. He waved me over. "Jim." He wore jeans, a waffle jersey, and a flannel shirt. "See, that's what's great about what you're doing," he said into the phone. "It's not just some guys dicking around on a dry lake somewhere." He shook his head for my benefit. "That's why you need to advertise it, so you—okay. No, I understand. Thanks."

He hung up, shook my hand, and said, "Welcome. You get pictures?" I nodded. He yelled "Jillian" to a woman who was on the phone across the room, and turned back to me. His expression was energy-saving, low eyelids and a sketch of a smile. "How's college? What are you taking?"

"Pre-law," I said.

"Mine was Italian literature," he said. "It's made all the difference."

The woman across the room got off the phone and came over. She was tall, with a sand-blond ponytail, in a chambray shirt, fishing vest, hiking boots, and jeans. Rensselaer said, "Henry, this is Jillian, your managing editor."

"The film," she said, and held out her hand. She was a few years older than I was. Her camping clothes and lack of makeup made her beauty seem like a knack, something she'd picked up along with fly-tying. Her face was friendly, but the gray eyes reserved the right to assess and make fun. There was the prospect of a radiant smirk.

I fumbled the four rolls out of my pocket and met her look as I handed them over. Out of nowhere I saw something, a room I'd never been in, with sunlight on a worn wooden floor, and the sound outside of a breeze over water. As I let go of the film I realized I'd made up a frame of her childhood, a lakeside house where she'd run through that room keeping up with a brother or two, as if she'd just told me about it. When she spoke again the image was gone. "Where do we have you staying?"

"Hotel Clayton," I said.

"Firetrap," she said.

"It is," Rensselaer said. "Although they make a turkey and rice soup over there that's . . ."

"Real turkey and rice lover's soup?" I said.

"Liker's," Jillian corrected me.

"You get interviews?" Rensselaer said. I nodded.

"You asked who their favorite sculptor is, right?" Jillian said. "We try to get that in."

"Definitely," I said. I gave her good odds of being the "Fuck you" woman.

My annoyance over Cliff being transposed to Florida, and me to Alabama, was from another time. I already loved the town, and I was liking the office more by the minute. Rensselaer stood at his desk like a guy grilling burgers on his patio. There was stained acoustical tile on the ceiling, and a Silex with half an inch of coffee getting crisp. Everything Gerald had specified for Troup's office had been shipped here instead.

Jillian showed me to a vacant desk, where I spread my notes out, turned on the computer, and went to work. I didn't have an extensive magazine-reading background to draw on—three issues of *Kite Buggy,* other kids' *Rolling Stones* and *Penthouses,* and the bewildering *Wooden Boat* while waiting in my underwear at the doctor's—but as I watched her walk back to her desk I decided to give it whatever I had.

Freddy Pasco's been waiting for this wind for two days—wind that blows a steady 35 mph, sandblastin' your face with half the Mojave Desert. He's killed the time doing some awesome Crazy Ivans. But now it's here.

Freddy's wind.

He's going 54 miles per when he starts to lift. Five . . . ten . . . fifteen feet over the lakebed, with his five-meter Ozone out in front of him.

You're back by the tent watching. You think he's just going to grab an airplane hangar's worth of air and come down. A day at the office.

Dude, you're wrong.

Freddy stays up there . . . and then he starts to turn.

When I looked up from what I was doing it was dark outside, everyone else had left, and I was hungry. I ate one of the three Lorna Doones in the break room and kept going.

The noise builds. People are yelling, but they don't know they're yelling. Nobody here knows if this is even possible.

And then the wind slacks off.

Freddy's wheels sink a foot. Two feet. Three. The crowd is so quiet you can hear a pin drop. Or Freddy, whichever comes first.

But you look at his face, and you don't see panic there. You look at his arms, and he's working his lines like a cowboy throwing a lariat over the hot Mojave wind.

His buggy rises a few inches . . . and keeps turning. Ninety degrees. But now he's falling again, even faster. Nobody can look. But nobody can look away.

And then Freddy Pasco throws his weight to one side, puts his arm muscles on turbo, and racks his kite across the sky like you or I can only dream of. He catches a gust, finishes the first airborne 180 anyone here has ever seen, and brings it down on the lakebed like a Huey. You can hear the cheers all the way at the Kite Buggy *office in Clayton Illin' Noise.*

It was four thirty in the morning and I still had to write up my interviews. I slept on the waiting room couch for two hours, washed my face, drank some Silex carbon, and went back to work with bursting silver spots in front of my eyes.

When the wind fell off, "I wasn't thinking about dying or getting hurt," Freddy says. "I was thinking, Look at that. Look how we're not in charge of our energy on this planet. It can change any time. If you don't change with it, you

I stopped there when Rensselaer came in. He leaned over my shoulder, read what I'd written, and said, "You've mastered the idiom, Henry. You should get out while you can. At least get yourself a malt cup. You look like hell."

He pointed me to the break room freezer, where there were chocolate malt cups like the ones at a baseball game. I started scraping one and went back to work. A few minutes later Rensselaer came over to my desk with a wiry guy in his sixties and said, "Henry, this is Arnold Dobey. He owns this place. Henry's writing the Buggy Break story."

The Dobey in Dobey Publications leaned over me and read my copy. "We should say how many spectators," he said. His voice went rat-a-tat and he wore a tight polo shirt that showed off his biceps. The combined effect was Popeye.

"There weren't really spectators," I said. "Everyone there was—"

"But people watched him do it, right?" Rensselaer said.

"Right, but they were the other—"

"But at that *moment*, they were, we would call these people . . ."

"Spectators," I said.

"Five hundred?" Arnold Dobey said.

I said, "No, there—"

"Three hundred," Rensselaer said.

Dobey said, "Four hundred."

Rensselaer said, "Done." Dobey pointed to the screen. After *like a Huey* I added *in front of four hundred spectators*. Rensselaer reached over me and typed in *breathless* before *spectators*. Dobey said, "Good," and went away.

"There you go," Rensselaer said. "You should come over to the press tonight and watch it come off."

"Tonight?"

"We're nimble here, Henry. We're trained professionals."

I went back to work, alternately eating the malt cup and holding it to my forehead. I finished at 11:00 A.M., went back to the hotel, slept till evening, ate turkey and rice soup in the deserted dining room, and went to see the press.

It was a big roomful of deafening machinery in an unmarked brick building near the bus depot. Rensselaer, Jillian, and three other staff people were already there. The four pressmen wore dirty blue aprons and paper hats made from page proofs.

The press had printed cereal boxes for twenty years before Dobey bought it. The millions of roosters and Johnny Unitases had worn out the color registration, so that kite buggiers were dogged by blue shadows, and the pictures on the afghans in *Crochet Life* looked like action paintings instead of Raggedy Anns.

The opening of my story came off, one of four pages on an uncut sheet. The press was as loud as a rock concert, not the way the audience heard it, but the way it would sound if you were the star onstage, with lights glaring on the mike stands and your finger in your ear for the harmony parts. The clay smell of offset ink was the marijuana. I didn't even see Jillian come over to me as I watched the copies pile up in the hopper. She had to shout to get my attention: "Are you wearing underwear?"

The six of us drove from the press to the Days Inn on the interstate at 3:00 A.M., sneaked around to the back, undressed to our underwear, and slipped into the heated pool. I breaststroked underwater, passing beneath Jillian as she floated on her back.

Rensselaer got out first and padded to the chaise where he'd left his clothes. I got out a few minutes later and sat on the one next to it. He went into his shirt pocket, and there was the marijuana for real. He lit a joint, drew on it, passed it to me, asked about my life at home, and hit the jackpot. I told him about Dad's pension, the web chairs, the frying, the proofreading, and Troup being buddies with the fencing-enthusiast lawyer for Controlled Dynamics.

"Yeah, these people all know each other," Rensselaer said. "They went to fucking-up-the-country school together. Trust me. I've covered state politics for a daily newspaper."

"Really?"

"Yes," he croaked, and exhaled smoke. "And the guys I covered? The bright young lawmakers? They're the *worst* fucking people. They're the Junior Chamber of Commerce guys you cross the street to avoid. It's like that in Washington, too. All the way up the echelon."

I sneaked a look at Jillian. She had kept her shirt on but clearly wore no bra. "Then you have the newspapers themselves," Rensselaer said. "If you work there, you're supposed to actually read the stories. Boy, do you get used to the stories. Pawnshops shedding seedy image. Retirement not just shuffleboard anymore. Kids' bookbags too heavy, experts say. Kids not getting enough exercise, say experts. You make an effort not to run those last two on the same day." He killed the joint. "That's why I'm not embarrassed to be working at *Kite Buggy* magazine. Would you be?"

"What? No," I said, and meant it, with the sudden conviction that I was fine and so was Dad, that there were pluses to being ancillary, that the people I was with would still be swimming in their underwear at three in the morning long after Freddy Pasco's rotator cuff blew out for good. I wanted to find a pay phone, call Dad, and tell him, but then I remembered that he had to be at the salad bar at 7:00 A.M.

I also decided not to try anything with Jillian that night.

Rensselaer's dope made my voice seem to come in by radio, and there was no telling what suave things I might say.

I got up early the next day and walked around town. There was a railroad switching yard that had once been busy, and a small college that supported two blocks of foreign restaurants and vaguely hip stores. At a meeting to plan the next issue, Rensselaer assigned me a story on the new breed of traction-kite designers.

"There's a new breed?" the art director said.

"We're breeding them right now," Rensselaer said. "In the back."

Boxes of the new issue came in during the meeting. Rensselaer said he knew I wanted copies for all my friends and relatives but that he had to limit me to forty. I said I couldn't take forty on the plane, but he kept pushing them at me and saying, "Be reasonable, Henry. Forty's the most we can spare. This isn't *Crochet Life* here. We run lean." I pushed them back, but he found my duffel bag and stuffed them in.

When it was almost time to leave, I saw Jillian go into the break room, waited a minute, and followed her. She was drinking guava nectar and doing the cryptogram in the St. Louis paper. She said, "Hey, Henry," and patted the spot next to her on the couch.

"Hey," I said, and sat down. "So, do you ride?"

"A little. I did a trip last year where you go through Banff on Appaloosas. It wrecks your butt but it's fun."

"I meant kite buggies."

"Oh. Yeah, I tried it once at the proving grounds."

"Are there actually proving grounds?"

"The high-school field. Jim and Devon and those guys go

crashing around in the test equipment. In certain circles it's called the 'Just What Are You Proving?' grounds."

"So how'd you get into this?"

"I was working down the hall at the title company and I kept hearing laughing." She put the paper down. "Will you be back to see us?"

"I don't know. I have school and everything."

"Yes, but Jim is very persuasive. I'm ever modest but he gets me to go swimming with everyone. But law school, right?" I nodded. "Isn't that like twelve years?"

"No, it's another five. You know, if I do it all the way." If you what? Wake Dad up and tell him *that*, jerk-off. "Do you ever get to California?"

"I haven't yet," she said.

"You should call me if you come out. I could show you stuff." Soviet dorms and Doctor Taco. You'll love it.

"That's so nice of you. I want to see Bakersfield, the home of Buck Owens. I mean, who knows when I'd get to go. But, yeah."

I dig the brother Buck Owens," Gerald said in the quad. "'I've got a tiger by the tail, it's plain to see.'"

"Me, too," I said. I was frying, proofreading, sleeping on buses, and interviewing the new breed of traction-kite designers from pay phones. I had so little time to study that the classes I made it to seemed like experimental theater. The last time I'd asked Dan Troup how the Controlled Dynamics case was going, he'd said it could be years before there was a verdict, "and at that point, of course, the appeals process chimes in."

"Most people would say San Francisco," Gerald said. "Or Hollywood. But Bakersfield, that's good. 'And all I've got to do is, Act naturally.'"

"Yeah. I've got to go to work," I said. "Fuck."

"What?"

"I missed Statistics."

"'It's crying time again,'" Gerald said.

Rensselaer, calling up about the kite designer story, showed impressive powers of retention for the complaining he'd heard, stoned, a month earlier. He asked how the lawyer with the collars was, how Dad was holding up, and whether my forearms were crispy good yet. When I told him, he said, "At least you know there's a job here if you want it."

"There is?"

"As of today, yeah. I caught Arnold just after he made some money."

"From our magazine, or the other ones?" I hadn't meant to say "our."

"No, on the Broncos," Rensselaer said. "He said I could hire an associate editor so I don't keel over. Not that you should suddenly move here. Hold on a second. Jillian wants to say hi."

Barney drove straight from Cal Poly to Doctor Taco and walked in at 11:00 P.M. I was thrilled to see him till I registered the expression on his face, which put me back in Rancho Cahuenga the day I spilled Sprite on his centrifuge.

I hadn't expected him to be mad—I'd told him on the phone a few times how slowly the lawsuit was going, and he hadn't seemed concerned—but the stare of concentration was a ray gun now. We sat at a table and he said, "I don't understand what happened here, Henry."

"I was offered a job," I said.

"A job?"

"At a publishing company." I told him the titles, which sounded ridiculous when I said them out loud.

"Is that what you want to do? People's hobbies?"

"The lawyer's still there," I said. "He's still doing the lawsuit. But it could be years before they have the trial."

"See, that's okay, Henry, because Mom and Dad are going to be alive for years, and they're going to need the money. You see how that works?"

"I screwed up college, Barney. I can't do what you can do."

"No, you're not doing what *you* can do. This was for you, Henry. The material in the experiment was you."

What a memory on this guy. I looked over at the phone. The Doctor Taco Hunger Hotline was for incoming orders, but employees were allowed to make calls for family emergencies, and this definitely was one. I could have walked over and left Rensselaer a "really sorry" on Dobey Publications' answering machine. Historically my threshold for Barney being mad at me was zero, and my stomach was killing me now, but I said, "I want to try this for a while."

Even Jillian patting the couch next to her couldn't explain what I was doing. It had to be that I'd finally found my town, a place that would demand no more of me than I could deliver, but how would you explain that to Barney, who could meet any demand you gave him out to the hundredth decimal place? He got up, went out to his car, and started it with a sound like an old photograph being torn down the middle.

The train was Gerald's idea. I had too much stuff to take on a plane and too little for a U-Haul, and if I slept sitting up in coach, the travel money from Dobey would cover it.

Mom had said on the phone that just because I was changing my mind didn't mean I couldn't change it back, or that I had to. Dad said I should do what I was interested in and not worry about him. Gerald said, "Stop feeling like shit," as we sat on a bench by the ticket kiosk and the train from L.A. rolled toward us. "Do we doubt for one minute what Buck Owens would do with a woman like this in the picture?"

"It's not just her," I said.

"Do we think those songs of his are just *songs*?"

"No."

"No. We're learning that, aren't we?"

The train stopped and we dragged my stuff over to it. Gerald had even advised me on what food to take: Pilot crackers, beef jerky, apples, and white cheese. That was what the forty-niners had brought to California, he said, and it was about time someone took it back.

3

at the second building I tried in Clayton, a chalk-green box called The Tradewinds, I rented an apartment with looming ceilings, light-sucking gold carpet, and an alley view. I unpacked, went shopping at a quart-beer grocery store, made a liverwurst and chutney sandwich, and slept on the floor, all in a dense new loneliness. In the morning I was at the *Kite Buggy* office an hour before anyone else.

When Suzanne came in she gave me a desk and an employee orientation packet containing a zero-tolerance drug policy and two pizza discount coupons. Rensselaer arrived a few minutes later, waved me over, and said, "Ever been to Glassell Park?"

Once, I said, when I'd gotten lost between Pasadena and downtown L.A. He opened a manila envelope and shook out some snapshots of six tough-looking Latin teenagers posing with two kite buggies in front of a graffiti-covered culvert. The guys wore wife-beaters, high-water khakis, and pompadours that looked like the Brancusi sculptures Gerald had stood me in front of at the L.A. Museum. The buggies were customized with chromed rails, pleated seats, and brass cutouts of the Virgin of Guadalupe.

"Low buggiers," I said.

"I love them," Rensselaer said, and pointed to a guy with HIJO DEL VIENTO tattooed on his shoulder. "Nacio Moreno. He wrote the letter." He read aloud from loopy red cursive on notebook paper. *"Let me tell you . . .* What's this word?"

"Ese," I said. "It means 'this.'"

"They call people 'this'? That's great. Hey, This." He poked me. *"Let me tell you,* ese, *the cops chase us every time we ride here, and we don't give a shit. Those beach boys come up here from Venice to ride and we send them back to their fucking beach. We think you have an outstanding magazine."* He put everything back in the envelope and handed it to me. "This is a story, *ese*. You must question these men closely."

I was on my way back to my desk when Jillian came in. "Henry 'Hank'!" she said. "Amazing. Where are you living?" I told her and she winced. "You should get your furniture at Massey's. Tell me when you go and I'll help you." She'd grown bangs, an unnecessary perfecting touch.

That night at the Tradewinds, I was making sardines when I heard a guy scream, "YOU SAID WE WERE HAVING SPAGHETTI!" loud enough to be coming from my oven. A woman yelled at him to stop yelling. He yelled, "I'M NOT EATING THAT! YOU FUCKING BITCH! YOU NEVER TELL THE TRUTH!"

I went into the hall, traced the yelling to the apartment across from mine, and went back inside. It went on for forty minutes before one of them slammed the door and pounded down the stairs.

When it started the next night I knocked on their door. It was opened by a woman in her forties with marsupial circles under her eyes, and dressed in the navy skirt and white blouse of a work uniform. Her son, sixteen and muscular, hung back and stared at me with Wanted-poster calm. Their place was blanketed with old newspapers and back issues of the low-impact enthusiast magazine *TV Guide*.

I introduced myself and asked if they could hold it down. The woman said, "We don't complain about you," and closed the door. A guy came out of an apartment two doors down, said, "He exposes himself, too," and went back inside. I ate my sardines, walked to the drug-and-discount store by the highway, and got stuck in a consumer warp where I couldn't find anything to buy but couldn't leave until I'd bought something, which turned out to be a purple towel.

I called Barney once a week, keeping him on the phone for three minutes that cost me $4.55 while I told him about my new life and he answered with short *Mm*s or silence. At work I took my associate editing seriously. My skills were modest, but a lot of the copy that came in was written by fifteen-year-olds and hard not to improve. I made frequent mistakes, though, getting names mixed up in captions or pushing the wrong button on the phone, saying, "Hello?" into Dobey's private calls and scaring his bookie.

Rensselaer said not to worry about it. "The economy runs on mistakes. You ever have a problem with an insurance company?" I said no. "But you've seen their big buildings," he said. "Every other floor is for making mistakes. The floors in between are for saying the mistakes are being straightened out."

I rationed the number of times a day I looked over at Jillian and the minutes I spent talking to her. After a few weeks she invited me to go with her and some friends to hear Ricky Skaggs play Paducah. The friends had all gone to college, most of them to the one in Clayton. Jeff, who raced kayaks and restored pinball machines, drove. I sat in the back of his Galaxie between Dina, a journeywoman plasterer, and Scott, a county computer administrator and upright bassist. Jillian introduced me as "Henry 'Hank' Bay," though I'd never used the nickname.

Dina asked where I was living. When I said the Tradewinds, Steve, who made artistic fireplace implements, said, "What for?" Dina flicked the back of his head and said, "That's real mature."

Megan, who sold dresses at Mode O'Day and sewed her own designs at night, said, "I'm going to Kenya in the fall for two weeks."

"Plush toy!" Jillian said, one of her terms of approval.

"I know," Megan said. "I'm learning Dahalo. It has the click consonant." She said a foreign phrase with two loud *pocks* in it. "That was 'Where can I buy fabric like you're wearing?'" Everyone tried it. Steve said, "When do the *pock* hyenas stop swarming?" and Scott said, "I will *pock* give you all my *pock* money for the antidote." I threw my jaw out.

Steve said he was being stiffed on some andirons he'd made for a movie producer and his wife. "Now I'm stuck with these stupid andirons with the little flute-playing Hopi guy on them. I have to send them to the houseware gallery in Chicago."

"What movies did he make?" Jillian said.

"I'm not sure," Steve said. "I think he did that one where the learning-disabled guy can talk to the dead."

"I'd love it if I could talk to them," Jeff said. "I always get nervous. Especially with the cute dead."

Jillian asked Dina if she knew a guy named Jack, who taught adult-ed bookbinding in Clayton. Dina said, "No, and don't fix me up with him."

"Me, either," Megan said.

"I called it first," Dina said.

"Lick rocks," Jillian said.

"She's always trying to fix people up for romantic bliss," Megan said. "She's terrible at it. Don't let her do it to you."

"I won't," I said.

The theater had a bar in the lobby, and all the friends drank Heilemans for an hour, especially Scott and Jeff. When the lights started blinking for the show, Jillian came over to them and said, "It's time."

"It's *time*," Scott said.

"Time to take control of your family's financial future," Jeff said.

"Time to decide if you actually like Elgar."

"And we can help, with our worldwide resources. Who are we?"

"Hell if we know."

"At this stage of the evening?"

"You should live the way we live now so long."

The friends seemed like sophisticates to me—that night, anyway—and I didn't talk much. When the show started I grabbed the seat next to Jillian's and smiled diligently at the music. In the fourth song, the let's-slow-things-down one, I put my hand on hers on the armrest. She gave mine a friendly squeeze and slipped hers away, but I didn't see anything going on between her and Scott, Steve, or Jeff, or between anyone else. Maybe the six friends had a ban on being more than friends, or maybe they'd already run through one another the first year of college.

I kept up the watch all summer, but saw nothing except a week of flirtation between Scott and Dina that was too ironic to go anywhere. I spent my evenings with all of them at Riddenhauer's Bar, trying to play pool and listening to Jillian say, "Lick rocks," when someone impugned her judgment or her car. It was a PG-13 imprecation that fit her perfectly, but she used it only with the five of them.

The answer to the boyfriend question came on a cold night in the fall, when we'd all gone to the movies. It was my first time alone with her and my first visit to her duplex, where she was lending me a book about the Swedish emigration to America. The place was a shrine to the friends, decorated with collages of group vacation photos, napkin caricatures, and notes they'd left under her windshield wipers.

She sat on the bed to look through the book before letting it go. I sat next to her and put my hand on her knee. She looked down at it and said, "Outside the clothes but below the waist."

"How do you mean?" I said.

"I miss the system," she said. "As soon as you grow up, it's supposed to be all or nothing. Who says you want to go all the way with everyone?"

"I don't want to with everyone," I said.

"See?" she said. "It was useful. You should be able to say, 'Here's someone who should be inside the clothes but above the waist,' or whatever." She lifted my hand like a derrick and put it on the bedspread. "How come you're not going to be a lawyer?"

I told her about Dad, Troup, discovery, and motions. She said, "Is this better?"

"I think so. Do you like working there?"

"It's okay." She paused. "You know, I lived with Steve for a year."

"I didn't know that."

She nodded. "It keeps trying to grow back. Do you like him?"

"Sure."

"Yeah. He's a fine young man. He'd do anything to be of help." She stood up, led me to the door, and said goodnight. Outside it was so cold and dry that I could hear dogs and car doors blocks away. I had three layers of clothes on, but I was from the desert and it was freezing here.

A week later, on the TV set at Riddenhauer's, a newscaster said that the bomber who called himself Freebird had blown up a lab that developed identification chips to be implanted under the skin of animals. "Sure, these are strictly for pets," he wrote in a communiqué to *The New York Times*. "Have you had a vaccination lately? A 'routine' blood test? Whose little pet are you?"

At work I interviewed Nacio Moreno, the low buggier, who said the L.A. kite buggiers feuded like surfers over the best riding spots. When I showed Rensselaer my interview with an African American buggier called Chief Boy R.D., he said, "Yeah, good, but I can't show that language to Arnold." I edited it so that a passage in which the Chief warned rivals away from his turf read, *"Some of these [rascals] are trying to [interfere with] our [activity] up," says the seasoned Compton buggier. "That [situation] is [messed] up. If they [interfere] with our [activity], we'll put a cap in their [actual] [body]. Go on, [disrupt] my [activity] up, [bad-hygiened] [rascal]."*

One day Dobey called me across the hall into his office, whose door said OWNER in the black-and-gold letters people stick on their mailboxes.

"Jim tells me you're doing this thing about the Spanish kids in L.A.," he said. I nodded. "That's good," he said. "Things get started out there. I just want us to be careful. He said there's some of this 'screw the police' stuff. We don't champion that." I said we wouldn't.

"Good," he said, and a few days later he took me to lunch at the Clayton Hofbrau, where no one else from work went, but several other Popeye-like guys did. "Do you think this is really going to be a sport at some point?" he said. "I mean, in the kinds of numbers like paintball?"

"It might," I said. "I mean, it could."

"Because the thinking was, all the other sports were taken. Look at the newsstand. You need a magazine just to go jogging."

"Here's how to tie your shoes," I said. He smiled and pointed at me. I felt a flush, happy and then annoyed at myself for being happy.

"What about long range?" he said. "Where do you see yourself?"

"I haven't thought too much about it," I said.

"You should. This business you're working for? Grew out of wedding invitations. School menus were a big piece of business." He paused. "I have trouble talking to Jim sometimes. I think he thinks all this is funny."

They'd had a few arguments in Dobey's office lately, their voices loud but indistinct from across the hall. "He works on it seriously," I said.

"That's good that you say that," Dobey said. "That's a good tact for you to take."

We went back to the office. As I passed Rensselaer's desk he smiled and said, "Count your change."

That night I walked in on Jillian and Steve in the back hall at Riddenhauer's. He was leaning on the wall, pulling her toward him, and she was saying, "This is how we get in trouble." He let go of her when he saw me. She said, "Hey, Henry," and pointed toward the room where the pool table was. "I've got losers."

A few days later, Rensselaer said, "Look at these," and dropped a handful of skateboarding magazines on my desk: *Thrasher, Transworld, Bow to No Man*. The stories inside were set in green type on orange background, and the photos of emancipated minors flying off handrails were spattered and solarized. The magazines offered not just a sport but an inverse world, where ramps and drained pools were the places of business, and the normal life squatting just off the page was the dangerous hobby. Sitcoms and Filofaxes, you take your life in your hands with that shit.

Half an hour later Rensselaer took the magazines back and went into Dobey's office. I heard their raised voices again. When Rensselaer returned he pointed at me and gestured across the hall.

"Have a seat," Dobey said when I entered his office. "This is what I mean, about Jim. He thinks this is the way to broaden the appeal." He held up the skateboarding magazines. "Let's hate all the regular people. Over-inked bullshit." He threw them in the garbage. "Remember we talked about where you see yourself going? That's where we are now. There's a chance here for you to step up."

So this was it: office politics, ruthless. Dobey wanted me to take over the magazine, but I couldn't do that to Rensselaer unless he'd had it here. Even if he had, was I ready? Maybe I was. I cleared my throat. "I think—"

"Have you looked at *Crochet Life* lately?" Dobey said.

"What?" I said.

"Cerise Lander does it. She could use some help. It's gotten a little stagnated. This is a year ago."

He handed me a magazine whose cover was split into four photos of crocheted throws muddied by the cereal-box press: a unicorn, a raccoon family, the letters saying LOVE from that painting, and Rip Van Winkle yawning awake. The cover line was EASY PLEASERS!

"Here's the most recent," he said. It looked like the first one, except that the throws showed a koala bear, a soapbox derby car, the eye-rolling angels of gift-wrap fame, and a leprechaun guarding his treasure chest. The line was DO-ABLE DAZZLERS! "You see what I'm saying?" Dobey said. "It's lost some snap."

Was this a test? A joke? If anything, I thought the koala bear had more snap than the unicorn.

"She's fine with someone coming in for a couple of months," Dobey said. "She's in Wellfleet, Michigan."

"I don't know anything about crocheting," I said.

"No. Well, you know. Rosey Grier. The Rams? Bobby Kennedy?" I had no idea what he was talking about, though I later found out it was needlepoint. "Eileen has your travel."

I went back and told Rensselaer what was happening. "Jesus," he said. "I can't believe I got you to quit school for this. I thought I was managing him." I said it was okay, but when I got to Rosey Grier and the unicorn, he said, "See, he's actually losing it. That's what I didn't count on."

Jillian came over and said, "Cerise is nice, but two months? God. When are you going?"

"Friday."

"I'll make you a kit," she said, and the night before I left we had dinner at the Thai restaurant on Stovall Street. It was the first time since the Swedish book night that I'd seen her without the friends. When she put down her menu she said, "Do you ever get this big feeling of well-being for no reason? Just really happy all of a sudden?"

"Yes," I said. "I think so. Like you go outside and everything looks perfect? I think I get that about twice a year for, like, twenty minutes. Is that the kind of thing?"

She nodded, but her look gave me the feeling I'd just blown it, that she spent whole seasons in that condition and that forty minutes a year was the record low score. She picked up a canvas knapsack from the seat next to her and handed it to me.

"Your kit," she said. Inside were three sweet potato mini-pies from the Lofton Street Bakery, a beer from Riddenhauer's, a George Jones CD, a novel about fly-fishing, and a topographic map of the area I was going to.

"Thanks," I said. "You went crazy."

"Not at all. It's the minimum of what you'll need." She opened the map and pointed to a whorl of elevation lines. "Megan and Steve and I camped up here. If you take this trail there's like fifteen waterfalls on the way."

"Do you go a lot?"

"As much as I can," she said. "Even if it's just over by Jonesboro in the Shawnee Forest. Sometimes just putting the big socks on gives me that feeling you were talking about. When people tell me their problems I want to say, 'Buy a pair of hiking shoes and call me when they're worn out.' Most of them would never have to call."

"I wondered about that."

"What?"

"When I met you," I said. "You were wearing that vest and the boots and everything. I was wondering if that was something you really did or, you know. A style."

"Lick rocks," she said, drawing herself up in the booth and

saying it with the same mock umbrage she used on the friends. I felt both anointed and doomed, as if I'd been grandfathered into those photo collages and stuck safely to construction paper, mugging at a bowling alley birthday party or making cowboy coffee in a national wilderness.

Later, though, when she was dropping me off and I already had the car door open, she said, "Henry?" I turned to face her and she was on me with a kiss that lasted twelve seconds and crossed the blood-brain barrier. When it was over I tried to do it again but she pulled back, shook her head, and said, "I don't know what that was. Call me when you get settled, okay?"

I went up to my apartment. It occurred to me that it couldn't have been Jillian who'd said, "Fuck you," to Rensselaer the first time he called me. She didn't talk like that. Maybe it was Suzanne.

I was almost at the ticket counter of the Clayton bus station when I realized that the clerk was the woman who lived across the hall from me, wearing makeup that made her look a little less spectral than she did at home. I stopped for a second but then continued to the window and said, "Hi, how are you?"

She said, "Can I help you?" as if she didn't recognize me.

I bought a round-trip ticket and asked, "How long is the return part good for?"

"One year from the date of purchase."

"Okay," I said. "Yeah, I might not be back too soon. I'm looking forward to getting away. You know, someplace quiet."

Now she looked at me like she knew exactly who I was and said, "That's nice, that you can get to do that," so that I had something to feel bad about for all seven hours of my bus trip to the least scenic part of Michigan.

• • •

Cerise Lander was in her fifties, a little stocky in a fleece top, stretch pants, and a space-helmet perm. She said, "Come in and excuse the mess," but her split-level house was spotless, with a La-Z-Boy, graduation pictures, squiggle-icing cookies, a thermostat set to seventy, and a dog scrabbling on the linoleum by the constantly spinning clothes dryer in the pantry. Her husband was a civil engineer.

Crochet Life had a small office in town, but Cerise did most of the work at the computer and yarn basket in her living room. "I've been talking to Arnold on the phone," she said, "but I'm not that clear on what he's asking for."

"I think it's mostly about keeping the snap going," I said. We looked at each other. "Maybe you could kind of walk me through what you've got coming up."

She showed me the next issue on her computer. I searched for flaws and said, "I wonder if the ladybug could be *doing* something." When I suggested adding a few more colors of yarn to the Weekend Wonder project, she asked if I'd ever tried crocheting, handed me some yarn and a hook, sat on the sofa with me, and showed me a basic stitch. In fifteen minutes I had a lumpy row, and a kind of calm was setting in.

Cerise took a half-finished throw with Monet water lilies on it out of the basket, sat down across from me, and started running off fast three-color rows. I tried to think of more suggestions for the magazine but it made me lose track of my stitches. Neither of us said anything until she asked if I'd like some lunch. Two hours had vanished, but I had eight rows I was pretty happy with.

I was surprised at how much I liked being in her house, as if I'd been briefly exiled from places like this and then repatriated. It was like a Klondike in Rancho Cahuenga, cost-effective rooms on a cul-de-sac. I'd fled all this a year ago, but after a few months at the Tradewinds, I couldn't get enough of Cerise's pocket doors and lazy Susans.

Over soup at the kitchen table she asked if I'd like to go to Belton, Ohio, to see a woman named Wendy Probst whose throws always got good reader response. "You'd just take some pictures of her new pieces and get any comments she has on them," Cerise said. "She and I can do the technical stuff later on. I still get letters asking for her Paddington Bear."

The next day I took a bus to Belton, a poor town with houses the same size as their satellite dishes spread out through thin woods. Wendy Probst lived in a red wooden house with a sagging flat roof, bandanna curtains, and a dirt yard inches deep in pine needles. When I knocked on the door, she opened it looking like I'd wakened her from a dream of falling. She was in her thirties, thin, in a worn yellow housedress, her breasts and hair going where they wanted. In her hands were a crochet hook and a nearly finished throw the size of a twin bed.

"Hello?" she said.

"Hi. Are you Wendy? I'm Henry Bay. From *Crochet Life.* Cerise talked to you?"

"Oh gosh. Yes. I'm sorry. Come in."

It was an enthusiast crime scene in there, with teetering piles of unfolded clothes, unopened mail, dishes, skillets, sketchbooks, shower caps, pets' leashes, and Midol bottles. Industrial-size balls of yarn, in twenty colors, were spread around the house like designer tumbleweed.

She put the throw on the couch. The crocheted picture showed an equipment yard full of pallets and forklifts. A man in a uniform shirt and ball cap was shooting a woman with a handgun, her blood spraying across the scene. Another man, on his knees, pleaded with the shooter as people ran away in the background. The detail was finer than anything I'd seen in Cerise's house or the magazine, but the style was blunt, the people's heads like swollen knees and their hands like sandbags.

"That was a workplace shooting last year at Belton Lumber Byproducts," she said. "I wasn't there, but I saw the coverage. Most of these things, I was there for."

I looked at the other throws lying around. They showed violence, sickness, arrests, and people weeping into pay phones.

"I don't know what happened," she said. "I was starting out to do some stuff for the crafts fair in Dundee. In Kentucky. I was going to make a geometric, but the first line across it came out crooked and I said That's how the ground looks out here. The horizon. That's how it started. I had a big bag of frozen drumettes in the house and I just kept going."

She bent over a pile of throws on the floor and flipped through them. "This is the kids from Washington Park kicking my nephew Danny's head on the curb. He had eighteen stitches. This is us waiting in the emergency room. This woman had a chest wound. This one is Danny after his bad reaction to the medication. This is a fistfight at my niece's First Communion. This is a dishonest lawyer."

She stood up. "I don't know what I was thinking. It's not like I can take these to the crafts fair. I'm sorry I got you all the way out here."

"No," I said. "I think Cerise will like these."

She looked at me like I was crazy. "Cerise will shit," she said.

I photographed them anyway. When I finished I said, "Can I get you anything? Some food? Do you want to go into town?"

"No thanks," she said. She'd picked up the workplace-shooting throw again. "I think I need to finish."

• • •

I walked out of her house and straight into one of those unearned euphorias Jillian and I had talked about. For some reason Belton looked beautiful now, with its doublewides and shot-up STOP signs, and a ripped page of arithmetic homework on Big Chief paper lying in a patch of dirty snow. I saw the ratty horizon from the crochets laid over the real one. When I spotted a pay phone I called Barney and said, "It's Henry."

He said, "Hi," but not "How are you?" a habit of his that usually started the first of several silences.

"I think I might be leaving my job," I said. I hadn't known it till I said it to him, but Dobey had me troubleshooting unicorns, Jillian thought our kiss was a freak accident, and that shaky yarn horizon was making the world look wider.

There was a pause. "Okay," Barney said. "I'm sorry it's not going well."

"I didn't say it's not going well. It's just going how it's going. There's a woman I don't think I'm getting anywhere with, either."

"Are you going back to college?"

"I don't know," I said. "Look, I know you're mad at me. I'm sorry about that. I just want to tell you what I'm doing."

"What are you doing?"

"I'm in front of a grocery store in Belton, Ohio. The sky is bright orange. It's pretty, but I don't think it's healthy. I think it's from a company called Belton Lumber Byproducts. What are you doing?"

"I was reading about nuclear division in strange cytoplasm."

"Okay." It was getting colder. "Do you remember when we went to the zoo in L.A.?"

"I remember we went there, yes," Barney said.

"Do you remember telling me what the animals' philosophy was?"

"Their philosophy? No."

"Yeah. You watched them all day, and then you said all the animals had the same philosophy. It was 'I think I'll go over here for a while.'"

Another pause. "How old were we?"

"I don't know," I said. "Young."

I took the bus back to Wellfleet, and in the morning I went to Cerise's house to show her the photos of Wendy's new throws. "This one is a social worker from the county," I said. "This one—"

"Oh my God."

"That's her friend's daughter. She was ten."

"Is she okay? Wendy?"

"I couldn't really tell."

"Well. We can send her a little money." She squinted at a picture. "How is she *doing* this? It's very fine yarn, but still."

"Is there something we can put in instead?"

She nodded. "I have some penguins I can move up."

That night Rensselaer called me at my motel and said he was quitting. I said, "How's Arnold taking it?"

"Really well. I said I'd stay long enough to finish the issue and he said to stay the fuck out of the building."

I told Rensselaer I'd been thinking of quitting too. "It's up to you," he said. "I think he's bringing a guy in from *Nine-Hole Golfer*. I feel bad about this, but, yeah, you might want to push on."

"Do you know where you're going?"

"A daily paper in Ellis. The, hold on, 'The Award-Nominated Voice of the Tri-County Valley.' I'll be doing state politics."

"That sounds good."

"Yeah. If you want, there's a guy I can talk to at *Ultra Running*. It's in Nevada."

The next day I told Cerise I was quitting and asked if I could leave her the negatives of Wendy Probst's throws and keep the prints. She said okay. I took a bus back to Clayton and walked into the office at 4:00 P.M. The receptionist looked alarmed and said, "Henry, you don't want to go—"

It was too late. Dobey came out of the inner office with a half-crumpled page proof in his hand and yelled, "You little *shit!* You have the nerve to come *back* here?"

"What?" I said. "Wait, what—"

He backed me toward the door, holding up the proof of the L.A. story. The noun *motherfucker* jumped out. I'd somehow put the unedited Chief Boy R.D. interview into type.

"This was on *plates*!" he said, backing me into the hall. "The *press* was turned on! The *truck* was waiting!"

"It was a mistake," I said. "On the computer. I sent the wrong—"

"I *know* what you did! Let's take what Arnold built up from printing eviction notices and piss it away! It'll be *funny*!"

"No. I'm sorry. It was—"

"I *live* here! I have to walk down the *street* here!"

I almost fell down the stairs, but I caught the railing and held on to it while he told me never to show my face there again. He did such a good job of yelling that he became the hectoring voice in my head for years to come—not Dad or Barney or Freddy Krueger, from my childhood, but the Popeye whose smeary invitations were the third choice of wedding planners even in Clayton.

When he finally went back to his office, I went outside and sat on a bus bench. Jillian found me there and said, "We would have caught it. He swooped in and read it first."

"Hi," I said.

"How long are you in town for?"

"I'm not sure yet. I have to find a job."

"You can stay at Megan's a few days. She's in Kenya."

We went to the bottomless-pasta place on Meader with the five friends, but I was too shaken by Dobey to eat, and it took Scott and Jeff to beat the house edge. Megan's apartment was filled with foreign fashion magazines and watercolors of her dress designs. I fed her cats, Housebrand and Co-Pay, and then opened the closet to hang up my jacket.

Masking-taped to the inside of the door were ten Polaroids of Jillian modeling clothes Megan had made. It was a designer's portfolio, ranging from benefit-dinner dresses to I'm-dinner lingerie. A lot of women, posing in the latter, would have looked down with a bashful grin or affected homicidal ennui like the pros, but Jillian's face, a clear sky, said, "Sex, I know. We're so lucky to have bodies that can do this." The pictures in the dresses said she didn't need a tertiary town at all, that she could move to New York or L.A. and be in charge there in a week. I got my camera out, took a picture of each picture, jerked off in the shower, got yelled at by Dobey for it, and tried to sleep.

Rensselaer called his friend at *Ultra Running* and faxed him my spring break and low buggier stories. They hired me at a lower salary than I'd been making at *Kite Buggy* but promised me first dibs on review shoes in my size.

The day before I left town I called Steve and asked him to

meet me for dinner at the Hotel Clayton. He said yes, though he sounded wary. I was a little nervous myself. We'd been avoiding each other since I'd walked in on him and Jillian at Riddenhauer's.

I spent the day dealing with U-Haul, U-Store-It, and Massey's Used Furniture, till I owned only what I'd brought to Clayton plus a purple towel and enough money to last till my first paycheck in Nevada. While Steve and I waited for our soup, I spread the photos of Wendy Probst's throws on the table.

"Wow," he said. "Are those knitted?"

"Crocheted," I said. "You sell your work in art galleries, right?"

"Houseware galleries. But I know those people, yeah."

I gave him the pictures and Wendy's phone number, and said the gallery people might have to explain to her why they were calling. Putting the photos in his pocket, he paused and said, "Is that what you wanted to see me about?"

"Yeah," I said. "I'm leaving town."

He nodded. "I'm looking at that myself."

An hour later I met Jillian outside the bus station and got her to go in and buy my ticket from my ex-neighbor. When she held it out to me, I pulled her in and kissed her. She pulled away and said, "Henry 'Hank,'" like I was full of zany surprises. I took a seat on the bus and watched her recede through the window.

I stayed at *Ultra Running* three months, then did ten weeks at *Row!* magazine, "The Coxswain That Comes in Your Mailbox," in Swint, Massachusetts, and moved on from there, associate-editing my way across the country. I never stayed anywhere long, and I was the civilian at every magazine I worked for. At *Ice Climbing* I was the only staff member who still had all ten toes, and at *Metal Detector Treasures* I was the only one without twenty rings on his fingers.

I kept calling Barney, and he kept being distant. The towns were small and slow, but they weren't Clayton. Maybe it had been the river air there, or the borrowed friends, or just the fact that it was my first real town, but I couldn't duplicate it any more than I could Jillian or Gerald. They all went in my loss column, along with Barney's blessing and the late-boyhood dream of saving Dad.

On the plus side, being in the enthusiasm business let me see people being happy, doing what their bumper stickers said they'd rather be doing, what they braked for. For a long time I was able to coast in the wake of that happiness. Winning the prize for biggest geode or scariest wipeout changed their faces, and I was there, writing down the shop talk of the work that's not for money. It was a country of fevers, and I only had to deal with the harmless ones.

4

A year after I left Clayton, Mom called to tell me that Barney was engaged to a woman he'd met at the University of Kansas. He had a grant there, folding proteins in his computer and researching stem cells.

"Her name's Deirdre," Mom said. "They're coming here next month. Maybe you could come then too."

I said yes and started looking for a Fun Fare. I was a little nervous about seeing Barney, but the conditions were probably as good as they were going to get. He and his girlfriend would be floating on sex and wedding plans, he'd want her to see what a model son and brother he was, and maybe she'd have a gentling effect on him. I pictured a cute Midwestern girl with a great laugh. With luck, she and I would be making affectionate fun of him before the weekend was over.

I landed in the afternoon and passed the Controlled Dynamics buildings on my way from the airport. An Internet startup was in there now, and the parking lot was full of cars on a Saturday, supposedly a buy sign for a company's stock. The Valleycrest Mall had come back to life too, but Dad was still working at the salad bar in Altadena. He was home alone when I got there, and we sat in the living room with beers and Cheese Nips.

"I do every aspect," he said. "I chop. I clean the sneeze guards. I'm physically dead afterward. You forget what that's like." He pressed himself back into his chair as if there'd never be enough sitting down. I thought of apologizing for leaving Troup, but I'd done that before and he'd waved it off. I let Sergio Mendes on the stereo fill the silence.

Barney and Deirdre arrived just as Mom got home from putting in fan palms at the Internet startup. Deirdre was pretty but sterner-looking than I'd imagined, with pale skin, long brown hair, a gray turtleneck, and a mossy-looking floor-length skirt. Barney had changed his style of clothes again, to scratchy forest colors and drawstrings, in line with hers. We shook hands, his new self clashing with the old foyer. He didn't smile at me but gave a little nod, as if the handshake needed certifying.

Mom squeezed Deirdre's hand and gave her a welcoming smile but said she needed a shower before she hugged anyone. She made an exception for Dad, though, and when they embraced I saw them locate the aches from the day's work and press closer together to ease them. They hadn't done that when he was corporate.

Mom came back from the shower in long pants and a shirt with buttons, dressy for her. Deirdre helped her with dinner and asked her about the succulents outside while Barney told Dad about his work, a tangle of biochemical talk. For a minute

I thought Dad was moved by the exciting things Barney was doing, but then I realized that what I saw on his face was nostalgia for being baffled by the scientists he'd managed.

We went into the dining alcove for quesadillas and a big bowl of work Dad had brought home. Barney passed it to me. When he'd left for college I was the family champ at reading him, but now I couldn't tell if the look he gave me over the bowl meant "It's your fault this is what Dad's doing" or just "Here's the salad. Try not to drop it."

Deirdre was an anthropology major specializing in folk myths and a mover in university causes—divestment, T.A. salaries, soy ink. She'd grown up in Kansas, and this was her first trip to California. "That was kind of scary, all that housing and stuff coming here from the airport," she said. "You can't believe there are enough people to fill it up."

"It's a crazy scale," Barney said. "You have to get away from here to realize it."

"All the people we went past were like, 'Look at my body, look at my car,'" Deirdre said.

"I always thought that was nice, when I came out here," Dad said. "It was like you have to have a car and a body anyway, so they might as well be colorful."

"Oh," Deirdre said. "That's kind of neat, when you see it that way. The ornamentation. Barney said you work at a salad place?"

"Just for now," Dad said.

"That sounds good, though. Making salads for people, and then you see the results of it right away."

"It's just temporary," Dad said. He was getting the transit look, and Mom jumped in, asking Barney and Deirdre how they'd met.

"A guy was lying down on my car," Barney said.

"They were protesting the stem cell work," Deirdre said. "A group called Fundament House."

"I was just standing there, but Deirdre came over and started talking to him."

"I just said, 'Okay, you're doing civil disobedience for what you believe in. Let's value that, but let's look at what's at stake here.' "

"She actually debated with him. I never—"

"No, you got into it too," Deirdre said. "When he said, 'Life is sacred,' you said, 'Exactly.' "

"I said one word."

"Yeah, but it was the right word."

Barney, loved, gave a little smile and shrug. Deirdre leaned her head on his shoulder and he kissed her hair. I'd always thought he would marry a fellow scientist, but she made sense. His work and her causes were going to fix the world. It didn't matter if their ideas went over ninety-nine out of a hundred heads, as long as their own heads stayed huddled together the way they were right now.

I wanted to have that with someone too, someone who'd come through the door like Deirdre and say, "Thanks, little California family, I'll take him from here." I hadn't met anyone since Jillian, but I hadn't looked much, either. At my recent jobs I'd spent most of my evenings at home. When your only tool is your ass, every problem looks like a couch.

I got up early the next day and took some work out to the patio. Barney was there with a stack of printouts and a scientific calculator.

"How's it going?" I said.

"Good," he said. "Hard."

"I really like Deirdre," I said.

He nodded. "I was spending all my time down at the cell level," he said, tapping his printout. "There wasn't that much I was interested in up here before I got involved with her. Now I kind of commute between the two. I'm down to like sixty hours a week in the lab."

"That's still a lot."

"That's the other thing about her. She understands why I'm there so much. This could end up helping with all kinds of problems. You could grow heart tissue. You could have people who can only move their eyes now getting up and walking around."

"That's great."

"If it works. First you have to run through all the methods that don't work. There are a lot of those." He rubbed his eyes. "Tell me where you work now?"

"Ice Climbing."

"What is that?"

I had a copy in my work bag. I handed it to him and he flipped through it, past the jargon, the ONE BADASS CRAMPON ads, and the beauty shots of climbers hanging off escarpments with the obligatory winter sunlight bouncing off the lens.

"People need a lot of stimulus now," he said. "Going to the park and throwing the football around doesn't cut it anymore."

"Not for some people, no."

"Do you go out and do this with them?"

"They gave me a lesson."

"How was that?"

"Okay. It was good." Especially getting back to safety. "I probably won't stay there that long."

He nodded. "I think I'm going to be in Kansas a while. I like the people I'm working with. We might be getting somewhere on spinal cord injuries. And Deirdre and I are going to start trying for a baby."

He closed the magazine and looked at the climber on the cover, a spinal cord injury waiting to happen, before handing it back to me. He hadn't brought up Dad and the sneeze guards, but waiting for it had put what felt like a weather front in my chest, and it was still there.

I put the *Ice Climbing* away and Barney went back to his calculator. He didn't stare at the backyard landscape anymore, so I did it for him.

5

I had my own America going, a huge room lined with doors. Behind each door was an enthusiasm, a noisy roomful of slang, spending, sanctioning bodies, factional intrigues, and Freddy Pasco–like stars who walked like gods in that room and like toner salesmen everywhere else. Most people went through only a few of those doors in their lives, but I crashed one wild party after another and came back for more.

There was always a reason to change jobs. The paychecks bounced or were so small they cleared, or the magazines merged, my career keeping pace with the golden age of cutbacks. If I didn't get along with someone I was always the one to leave. Why should an enthusiast go and a civilian stay? All those hang gliders, storm chasers, and battle reenactors had found a way to stop time that I hadn't, but I had a vocation watching them do it.

• • •

Dad got lucky on the escalator. Exploring the mall on his break from the salad bar, he spotted a Franklin Covey store that sold motivational books and time-management systems to the determined. He walked in, got talking with the manager, and a few visits later he was hired to work the floor.

The customers could tell he'd once fought his way to the middle, and he clicked right away. Soon he was giving store-sponsored seminars where people came to a hotel meeting room and took down what he said in action-item binders he'd sold them. He would mention that he'd once managed forty scientists, say "*Talk* about herding cats," and move another eight hundred dollars in product right there in the room. Barney softened up a little toward me on our phone calls, though it might not have been because of Dad's new job. Deirdre was pregnant.

The day Dad gave his first seminar I was working at *Country Ways* in Destination, Nebraska, editing a farmer's article about hip lock during calving. Around the passage *Think of this in lieu of how you would feel if someone were to put a couple of forceps on you and yank you straight out of the vulva. You would squeal with justification!*, I decided I needed coffee.

I took a chance, going over to the wood stove that heated the Editorial Department's half of the barn and shaking the enamel percolator. It didn't slosh, and there were witnesses, so I had to make a new pot. Country ways meant sustainable farming, energy independence, and colon health, but above all self-reliance.

I put on my coat, scarf, gloves, and galoshes, got a cup and a pail and walked out into the snow. When I'd arrived in the fall the air had been filled with the strong contradictory smells of cider, pigsties, alfalfa, baking, organic fertilizer, and thrip-fighting garlic. Now there was only the cold, which sprung my eyes and mouth open like I was hearing bad news over and over.

I went into the main house and stumbled to the pantry with my glasses fogged up. Someone had roasted coffee beans, saving me twenty minutes of fire-building and cranking. I filled the cup with them, pumped well-water into the pail, and went back outside. Crossing a tractor path, my boot broke through ice into mud and I almost lost the coffee beans.

Rudy, from Circulation, was smoking a cigarette in front of the barn. "Coffee," he said. "Good man. Is there milk?"

I nodded. "Jesse milked."

Irena, from Art, came out shivering in two sweaters and a watch cap pulled low. "Oh, Henry, you're great," she said. "Coffee. That's arduous. Rudy, can I have a cigarette?"

He gave her one. She lit it, took a drag, and said, "These are good."

"Thanks," Rudy said. "Yeah, you know what it was before? I was curing it too hot."

I went back inside, made coffee, finished calving, and started on worming. My computer ran out of solar at three and I had to pedal the bicycle generator for twenty minutes to get it back up.

On my way out after work I passed the ad sales guys having a sorrel wine happy hour. "Now, he was a man," one of them was saying. "He could sell two pages to a stranger at a cattle auction. I've seen him do it one time." They raised the jar at me, but I said no thanks. I had to attend a class outside.

My third day there, I'd gotten lost on the farm roads and come in late. Thad Anderson, who owned both the farm and the magazine, had responded by putting me in charge of the "Survive It Yourself" column, written by a retired forest ranger in Montana. Every Friday Thad gave a wilderness lesson to me and whoever else was interested. So far we'd covered edible weeds and learned how to improvise splints and poultices.

Tonight there were five of us. Thad shined his flashlight at the Big Dipper on a star map and said, "Somebody show me that in the sky." He was fifty and barrel shaped, in overalls, canvas coat, and Carl Perkins hair.

Rick, from Production, pointed at the sky. "Okay," Thad said. "You go up from those two stars on the edge of the cup, about five times as far as they are from each other, and there's the North Star. Everyone got it?"

I nodded, but I could never pick out constellations or understand how the ancient audience had convinced themselves they were up there. My mind was on dinner at the Indian taco place in Destination's two-block downtown, where it would be warm.

"Good," Thad said. "And that'll always be north." He drew a circle in the snow with his finger. "Say you want to go east. The star's north, so east is here." He poked a hole in the snow. "You start walking, and you keep checking on that star as you go, so you stay in one direction. Every year you hear about some guy that died half a mile from the trail, just going around in circles."

The cold eased up a few weeks later, and Thad gave a morning woodlore lesson wearing fleece instead of down. "It's false spring, but I'll take it," he said, showing Rudy and me how to find directions in the daytime by putting a wristwatch on the ground and sticking a twig into the dirt beside it.

"The stick makes a shadow so you can line up the sun with the hour hand," Thad said. "Halfway between the hands is south." I wrote it down, and when I looked up from my pad he met my eyes. "I'm afraid I've got some bad news here, Henry. We're going to have to let a few people go."

I nodded. I was used to layoffs, and as the last hired I'd be the first to leave.

"Haven't had the greatest circulation this year," Thad said. "Some years it starts shooting up in April, and by June you can't believe the size of it. It's from people in cities, thinking, 'What in God's name are we doing sitting here in traffic for five hours to go to the seashore? Oughta buy some land and put up a dome.'"

"Newsstand gets up to here," Rudy said, stretching his arm toward the sky. "This wasn't one of those years, though."

"Well, it's weather," Thad said. "Everything's weather."

I told them not to worry about it, and after lunch I went home to start calling around for work. Four days later I was in Trask, Oklahoma, shaking hands with Dean Laswell.

"Hell, did I go and hire you?" he greeted me. "Your résumé sounds like a man of experience, but you're a kid. You're from the kiddie brigade. You're a young kid."

He owned and edited *The Short Sheet*, a monthly for shortwave radio enthusiasts, and had written thirty-two books about medical breakthroughs being kept from the public, the hard science proving that all NASA missions were faked, and the unconstitutionality of child support. Laswell published the books himself and sold them by mail to conspiracy buffs and easily amused college kids. He was in his loud, hearty sixties and came to work every day in green corduroy pants and an ARMY sweatshirt. Like one of my professors at Los Nietos, he wore a full beard and no moustache, a look that Gerald said "puts the 'Amish' in 'squeamish.'" Everything in the office, down to the pencils, had STOLEN FROM DEAN LASWELL printed on it.

The first nine pages of every *Short Sheet* were devoted to Laswell's editorials, which mentioned shortwave only occasionally. They were illustrated with photos of Laswell trying to look pensive, taken by Perry the one-man art department, a scowling burnout whose previous credit was airbrushing T-shirts on the boardwalk in Virginia Beach.

Between the editorials and his books, Laswell wrote thirty pages a day. The shortwave radio was always on, its high-frequency squeals sawing at my brainstem as I fought it out with his spelling and punctuation.

A "new world order"? Laswell wrote. *Sorry, no joy. Try "invisible old order" and you're a-speak-a my language, pilgrims. All the agencies that have their greasy thumbs in this thing, from the Joint Chiefs on over to the Federal Reserve, are shot through with 33rd-degree Masons, straight up the chain of command—you could look it up. A secret handshake is one thing, campers. A secret stranglehold is a whole 'nother kettle of grouper.* His assistant, Cheryl, forty and pale, talked nonstop about recipes, the weather, and Brinkman's department store having some nice things but being way over in Crowder's Ridge, distracting me from the shortwave that distracted me from work.

Laswell got up every half hour to change the station, skipping past the Catalan Friendship Hour to the ranters in the clandestine part of the shortwave band. In a good week he pulled in Freemen, militias, survivalists, income-tax deniers, Holocaust deniers, moon-shot deniers, dollar-bill decipherers, and a lady who hated the Bureau of Weights and Measures. His favorite was a guy with a flat western accent and a colleague named Ernie, who either was off mike or didn't exist.

"Big news story, Ernie," the guy said one day. "This is all they're talking about. One of these white-coat boys was in his lab, somebody mailed him a little present, and the present blew up on him. Feebs thinks this guy Freebird did it, but there's a lot of these lone rangers out here, it could be—what, Ernie? Ernie thinks I'm talking about the guy that had Tonto. No, this—these are people, they're working on their own hook, okay? Not mixers. No one can tell on 'em 'cause nobody knows.

"But these white-coat boys, they're getting called to account now. They've been working on all these fun deals like cloning animals and tracking everyone's whereabouts, and the sheeple out there, they see that white coat, they don't ask any questions. That's science, okay; leave that alone. Only guy I ever see in a white coat's the doctor. You see that white coat, the rubber glove's not far behind, it's *right* behind. That's what *all* these boys are up to. Quit laughing, Ernie. This is serious business here."

I bought a newspaper on the way home. A mail bomb had been sent to a human genome sequencing lab, killing the lead computer programmer. The front-page photo of cratered lab benches and fried instruments looked like Barney's room at home after an airstrike on Rancho Cahuenga. Freebird was suspected, but there'd been no communiqué yet.

I went online, where Freebird was an industry. First I found the chat rooms where people said they agreed with his theories but deplored his methods, and then, with a sinking feeling of discovery, the ones where people said his methods were the part that rocked.

It wasn't just Freebird or the shortwave guy who hated the white-coat boys. There was one website after another about scientists playing God and enslaving the trusting sheeple. I thought of the kids at the science fair in Chicago, the ones Barney relaxed around, who got giggly talking about nonferrous magnets. They were guileless, a bunch of absentminded professors in waiting, the mildest crowd of enthusiasts I'd ever seen overrun a Marriott. Whose enemy could they be?

Someone's. The bright boys were concocting designer plagues, I read, cloning livers for rich drunks and heating up the climate so the usual bankers could snap up the failed farms. They needed a good shot to the head. They needed their names and home addresses listed online, with a line through the genome guy who'd gotten the bomb, a list that kept getting shut down till it moved to a server in a no-questions-ocracy where free speech was still for sale. Barney wasn't on the list, but was that Asian name the polypeptide girl from the science fair, or that Jewish one the Bronx Science guy, the kids we'd run down the stairwells with?

I had a hobby. I hated looking but I kept going back, night after night. Only a few people could have believed the doctrines on my screen, but how many did you need?

I called Barney. He said, "Yeah, we got a thing that said to verify packages before we open them. They had security guys at the last few conferences. I don't know what else you can do." I called the FBI, too, to ask if they were seeing what I was. The bored lady at the 800 number took down what I told her, but answered my questions by telling me what information they didn't give out until I felt like a bad pet named Sir.

Two weeks later I arrived for work at *The Short Sheet* and found Cheryl and Perry out in the hall looking at a padlocked door and a notice saying the premises had been secured by the Sheriff's Department for nonpayment of debts. Cheryl turned to me with tears in her eyes and said, "They've silenced him."

I hadn't realized she was a believer. I thought Perry would snort at her, but he nodded in solemn agreement. "Did he say who we should call if this happened?" Cheryl said.

I pictured a red phone ringing inside a hollow mountain, the secret headquarters of the crank command. I shook my head. "He said to just walk away," I said, with a gravity I didn't have to fake because I was out three weeks' pay.

I went home, called around, and found a job. A few days later I was packing up my apartment when the phone rang.

"Henry Bay?"

"Yes?"

"Mr. Bay, this is the fourth phone number we've called in our attempts to reach you. It seems you've been moving a great deal. That won't protect you from meeting your obligations, Mr. Bay. When we have a matter to collect on, we collect. What people like you don't seem to realize is that we are everywhere. Our agents forswear sleep."

"Gerald?" I said.

"You *flight* risk."

"Hey."

"*Hey*, baby."

"Where are you?"

"I'm in New York City. That was true about the fourth phone number, by the way."

"I know," I said. "And I'm moving again."

"When?"

"Sunday. To Albany, New York. I've got a job at *Martial Arts World*."

"Oh, that's wonderful. *Martial Arts World*. Now, have you hired professional movers to break your belongings?"

"I'm getting a U-Haul."

"And sir, you are aware that the vehicle may have higher clearance than you're accustomed to."

"I just need you to initial here and here."

"I'll have your contract and all that good stuff in just a minute," he said. "Don't you hate that? 'All that good stuff'? That's worse than 'puppy.' 'We'll have this puppy wrapped up by close of business today.' You want a hand with those boxes?"

"Seriously?"

"On a Sunday? In Albany? I'm all about helping, big boy. I'm all about helping with the boxes."

"That's great."

"That's another one. 'I'm all about.' Fucking horrible."

My new apartment was in a three-story building five blocks from the state capitol. I got there on Sunday afternoon, parked the U-Haul van, and waited for Gerald, who came speeding up the street in a two-year-old Lexus, braked hard to stop nose to nose with the van, got out laughing, and embraced me in the gutter. He'd dropped the ex-GI look for a blue blazer, white business shirt, and tropical-weight khakis, and he looked like he'd seen nothing but good luck and health since college.

He stepped back and assessed the building. "We'll need to go in that window," he said. "We can do block and tackle. I hate to bring in the crane unless it's completely necessary."

"The union comes into play," I said.

"Look at you!" he said. "*Martial Arts World*! They say Henry Bay knows the way of the Shaolin masters. They say he knows the way of fighting that is not fighting."

"Yeah, I'm great at the not fighting." I opened the back of the U-Haul. Gerald jumped in, hung his blazer on a hook, and picked up the back of a leather armchair I'd bought used in Massachusetts.

"Chair like this is indispensable," he said. "A man subjects himself for ten long hours, he comes home, he needs this chair.

'It's all going to greater metropolitan Hell out there, honey. I'm not talking about in the streets. *That* battle is *long* lost.'"

"'I'm talking about what at one time was a *business*,'" I said, taking the legs.

"'What we liked to think of as a certain set of *standards*,'" he said. "I say that to my woman every night. You need a chair like this to say that in."

"Who's your woman?" I said.

"Chloe," he said. "She's wonderful. You'd love each other. She'd leave me for you like that." We carried the chair inside. The little lobby was dim and mop-smelling, the brass mailboxes tarnished almost black. "She's in graduate school. City planning. One man to another? She has the largest student loans of any woman I've ever seen."

We took the chair upstairs on a groaning lattice-caged elevator. As I unlocked the apartment a guy came out of the one next door and said, "Hello, I'm Robert. Are you fellows moving in?"

"I am," I said. "I'm Henry Bay."

"Gerald Hauser. I'm just advising."

We shook hands with Robert, who was in his seventies, with two thick brown growths on his forehead and his pants up on his stomach under an old cardigan. "Glad to meet you," he said. "Now, are you in government?"

"No, I'm going to be working for a magazine," I said. "*Martial Arts World*."

"*Martial Arts*. No, we never sold that one. I was the concessionaire over here in the capitol building for many years. But that's the karate." I nodded. "There were times when I could have used that," he said.

Gerald said, "Someone told me that *karate* means 'the empty hand.' It's from the same root as *karaoke*. That's 'the empty orchestra.'"

"Empty orchestra," Robert said. "Oh, because it's just the music playing. That's good."

"Isn't that nice?" Gerald said.

"I went to one once," Robert said. "One of the lawmakers was retiring, so they had a big group and they asked me to come along. I wouldn't get up. They said Robert, Robert, but you couldn't get me up there."

"No, you don't want to do that," Gerald said. "If the orchestra's empty, that's their problem."

Robert smiled. "That's very good. Now, are you in that business also, the magazines?"

"No," Gerald said. "I buy and sell metal."

"Oh, boy," Robert said. "I had a car that I let them do that with. I took it out there and watched them pick it up with that machine and drop it on all these other old cars. All the way there I was thinking, This is terrific, I'll get a bus pass and to heck with this thing, but boy. I didn't think it would affect me, but it did."

"It was part of your life," I said.

"No, I wouldn't say that," Robert said. "Well, I don't want to hold you fellows up. I just wanted to welcome you. This is a good building. We don't have any of the lawmakers themselves, but there are a couple of gals downstairs that are legislative assistants. They serve as the front lines very often. Okay. Gerald and . . ."

"Henry," I said.

"Okay." He went back inside.

I'd found the apartment online. It was my usual, but with Gerald there the standard features—armchair ghosts on the walls, phone wires painted lumpily to the moldings—shone with sordidness. I hurried the move and we got into his car to go to dinner.

"Concessionaire," he said as he started the engine.

"The unique vocal stylings of the Concessionaires," I said.

"Yeah, they were unique. Do we know where we're going?"

"No. I thought we'd just look for something." We pulled out. "What kind of metal do you buy and sell?"

"Strategic," he said. "I play the palladium. Although gallium is more and more on my mind these days. They use that in your silicon chips. You can't make a karaoke machine without it."

We circled out from the dead downtown and finally found a brightly lit storefront restaurant with a neon sign in an alphabet I didn't recognize. There was one other customer, a woman eating a pink entrée and reading Richard North Patterson. The waiter, who could have been Indonesian or Inuit, brought menus. When he left I said quietly, "Do you know what cuisine this is?"

"No, and I live in New York," Gerald said.

The menus were in the same alphabet as the neon, with semi-translations: *Chicken pektânnu. Beef pektânnu.* We both ordered the chicken. "Spaetzle or taro with that?" the waiter said. We said taro.

"How's New York?" I said when he left.

"Well. You've been there, right?" Gerald said. I shook my head. "Wow. Well, you owe it to yourself. And they're ready for you. I moved there the day after I graduated; I gave them no lead time at all, and they were ready for me anyway. By my third day of walking to work I had my coffee guy, my bakery guy, and my fruit guy. The whole city runs on guys. It's like polytheism with immediate rewards.

"You know how your big cities are supposed to diminish people? You're supposed to feel small in the face of it? That's bullshit. You walk down the street in New York, you see all these sagas going on, you smell thirty smells in a block, and you *snowball*. These things are *added* unto you. If you want people to feel small, you have to put them in the suburbs. They drive those cars that look like dump trucks to make up for it. They put on weight so they won't blow away."

The food came, a greenish stew and chunks of steaming, soap-like vegetable. "Have you heard this music that's coming out now?" Gerald said.

"Probably not," I said.

"They've got a guy rapping, and then there are these little snatches of talking and like Arabic wailing going in and out. I didn't know what that was about till I moved there. Because two hundred years ago, you went for a walk and you heard the birds singing and you went home and wrote the *Pastorale*, right? But New York, you go outside, it's like a radio that gets every station at once, plus the bonus cursing-nanny channel. So you go home and write that." He jabbed at an air synthesizer, "'I was a, I was a, *what* is a, *you* were a,'" scratched a turntable, "*Wheersht wheersht*," and jabbed a key again, "'Kali *zulfon*, I was a.'

"But then you turn onto a desirable side street? And there are the birds! The birds haven't gone anywhere! There are trees with little rubber collars on them. There are doormen. There are gifted children. You want *Pastorale*? Your guy has some nice *Pastorale* today, no problem."

He was leaning back in his fiberglass chair, draping himself over it like a high-finance guy in an interview photo. I congratulated myself on having been right about his future, a gold rush with hipper minerals.

We ordered coffee. It came in jelly glasses with straws, and Gerald's had an umbrella. "So," he said, "the publishing game. I hear that's a sweet racket. I hear you boys talk into Dictaphone machines and drink Martini cocktails. I hear you get your collars made to order."

"It's all true," I said. "Actually, I don't think I'm getting anywhere."

"No? But you work with people who devote themselves to things, right?"

"Are you kidding?" I told him a few enthusiast stories, and every time I finished one he made me tell another. He couldn't get enough of people who got interested in something and looked around one day to see that the something was everything.

"I take all that back about New York," he said. "You don't need New York at all. That's wonderful, what you're doing."

"Why is it wonderful?" I said.

"To help people give themselves over? If you live in Japan, you see the monk with the begging bowl, you put something in there, because he's not just trying to get *his* parking validated. He's doing it for everyone. It's like, 'I have a tea guy, a rice guy, and a guy who touches the essence.' But Japan's got nothing on us. We don't just go in for things, we go in and never come out again. Skydiving. Model trains. Wars. Whatever's handy. And you're right in the middle of it. You should take some national pride."

"You saw my apartment, right? That's a bad apartment."

"No question. You're doing public interest work. You always wanted to. Don't worry about the apartment. Those things will come."

He dropped a twenty on the table and drove me back to my building. As we idled at the curb he handed me a business card and said, "Now, Henry, this card has my telephone number on it. Anything you hear that might help us solve this thing, day or night, I want you to call that number. You understand?"

"Take me with you," I said.

"Get your toiletries. You'll love it. They'll love you."

"Yeah. I'll come down and see you, though."

"I should fucking well hope so. We'll have a large time."

"Okay."

"That's another one," he said. "'A large time.' Don't you hate that?"

I said I did and went up to my apartment. I was too tired to unpack my sheets so I slept in the chair.

The job at *Martial Arts World* was okay except that I kept finding myself on the floor. Jerry Wing would say, "Henry, look at this layout a second," or Lisa Schneider would say, "Henry, quick question." I'd start walking with them, then feel a light pressure behind me and my weight lifting off, and then I'd be looking at the ceiling, amazed that I'd gone for it again. Bill Lam, the editor in chief, would say, "Dojo's down the hall, boys," being extra cool by not looking up from what he was doing.

I put off going to New York to see Gerald because *Martial Arts World* was understaffed and I worked on weekends. When we hired some new people, the weekends cleared up but the new people made me superfluous. I found a job at *Rock Hunter*, in Peking, Kentucky, and when I packed I put Gerald's card in with my pictures of Jillian.

6

In my ten years on the road I never got two hundred dollars ahead, and I ran up a long list of places I didn't need to see again. Evenings fell hard in those scraping-by towns. You could chart my lack of progress by the cars I drove: a Sidekick, an Escort, a Protégé, a Kadett, an Aspire, a Justy, and for six awful months a Flurry, one of the most entry-level cars ever made by a Big Three manufacturer.

The TV commercials for the Flurry had shown college-age kids, braless and Fugee-haired, silently laughing it up as they drove down a mercury vapor–lit expressway with Scottish techno on the soundtrack. In real life Flurry was a perfect name for the car because it weighed nothing and a gust of wind could move it over a lane and a half. There were two recalls after I bought it, one for its gossamer steering linkage and one for its Molotov gas tank. Mine was stolen twice, but viciously turned up a few blocks away both times. My model was the Hatchback GS, but if they'd called it the Associate Editor I wouldn't have argued.

I had the Flurry when I worked at *Spelunk*, in Silica, Missouri. For the first five weeks I managed to duck my caving lesson, but the day came when I had to get up at 4:00 A.M. and put on orange coveralls, Wellington boots, abseiling gloves, and a helmet with two headlamps and a chinstrap—all new items sent to the magazine for review. I looked like a guy in a ballet about a mining disaster.

Geoff Florian, the other associate editor, picked me up at five in the company Willys. "Morning, lad," he said as I got in. He had a lower-middle-class English accent, a little social grievance in every vowel. His skin was pink going on purple, his straw hair flyaway, his belly a placidly rising and falling dome. He was wearing the same outfit I was, but his had been in caves.

Years ago, in London, Geoff had written columns for the celebrity magazine *Hullo, Then!*, the travel magazine *Off You Go!* and the fashion magazine *Good on You!* Then he'd gotten caught up in some journalistic scandals, the fake Hitler diaries and the morphed Kiki Dee nude photos. He'd taken a long slide, passing through the Hollywood overseas press corps and two Yeti tabloids in Florida before bottoming out here.

"Sleep any?" he asked.

I pointed across the street at the Silica Tavern, home of the bottomless beer pitcher and a 1970s cover band whose patch-cord thunderclaps had trained me to dream fast. "They were racing their trucks all night," I said.

Geoff pulled out, shaking his head at the view of stubby black mountains under constant storm heads. "Never quite believe this is where I've come to," he said, smoking a Merit down past its logo and starting another with the Willys' ancient, spark-dripping lighter. "*Mmf.* I'll confess, though, Henry, there are times I feel it was waiting for me all along. Silica, Missouri, lying there so quiet I never heard it. 'We're ready when you are, Geoff. No, take your time, we brought something to read. What is it? An entire magazine about people who go about in caves. Oh, you laugh now. Laugh while you may, Geoff. We'll wait.'"

It started to rain as we got onto the state highway and kept it up most of the way. Twenty miles out of Silica, Geoff said, "Possibility of our being sold, by the bye. Nothing confirmed, but you want to keep your feelers out."

"Really?" I said. "Who would buy it?"

"Company in California. San Jose. That's in the Silicon Valley, isn't it? Modern marvels. Fit all the world's wisdom in a handy suppository. Off you go!" He flicked a finger. "Any rate, that's where they are. Outfit called Clean Page. Plan is to buy every enthusiast title on the rack, sell the ads from one shop, and own the trade shows as well. Maximize efficiency, like Henry Ford. Rivet number two-eighty-three, day upon day, it's all I know and my father before me. Downsizers, naturally. Find ourselves in Miami, covering the hound dog races."

In the afternoon we got off the highway west of St. Louis, followed a two-lane road into low scrub-covered hills, parked under a pin oak, and put on backpacks full of ropes and gear. It had stopped raining and the air smelled like metal. Geoff checked a map and found the cave entrance, a five-foot crack in a hillside half hidden by trees. The cave was prized for its tight passages, icy mud storms, and swarming bats.

We lit our carbide lamps and stepped from the muggy world into a cool hallway of rock just tall enough to stand in. "Nice phreatic passage," Geoff said. He'd been an amateur caver in England, "just mucking about at Swildons Hole and Easegill. Into the hollow and get the damp on you. Sexual, I don't doubt."

To me it felt more like walking around inside an eggplant. Half a mile in, Geoff yanked me back at the last second from a thirty-foot hole and shined his lamp down a metal rope ladder bolted to the rock. "Thoughtful of someone," he said. "Won't be needing the descenders."

At the bottom of the ladder we walked down another corridor, this one with a stream in the middle of it. Geoff pointed out cave pearls, calcite straws, and degenerate-eyed fish. When I got my head stuck in a tight passage, he barked at me to relax till I scraped free. Just past the squeeze, we came into a room-like chamber twenty feet across.

Geoff turned in a slow arc, his headlight illuminating a bedroll, sealed food containers, aluminum dishes, a hibachi, and a milk crate full of folded clothes.

"Dweller," he said.

I shined my lamp around too. There were clothes soaking in a washtub by a pool of water, and a pair of tan pants hanging from a clothesline attached to the walls with pitons. Beside the bedroll were worn paperbacks of *Centennial* and *Shogun* and a magazine called *Wet and Ready*, from an old heritage of enthusiast titles.

"Current," I said.

Geoff nodded. "Shame no one's home. Readers love it. Living the dream." We started back the way we'd come. "See it in England now and then, front page of the *Sun*—THE NEW TROGLODYTES! Filthy little face peering out at the camera, mental as anything, of course—"

He stopped suddenly, and I looked up from the cave floor to see a guy pointing a handgun at us. We threw our hands up, yelling, "Hello! Sorry! We're sorry!"

The guy was in his thirties, a little beefy in twill pants, a white business shirt half-soaked with sweat, a small backpack, and a caving helmet. "Who are you?" he said in a Missouri twang.

"Very sorry," Geoff said. "Let's be calm. We must have given you a start. We were—"

"I *said*, Who are you?"

"Right. Sorry. I'm Geoffrey Florian and this is Henry Bay. We're with *Spelunk* magazine. About caves?"

"I don't think I've seen it," the guy said.

"Not important," Geoff said.

My voice shaky, I said, "We can just—"

"I don't suppose you'd like to talk to us," Geoff said. "A short interview?" The guy's eyes narrowed. "It's just that our readers are always interested in people who've actually made their homes in caves. Or we can be on our way and sorry for the interruption. Entirely up to you."

"It's up to me? The guy with the gun? Amazing." He lowered it, though, and thought for a minute. "You can't put my name in there. Or where this is."

"No, no," Geoff said. "Complete discretion." I had no idea where he was getting his calm from. Either the Kiki Dee thing had battle-hardened him or Silica had gotten him past caring.

The guy thought some more, then nodded us back to the room we'd found. When we got in there he put his gun and backpack on the floor, scooped water from the pool, drank, and sat down on a rock.

The three headlamps brought the light up to winter gloom, and I could see a drawing that covered most of one wall. It had the plain dark lines of an Altamira mammoth but it was some kind of flow chart, ovals and rectangles with names in them. Some of the names had been crossed out. I wondered if they were serial murder victims.

"Sir—" Geoff said.

"Larry," the guy said.

"Larry. It's good to meet you, Larry." He took a tape recorder out of his pack and held it up. "I could use this or it's perfectly fine not to." Larry shrugged. "That's very kind. Thank you," Geoff said, and pressed Record. "So, to jump in, then, ah, how long have you lived here?"

"Few months," Larry said. He squirted lighter fluid on the coals in the hibachi and lit them.

"Have you done any mapping of these caves?" Geoff said. "Or animal counts?"

"Nope. I bet that would be real engrossing, though."

"So, in general, then, what would you say led you to, uh, live here?"

"What led me. Yeah." He stared at the fire for a minute, shook his head, and turned to us. "How much do you guys know about market research?"

We looked at each other. "Not that much," I said.

"Yeah, well, that's what led me here. Market research. Working at a company in St. Louis. We broke the population down into groups and found out everything about them. What they bought, what they wore, what they watched, what they drank, how they talked. We started out with all the old classifications, like Sustainers and Achievers and I Am Me's, and then we broke them *way* down. We had eighty subgroups. Nobody's Homies, Dior Christians, Home Despots, Shaft in Golf Pants. The energy just to think up the names would power a small city. But the data were beautiful. The ad agencies? Political parties? Wanted to marry us.

"I did interviews. I ran focus groups. These women would come in to talk about hair extensions, or diet shakes . . ." He trailed off, studying the fire's shadows on the cave wall.

"It's harder to hit on women now than it's ever been before," he said finally. "I don't have the numbers in front of me, but it is. You almost have to be from the same little tribe they are, and like I say, there are eighty. You can have a conversation, but you both know nothing's going to happen, because she's a Guyless in Prada and you're a Keg with Legs."

The flames had died down and the coals were glowing. He opened a food canister and put some lumps of raw meat on the grill. "But I *knew* these women," he said. "From the research. I knew how to talk to them. I don't mean the ones that came in for the groups. I was strict about that. Fairly strict. But I'd see other ones out there that were just like them. I knew their psychographics. I knew which commercials made them mist up. I knew where they lived and I knew where their kids went to school."

He plucked a piece of meat off the grill, waved it around to cool it, and ate. "The first time was at the mall. Naturally. My wife is shopping and I wander off and I see this kiosk girl. I see that little hand working the jewelry pliers, the little tank top and the four pony tails . . ." He looked at Geoff. "Tell me you never wanted kiosk. But you didn't attempt it, right?

"I look at her and I think, 'Yeah, you're an Emulator, aren't you? I can see your apartment from here. It's bad but it's near water, your desk calendar's got angels on it, you splurge on underwear, you listen to K-101 regardless of what city you live in, and you're taking a class, screenwriting, songwriting, greeting card writing. You've got half a dozen start-your-own-business ideas, but people are unfair. They screw over your dreams, but you don't give up. You're upward-aspiring. Guess what I'm aspiring up.'

"Emulator sex. Boy." He shook his head. "It's like a movie where they're overacting, but that's what's great about it. The curtains are blowing in and out and there's screaming.

Afterwards she goes to get beers and she goes, 'You stay right there, you.'" He pressed a playful finger, covered with charred fat, to an invisible nose. "Just poignant, because you both know you're going to have to talk her down at some point.

"I'd never done anything like this. My wife was only my third sex partner. But I had the *keys* now. I'd see a Tightie Whitey in a sweater set and I'd be like, Guess who's getting into *that* gated community." He saw Geoff look down. "Am I offending you? Is this a little coarse? I'm sorry. I live in a cave, okay? Wolves are raised by *me*."

"Right, no, I—"

"I got kiosk, I got arthouse, I got sales conference. They were stashing the kid at phonics. They were flying in an hour early and meeting me at Embassy Suites. The clothes were *sailing* off. So many opening nights. And it's only opening night once, right? And you do not get jaded. I don't know who propounded that shit. My heart was going louder every time. Like, look at this, I'm getting it *again*! I escaped from all my troubles. Actually, I didn't *have* any troubles, going in, but I escaped from the troubles I was making for myself by escaping. Or maybe I escaped from how we're all going to escape for real one day. That's what they say about sex, right? Like I needed to know what they say.

"So naturally I fucked it up. I just had to have a Sustainer. That's the group where they're just getting by. Crisis to crisis. Heavy users of paycheck advance stores. This was some seriously forbidden-assed fruit. Sustainer sex is a crisis in itself. You feel like an asthma inhaler.

"Week five, she comes to the house." He sighed. "We were having people over, some Peaked in Colleges my wife, Kelly, peaked in college with, but that was no barrier to entry, right? Dolores, the Sustainer, comes in sobbing. She'd confessed to her husband and she prayed that Kelly could forgive her someday although she'd never forgive herself, and so on. So forget the marriage. I had zero money. I'd been out here and seen this cave . . ."

Geoff said, "You lost your job, then? For using the information?"

"No, I still work there. But every dime goes to her. And I'd kind of drained out our savings. There were some trucks."

"Sorry, trucks?"

"I bought a few women pickup trucks. To get things going."

"Ah." Geoff paused. "I'd thought it was just by talking to them."

"Wake up, cave boy," Larry said. "You'll be late for school. The bus is down by the Millers' house."

"Right," Geoff said.

"It's knowing who would *want* a truck."

"No, of course."

I cleared my throat and said, "Do you think living in a cave has influenced the way you look at life?"

"Yeah," Larry said. "I mean, if you look at the manhood signifiers that are available out there? Like watching football? That's supposed to be manly because *I'm* not knocking into anyone, but these little millionaire men are knocking into each other *for* me, and they have to douche with steroids to do it, but I scream at the TV set, and somehow that's manly of me. But a cave? *Mm*-hm. Like at work. I never even tried to advance before, and now I'm going for department head." He pointed at the names on the wall. "That's everyone that stands between me and the job. Some of them don't anymore. Out-politicked. That's a cave thing. You're not finished hunting till you paint it on there." He nodded at me. "Why don't you come in there with me tomorrow and see? Tell people you're interviewing me for a business magazine."

Geoff said, "Right, I don't imagine you tell people where you live."

"Sure, I do," Larry said. "I ridicule someone's presentation so bad they have to go in the bathroom for half an hour, and people go, 'Okay, wow, well, you really had some questions there.' I go, 'Hey, sorry. You know, I live in a cave.'"

"What do they say?"

"They laugh." He did a joyless office chuckle, nailing it, so you could see a file folder clutched nervously to sweatered breasts. "Ah ha ha ha." He shook his head. "That Larry."

Geoff killed a Merit in three drags as we walked back to the Willys to roll out our sleeping bags. "Not really a *cave* story, is it?" he said. "I'll drop you and him at his office tomorrow, go back down and find some insects to photograph, if he hasn't eaten them all."

In the morning we drove Larry to an office park of one-story stucco buildings on landscaped rolling hills. He looked around as the Willys idled and said, "Perimeter check. That's a nice thing about caves. You don't see a lot of the irate-husband demographic down there."

He converted his backpack to a soft briefcase as we walked to his building. "What's the deal with you and the English guy?" he said, watching Geoff drive away.

"How do you mean?" I said.

"Who's got the better title?"

"Neither. We're both associate editor."

"Yeah? He acts like he's over you. Who's going to move up? Who's going away in a cutback? You're not thinking about that, are you? He is."

"I don't think there's anything like that going on."

"I know you don't. I'm three questions away from knowing your subgroup. If I had to guess right now I'd say you're an Oil Case."

"What's that?"

"It means you have a car that causes you to buy oil by the case, and everything else pretty much flows from that. The Oil Case doesn't go for what he wants. The Oil Case thinks things will work out on their own. While they don't, the Oil Case crams our nation's landfills with empty cans of forty-weight."

The atrium lobby of his building had a juice bar, a newsstand, and a dry cleaner. In the open-plan offices beyond it, people in business-casual clothes strolled purposefully around with tall coffees and bound reports. We passed a daycare center full of toddlers, a gym with people on Stairmasters, and an indirectly lit cafeteria with three-dollar Chinese chicken salads. On the walls were paintings I could tell were good. Larry saw me looking around and said, "Fucking rest home."

He had a private office, third from the corner. His assistant, a ninety-pound guy my age with a soul patch and a phone headset, sat at a desk outside it. "Anything?" Larry asked him.

"Friedman wrote an e-mail," the assistant said, "saying we should focus more on packaged-goods business."

"You're saying Friedman walked out in front of a bus?" Larry said. "You're saying Friedman ritually disemboweled himself? The poor blighter."

"I know," the assistant said. "Total blighter." He handed Larry some phone messages.

"You see how he hands me the messages?" Larry said to me. "You could learn to do that, right?" The assistant made threatening kissing noises at me like a Pachuco in a prison movie.

Larry and I went into his office. There were no decorations, and only two pieces of paper on his desk. The window framed a green rise with three birch trees on it. Larry threw most of the phone messages away. The intercom buzzed and his assistant said, "Stan's out here."

"Good," Larry said, and pointed at me like "You're on." I pushed Record on the tape recorder as a guy about Larry's age came in.

"But what you've done, really," I said, "is to reinvent how these groups are seen."

"Yes," Larry said. "I had input from other people here, but yes. Stan, this is Henry."

"I'm from *Fast Company,*" I lied. "We're doing a story on Larry."

"Really?" Stan said. "That's great." He looked like he'd been shot.

"What's up?" Larry asked Stan.

"Uh, nothing. You guys are into it. I'll get you later."

He left. After a few minutes I went out into the open plan. Stan was at a coffee station that had French roast and Power-Bars. "How's it going?" he said as I poured a cup.

"Good," I said.

"Great. Yeah, I was just curious, how did you guys kind of hone in on Larry?"

"Sometimes someone's name keeps coming up," I said. "My editor said let's not be the second place to do him."

I was surprised at myself. Larry was no one to me, and Stan wasn't my enemy, but I was more than willing to do this office karaoke. It was the building, I realized, with its subsidized salads and uninsulting paintings, a building that would look with pity on *Spelunk*'s two-room office and all the similar dungeons I'd worked in. I would die without ever working someplace like this, but at least I could participate in the cave painting. I could help draw a line through Stan here. I put a heat sleeve on my coffee, pointed the stupid "Later" finger at him, and went back to Larry's office.

At ten there was a focus group, and Larry and I sat in the control booth with two of his colleagues. Across the one-way mirror, six pink-collar workers talked about mid-priced cosmetics over doughnuts and Sunny Delight. The facilitator let them spend the first few minutes saying how great this place was, how they'd never get their kids to leave the daycare room and they guessed they'd just have to move in.

"Sustainer humor," Larry said, staring through the mirror. When I caught his eye, he nodded at the glass and said, "In the yellow," and I realized I'd been looking at her, too. When I got back to Silica I called Jillian for the first time in over a year.

She was friendly, as always, and when she heard where I was living she invited me to drive over and see her the following Sunday. For the rest of the week I pictured the two of us walking around downtown Clayton, the streets steaming after a morning rain. We kissed on the corner by the tackle store and she said, "God, look at us, and I'm ever modest." Then we were back at her apartment, and Megan had let her keep the clothes from the Polaroids.

Someone takes a trip overseas and brings you a fifty-something banknote as a souvenir. The familiar aspects of money (denominations, serial numbers) crash into the strange ones (pink scrollwork, a purple dictator), so that you're holding an object out of last night's dream.

That's how it felt to come back to Clayton after six years away. My accurate memories collided with the ones I'd scrambled and the few actual changes on Lofton Street, where the steam I'd been picturing curled up from the pavement to be blown away by the Flurry's grille.

I'd driven seven hours, stopping once for gas and twice for oil, and it was late afternoon when I got to Jillian's. She opened the door in her usual jeans and denim shirt, pointy new boots and turquoise jewelry. Summer had darkened her freckles and put highlights on her bangs. "Henry 'Hank'!" she said, and hugged me. "This is so cool. Come in."

"You look great," I said. "Your place looks great."

"Well, thank you. I don't think it's any different. Oh, this is new." It was a photo collage of herself, Scott, and Dina posing by camping gear and twisted trees. "Joshua Tree Monument. We went last fall. It was amazing."

"Did you get to Bakersfield?"

"No. I was crestfallen. Scott had to come back and work. Let me get my junk and we'll go somewhere."

We drove toward the river in her Jetta. "You left at the right time," she said. "Arnold finally figured out there was no money in *Kite Buggy* and he folded it. He keeps trying new ones. I'm working on *Rug Hooking* and *Stick Fighting* now." She paused. "Steve moved to Chicago."

"How come?"

"Nearness to the galleries. Plus I finally drove him nuts." She downshifted, her shoulder flexing under the denim, as she turned onto a riverside street and parked by a sandy path.

We walked by the river as the sun went down. "Do you realize where Jim Rensselaer is now?" Jillian said. "The Washington bureau of the *Kansas City Star*. It's hilarious. He goes to cocktail parties on Embassy Row."

"That's great," I said, and stopped walking. "That time we went to the Thai restaurant and you kissed me afterward. Do you remember that?"

"Of course."

"What was that about?"

"It's when a man and a lady like each other very much."

"Did you?"

"Yes," she said. "You know that."

"No I don't."

"Well, I did."

"Me, too," I said.

She started walking again. "I mean, it's not like I planned it. You know those things where they give the spiders all different drugs and they try to make their spider webs and the webs are hopelessly screwed up? That's what my plans are like."

"Okay," I said.

"I don't know, Henry, it's . . . if you sleep with people you don't care about, you don't feel so springtime fresh afterward, and if you sleep with people you do care about, it's like, how do you steer this thing?"

"Maybe you don't."

"I *definitely* don't. That's what I'm saying." She stopped walking and took my hand as the sunset blazed over the fine hairs on her neck. "You're making me do the part I can't do," she said.

"I can't, either," I said. "We could build on that."

"Build on that? Henry, you're a bigger spider on drugs than I am."

"No, I'm not," I said. "Why do you think I drove up here?"

I put my hand behind her head and tried to kiss her. She pulled away so sharply that I felt like some kind of abuser. For a minute we looked at each other as if we were on opposite sides of the river.

"I don't think we better," she said. "I'm sorry. I don't think we can."

"Should I still call you?"

"Of course. And I still want to see Bakersfield." The change of subject steadied her voice. "Look at *their* personal lives. And yet they soldier on."

"Who soldiers on?"

"Buck and Merle and everyone. I think that's why I look up to them." The copper gleams from the river were blinding. As I turned back toward the car she touched my arm and said, "Everyone liked you here."

It took me all night to drive back. The Flurry's radio was working for once and I got an all-news station from Jefferson City. A family planning researcher in Maryland, heating up soup while his wife and kids slept, had been shot through his kitchen window. The authorities had no leads. When I got back to Silica the band with the patch-cord problems was singing, "Brandy, you're a fine girl." I only got a few hours' sleep, but I was glad I had a job to go to in the morning.

Except that I didn't. *Spelunk* had been bought by Clean Page, the company in San Jose, as Geoff predicted. Larry was right too: Geoff survived the transition and I didn't.

I went home and started calling around. Laura O'Connor, the art director of *Row!* when I worked there, said she thought a friend of hers named Agnes in the Hudson River Valley might want help with *Cozy, The Magazine of Tea*.

"Tea like you drink?" I said. "Like at Chinese restaurants?"

"It's better tea than that," Laura said. "But yes."

Two hours later, at the biggest newsstand in St. Louis, I read the want ads in *Editor and Publisher*. All the job openings required a knowledge of news, politics, or the kind of sports that people leave their homes to watch. I put it back and moved on to the enthusiast titles. The Clean Page logo, a smugly meaningless swoosh, was on every sixth one.

I bought a copy of *Cozy* and took it home. It had photos of chintz-filled tearooms and people walking around Kenya with baskets on their heads, and a list of places you could call to book a six-hour Japanese tea ceremony. It didn't seem any crazier than anyplace else I'd worked, and I called them in the morning.

7

"Cozy. This is Agnes," the woman who answered the phone said. I'd expected an old lady's blown-speaker voice, but hers was strong. I told her how I'd heard about the job opening. "Oh, good," she said. "How's Laura, is she painting?"

"Part time," I said.

"And you're an editor?"

"Yes. I could send you my résumé, or—"

"No, no, that's okay. Do you want to come out here?"

I said I'd drive up, and she gave me directions from Philadelphia on. It took a while because she threw in stops for hero sandwiches, apple cake, waterfalls, a motel with Magic Fingers, and a Russian Orthodox church. "I'm just giving you highlights," she said. "You'll probably find a whole other set of things. Just call us when you're close."

I followed her directions through scrapyards outside New

York City and onto a green highway, where I glimpsed the river's palisades between beeches and maples. In her town, streets of old cottages crabbed their way up the steep riverbank and met in six-way intersections. I found her mailbox at midday on a two-lane road outside of town. Fifty yards up the driveway was a turnout with a GUEST PARKING sign and a wastebasket full of cane umbrellas.

I parked and walked from there. The woods gave way to a garden full of hot flower smells, and then a garage with an old Jeep, an old Vespa, and walls hung with garden tools and snow shovels. The house was a two-story bungalow, climbed by flowering vines, with long eaves and a wraparound porch.

Agnes was sitting in a sling chair on a sundeck that stuck out from the porch. She smiled and said, "Henry?" as I came up the steps. She was in her forties, with brown hair to her shoulders and a reddish round face, and wore a rose leotard, blue jeans, and wrecked purple espadrilles. On a table beside her were an iron teapot, a ceramic bowl of tea, a cordless phone, and a marble-covered schoolkid's notebook. "Tea?"

I said yes, though it seemed hot for it, and followed her into the house. I paused in the living room because it looked familiar, and then realized that it looked like the room I'd pictured when I first met Jillian, with a sunlit wooden floor, white walls, and plain maple wainscoting. "Richard?" Agnes called upstairs. "Henry's here."

In the kitchen were six more iron teapots, a dozen ceramic bowls, and thirty steel canisters with labels like DARJEELING SILVER TIPS and TAI PING MONKEY KING. "There's Kemun in the samovar," Agnes said, pointing to a big silver urn with an eagle on top of it, "but we can do anything you see there."

"No, that sounds good," I said.

"Oh, it is. I haven't left it alone all day."

She filled a teapot from the samovar and waved at the bowls. As I picked a blue-and-gray one with red streaks, a tall thin man walked in carrying another teapot and a black glazed bowl. He was Agnes's age, in blue jeans, bare feet, and a white button-down shirt with a teaspoon in the pocket. He said, "I'm Richard," and we shook hands.

Agnes pointed to my bowl and said, "Henry went right for the rising moon."

"Henry's no fool," Richard said. "I'm making the big move to Nilgiri here." He put a kettle on, opened a canister, smelled the tea, said a silent "Oh," and spooned some into a teapot. "So you're friends with Laura?"

"We used to work together," I said.

"She seems very fond of you, Henry," Agnes said.

"Ah," Richard said.

"Laura did a series of paintings that were all scenes from jokes people told her," Agnes said. "It was wonderful. Everyone does their dreams, but these were much weirder."

Richard made his tea and we all backed through the screen door with our hands full. Agnes went back to her sling chair, I took a plastic one, and Richard carefully placed an Adirondack in a thin slice of sunshine between the shadows of a tree and a porch post.

"He loves to get that one ray of sunshine on his bowl," Agnes said.

"I do," he said. "Look at that. It's like it's splitting the atom." He took the teaspoon from his pocket, filled it with tea, and slurped it loudly.

"You do that for the oxygen," Agnes said. I tried to slurp mine. "What do you think of that?"

"It's good," I said. It was like Chinese restaurant tea with three extra flavors and a gag reflex.

They asked about my previous jobs. I told them about *The Short Sheet*, with Laswell writing anti-Mason editorials and the paranoia pouring out of the radio.

"We should get some angry things like that in the magazine," Richard said. "Tea is actually very violent and bloody. The Opium Wars were about tea. The English were getting their tea from China but they couldn't pay for it because they didn't have anything the Chinese wanted, so they brought in opium. Guys were lying around in opium dens, and the Chinese said, 'What are you doing? You're turning our people into junkies.'

"But the *reason* the English did that was they were junkies too. All those ships burning up and guys in great naval uniforms getting shot in the face, that was all about the fifteen seconds when the civil servant has the first sip of tea and he goes, '*There* we are, few hours to go, nothing a chap can't handle.' They had a whole war over that fifteen seconds. Because otherwise, the civil servant, never mind, you know, the hapless guy that *picks* the tea, they weren't going to make it."

"To even think about the hapless guy that picks the tea," Agnes said, "you need the very finest in hapless-guy-picked tea." She drank. "We should be careful. We're going to turn Henry off on the whole thing."

"No, no," I said. I did have reservations, though. It wasn't that the magazine was about something I couldn't believe there was a whole magazine about. That described most of my previous jobs. At those jobs, though, we were usually a week behind and panicking. "Is this kind of an off day here?" I said.

"We don't have off days, Henry," Richard said. "That's how it is when you have your own business." They both laughed. "You mean when do we work?"

"No, I just—"

"Have you seen the magazine?"

I nodded.

"That seems to be what people want. That isn't so hard. If people wanted something great, we'd be running around and yelling."

"God damn it!" Agnes said experimentally.

"We're fucked. We're *fucked!*" Richard said. "That's fun."

"No, but we run around and yell sometimes," Agnes said. "Like the thing a few years ago. We have a feature every month, pictures of tearooms, because a lot of our readers are these ladies—"

"Let me get it," Richard said, and went inside.

"We found this guy who's a caterer-slash-florist in Mississippi," Agnes said, "in an area where that's about the only thing a gay guy can do, and he was supposed to take the pictures that month. We sent him some antique teapots, and he was going to give a party and shoot the teapots with people—"

Richard returned with a manila folder. "The deadline comes and goes," he said, "and the pictures aren't coming, and we keep calling him—"

"—not realizing that he's an alcoholic and he's gone into a complete—"

"—just shitfaced—"

"—implosion, but he sounded great on the phone. He'd say, 'I'm just waiting on this cake, there's this woman in,' you know, Dred Scott County—"

"Because they know now that alcoholism is genetic," Richard said, "and apparently the gene for alcoholism and the gene for sounding good on the phone are right next to each other. And then finally the pictures come." He opened the folder and handed me an eight-by-ten print. "The best thing is this macaroni salad," he said. "It's not from a deli—"

"It's not even from a deli *department*—"

"It's like from the refrigerator case in the liquor store, and it's still in the shape from the plastic container, he didn't even take a fork and—"

"—with this radioactive color from the mayonnaise being left out—"

"—and I'm staring at these things, and I realize, these are Slim Jims—"

"But the *people* are what's—"

"We think he found the people at the liquor store in the middle of the night and put hats on them. As long as he's there buying the salad—"

"This poor woman—"

"—acute alcohol poisoning, but the hat makes all the—"

"So we had no backup, and it's getting dark out, and we realize we're going to have to disguise our living room as one of these places—"

"—three A.M. and we're baking scones and waking up all the women we know up here and making them dress like—"

"—and it hits us that we're just reliving what he did twenty-four hours earlier," Agnes said. "And at that point you just feel for him. I mean living there, and he's like their pet, but really having to toe the line—"

"—and the possibility of his getting stomped by other segments of the community is always there," Richard said. "I would drink."

He poured more tea and opened a back issue of *Cozy* to a two-page photo of their living room. The furniture had been covered in vertigo fabric and the tables were crowded with teapots, cozies, fancy tableware, and pastries, their glazes liquid in the faked streaming-in sunlight. Women held teacups and mimed gala-planning conversation in hats with wildlife on them. I wasn't the market but I could see how someone, say Cerise Lander, would feel a perfect welcome. The picture was credited to the guy in Mississippi.

We talked and drank tea all afternoon, rotating from kitchen to bathroom to deck. Sometime after my sixth cup I realized I'd been staring into the garden for twenty minutes. I discovered that focusing on one spot and then another, a flower to a leaf to a branch, felt like flying. I wondered why I'd worried about Richard and Agnes not working, and why I ever worried about time at all. There was plenty. Bees and butterflies, slow in the sun, drank from the flowers as we laughed about ice climbers and tea traders. At six Agnes said, "Is anyone hungry?"

Richard went inside while I followed Agnes to the vegetable garden and helped her pick lettuce, tomatoes, corn, and onions. When we went in, Richard had water boiling and was getting ready to grill fish. I cleaned the corn while Agnes made a salad.

"So, Henry," Richard said over dinner, "are you in?"

"No, we have to agree on money," Agnes said.

"Oh, right. We haven't really hired anyone before. What was the last place paying you?" I told him. "Thirty a week more?"

I said yes. Alice opened her notebook and wrote, "CONTRACT," in decorative letters with a fountain pen. "I'm saying either party can terminate at any time," she said, "and when you leave, we'll give you some extra money and a suit. Like getting out of jail."

"I should find a place to stay," I said.

"A friend of ours in town has a room over her garage," Agnes said. "Janice. You'd have privacy and a basketball thing. Should I call her?"

I said yes and we went back to eating. I hadn't stopped for

lunch on the way there. I had seconds of everything and three glasses of iced Lapsang Souchong.

It was eight thirty, just cooling down, when I parked on Janice's street. She lived in the flats by the tracks, ten blocks below the Fourth of July–looking town center with its gazebos and clock tower. There were no sidewalks down here, just small houses with fading shingles and blistered siding. Some kids were running under a sprinkler on a weedy lawn and a teenager cruised by on his bike, advancing a tennis ball with a hockey stick.

The garage next to Janice's house had a second story with a peaked roof and a dormer window. I climbed the back stairs and found a key under the flowerpot she'd told Agnes about.

The room was a stoop-ceilinged oven, its air a sour concentrate of old wood and fabric. There were scorch marks around the electric outlets on the dirty walls. Sallow bedclothes were folded on a steel cot's thin mattress. There was a hot plate, a mini refrigerator, and a bookcase full of Zane Grey, *Your Erroneous Zones*, and other discards from the house. On the cot was a handwritten note:

Welcome Henry!

This room has always been a special place to me, a place to think and dream. I hope you enjoy it!

Please be careful as far as using the electric things, if you use more than two at once the wiring acts weird! If you're using the hot plate, ONLY use the hot plate, no other electric things. Using overhead light and fan at the same time is usually alright.

Please keep showers short *so floor doesn't leak. We are working on this one (grin)!*

I know Agnes explained the arrangements to you as far as rent, but if you have any questions, you can come over and knock until about 9PM at night.

Janice

In the shower I heard the water drip through the lumpy caulk and into the garage as soon as I turned it on. I made up the cot and tried to sleep but spent most of the night getting up to go to the bathroom and then lying awake, wondering what I was doing at this job. Three hots and a cot, yes, but this actually *was* a cot. Barney had a wife, a house, two kids now, and a job doing things so scientific they made Controlled Dynamics look like a pottery class, while I was working for people whose hearts opened like parachutes for gay caterer-slash-florists but who'd packed me off to Janice's hell garage without a second thought. Sleep wouldn't come, and at 3:00 A.M. I realized it was the tea, that my sweats and insomnia were blowback from my fit of contentment on the porch twelve hours earlier.

My urine foamed in the rusty toilet, a bubble bath of exploited-Asian bile. Richard and Agnes just wanted someone to get high with, like Rensselaer, who'd traded Freddy Pasco for Orrin Hatch and left me holding the tertiary bag. I pictured a news photo of Rensselaer and a senator in overcoats on the Capitol steps, leaning their heads together, the senator chopping the air for emphasis while Rensselaer took notes. Then I saw it on the front page of the *Clayton Herald*, and Dobey picking it up in his driveway and looking like he'd been punched, and finally I got a few hours' sleep.

• • •

I woke up at eight with a suicide headache. On the way to my car I saw a klepto wire running from the base of a public lamppost to the back of Janice's garage.

I stopped at a 7-Eleven for a bear claw and a Daily Pak of vitamin pills, a product I remembered to buy about every six months. There were eight different pills, making me feel like the dying millionaire who summons the private eye. Please excuse these vials, sir. *Kaff kaff.* My children are vultures. I considered buying a quart cup of Silex coffee and bringing it to work as a subtle act of rebellion, but the smell made my stomach flare up. I bought a canned milkshake instead and drank it while looking at the magazine rack's awesome abs, monster hot rods, and rampant Clean Page swooshes.

Agnes was gardening when I got there. "Good morning," she said. "Tea?" There were teapots and bowls sitting on a retaining wall. I gave in and drank some, and half my headache went away. "How was Janice's?"

"Okay," I said.

"Don't stay there if it isn't good. I've only seen it from the outside. I like how it's up in the trees, though. Does it feel like a tree house?"

I thought about it, and there had been some trees. "Kind of. Yeah."

Richard came down the gravel path wheeling a cart with six potted plants on it. He said, "Hey, Henry," and told Agnes, "I'm going to put these in over there."

I drank more tea and said, "Should I help you with that?"

"Sure, if you feel like it," he said. "We should start on the magazine soon."

As we dug holes, Richard asked about Janice's place and I told him about the electricity. "Yeah, worthless Herbert rigged all that up," he said. "She's got a restraining order on Herbert. He dislocated her shoulder."

We worked in the garden all morning, spreading gravel on a balding path, working soil amendment into a vegetable bed, and turning over a hundred pounds of fissioning compost. At ten we switched to iced Oolong, and at noon Agnes's phone rang while she was pruning roses. She took it off her belt and said, "*Cozy.* This is Agnes. . . . Hi, how are you? Give me one second and I'll bring that up on here." She smiled at me as her imaginary computer found the data. "Here we go. I show you having half a page through January. . . . Sure, let me just—" She talked as if she were writing it down: "New . . . invoice . . . for Fran. Got it. You, too." She rang off and said, "I guess we should do some work."

We made eggplant sandwiches for lunch and ate them on the deck. I had thorn gouges, a sunburn, and arms of throbbing rubber. The garden looked beautiful in a different way now, a map of temporary victories. Agnes made phone calls, Richard did layouts on his laptop, and I cleaned up "From the Strainer," the front of the book. I had to ask a lot of questions, but they were happy to answer them, especially when the answer involved making me taste another tea.

That night I knocked on Janice's door. She opened it, smiled, and said, "Hi. Are you Henry?" She was in her thirties, short on chin but otherwise nice-looking.

"Yes," I said. "Hi. I was wondering, I was thinking of moving a few things around up there and maybe painting a little, but I wanted to ask you first."

"Sure," she said. "That's fine."

I'd left the dormer window open in the morning and the

room was cooler this time. I didn't actually know what I was planning to do to the place, or why. I'd lived in a lot of bad apartments by then, but it had never occurred to me to improve one.

The next day we were tasting Indian teas on the porch when an old wood-trimmed Country Squire station wagon pulled up. The driver got out first, a guy my age in a western shirt. Then the passenger door opened and a thin man in his forties emerged, with curly hair, a creased wary face, black jeans, old boots, and a close-fitting black jacket over a seersucker shirt. I blinked, thinking it couldn't be who I thought it was, as Agnes said, "Tom, hi."

I had eleven Tom Foley CDs back in my room. There'd been a time, after my last visit with Jillian, when I'd listened to nothing but the long songs from his fever-dream period, in which characters from old movies and American history, plus half the cast of the Bible, yelled cryptically at one another while doom and redemption slugged it out in the background. These songs were interpreted exhaustively in music magazines and on the Web pages of self-proclaimed "Foley-ologists." When interviewed, Foley said things like "I'm just watching certain movies take place. Then I go out in the lobby by the popcorn stand, tear down the poster for next week's attraction, turn it over, and write down what I just saw. Then I sing whatever it says on there."

A couple of years before I came to *Cozy*, though, he'd abruptly started releasing bafflingly straightforward songs about the pleasures of walking around woods and towns, watching streams go by over stones, and going home to fix lunch. The reactions in the music magazines had ranged from "his deepest riddles yet" to "full frontal lobotomy." I liked music, and one of the few things I'd ever known better than to do was to work at a music magazine.

He came up the porch steps. I shook his hand and managed to say my name. He shoulder-hugged Richard and Agnes and introduced the guy in the western shirt as James. Richard said, "You guys are just in time for some south Darjeeling."

I went to the kitchen to get bowls for them. When I came back everyone but James was sitting down. Foley was in the chair where the sun split the atom. I held a bowl out to James, who said, "Oh, no thanks."

Richard, pouring, said, "What you're going to taste here is changing weather. Where this tea is grown, the frost happens at only the highest altitudes on the ten coldest nights of the year. By noon the temperature is tropical. It's that change that produces the flavor."

"Change in the weather," Foley said. He tasted the tea, closed his eyes, slowly lowered the cup, opened his eyes, and said, "Richard, that's . . . *hoo*."

Richard laughed. "You might notice a note of eucalyptus," he said. "The eucalyptus trees actually spread their molecules through the soil to the tea bushes."

Foley said, "Have you been there? Where they grow this?"

Agnes nodded and said, "In India. The most beautiful mornings. There are tigers and elephants walking through the tea bushes."

Foley took another sip and said, "Yeah, I think there's a note of elephant in there too." Everyone laughed. He drank again. "No, that's great tea. You know what that does, Richard?" He put a finger to his temple. "It makes you twice as right here." Richard nodded. I drank more, trying to see what Foley was talking about.

"I was over there in India one time," he said. "I had quite an unusual experience. I was reading this book on my way there—" He frowned. "James, have I got anything to read tonight?"

"I don't think so," James said.

"Can you go into the local town here and get something?"

"What kind of thing?"

"I don't know, James. Disused poetry. Reckless true criminals."

"I've been reading something wonderful," Agnes said. "*The March of Folly.* Military history. The Trojan War and the Boston Tea Party are both in there."

"Get that," Foley said. "And anything else they have like that."

James got his keys out and said to me, "You want to show me where it is?"

It could have been the fact that I'd gone to get the bowls, or just the underling gas I gave off. I wanted to stay and listen to Foley, but I got in the car.

In town James bought *The March of Folly* and eight other books. On the way back I said, "That story Tom was starting to tell sounded interesting. About India."

"They lost his luggage," James said.

"Oh," I said. "Has he been interested in tea for a while?"

"Couple years. Since he stopped everything else. Except incense. You should hear people talk about different kinds of incense for an hour and a half sometime. Jesus Christ."

I was still hoping to hear the end of Foley's India story, but when we got back he was saying, "What kind of gas mileage does that car of yours get, Richard?"

"I'm not sure," Richard said. "Twenty-five?"

"That's pretty good gas mileage," Foley said. "This Country

Squire here gets terrible mileage. I think about trading it in sometimes."

"But the wood and everything," Agnes said.

"That's not real wood. I just keep it for the name. The Country Squire. The country squire checks his tires."

"There you go," Richard said.

"We may be present for something here," Agnes said.

"Naah," Foley said, and stood up. "We should get going, James."

He picked up a few bags of tea from the table, hugged Agnes, shook hands with Richard, nodded at me, and got into the car with James. When they were gone, Richard said, "He seems good."

"Pretty good," Agnes said. I asked her how they knew him. She said, "Oh, we all lived in New York at the same time."

There was company almost every day, including tea traders and importers who drank twelve cups of *matcha* or yerba maté a day and walked around six inches off the ground, speaking in giggles and sighs. Foley was the only visitor I'd heard of, but there were others I should have, artists, musicians, and writers. Old Volvos and taxis from the train station came up the driveway all week long, especially on Friday nights. Some guests drank tea, while others brought liquor even when they came for breakfast.

These people came to get away from their work, but that was impossible. They'd talk for forty-five minutes about what they were doing, and then say, "I guess I can't really talk about it." A musician came up one Friday, excited about a new song cycle he was composing. "It's unbelievable," he said. "I work on it for twelve hours and then I go stand in the street and just feel my brain growing." Two weeks later he came back, fell into a chair, put his head in his hands, and said, "It's okay. It's okay. It's this fucking song cycle." Their work kept them sleepless for days, sucked them into rival camps, and caused them to wake up divorced and leave things on the subway. They made all the other enthusiasts I'd met look like rank beginners.

Some of them lived in a reverse world, where hit movies and TV shows were esoteric. One night a woman who translated Spanish fiction said, "Yes, there's one now, I don't know what it's called, but there's a group of cops and they let them say 'asshole.'"

"*NYPD Blue*," a sculptor said.

"That's terrific that you know that," the translator said.

"That's not terrific. I have it on when I'm welding. It's not like it's something you have to go to Bern and study."

"It is to me," the translator said. "*The Blue P.D.* That's wonderful."

Work on *Cozy* fell into gaps between gardening, cooking, and the ongoing party. Sometimes, close to deadline, the visitors would help. An article on doilies was illustrated by a photo of a ballerina from Beacon wearing two of them as a bra. A New York poet slipped the phrase "an unmistakable hint of cirrus clouds passing over Melina Mercouri's head" into a review of some Harmutty Assam tea.

On a Friday night in September, with warm rain outside and a crowd growing in the living room, Richard welcomed a carload of people at the screen door: the sculptor, the ballerina, the guy who'd taken her picture, and a woman I hadn't seen before. She was in her thirties and skinny, in red pants, black Keds, and a black sweater, with an "unconventionally" pretty face, the kind they didn't usually put in movies until the seventies, although those little disproportions must have been making people horny for centuries beforehand. Richard said, "Hey," when he saw her, a soft exclamation. She hugged him, folded her umbrella, shook my hand, and said, "Hi, I'm Carol."

"This is Henry," Richard said. "He does the magazine with us. Carol plays saxophone. How's it going?"

"Good," she said. "I'm doing some things at the Difficult Listening Festival. You should come."

"Yeah, we should get down there," Richard said, as Agnes came over. She and Carol said hello to each other with measured smiles.

I remembered I'd left a fax unsent, went upstairs to the office, and found the song cycle guy lying on the floor, his eyes closed, a half-full rocks glass on his chest. Classical music, a solo piano, played on the bookshelf stereo. He heard me come in, opened his eyes, and said, "Richard Goode. He says, 'Look, I can get you in the room with Bach, and the two of you work it out.' Not many people can make that offer." He closed his eyes again. I listened to the music for a few minutes and went back downstairs.

A Japanese American guy who taught the tea ceremony in New York had arrived, and there were a few conversations going on in the living room. *See, but there's a straight line from the teahouse in Japan to the tearoom in America, She was living with some people in a house in Tangiers, Oh I know who you are, because you have all these stories about the Japanese leaders coming to the teahouse and bowing through the low doorway, I'm trying to lose a pound,* everyone talking but Agnes, *and who are the leaders in the Biggest Little City in America type of town,* I saw Clayton's stunted skyline, *is it the idiot nephew mayor? You'd better hope not,* Richard took a sip of Carol's wine, *No, it's the ladies, You can go down to the marketplace and buy opium, the hospital and the museum would go broke if the ladies didn't put on a,* Carol looked at Agnes but Agnes didn't look back, *the one perfect morning glory in Kyoto or the big vomit flower arrangement in Atlanta somewhere, it's the same deal.* I'd tried to hear the guy leaving me in the room with Bach, like I'd tried to be twice as right there when Foley talked about it, but I didn't know how. I'd had poor skills at my other jobs too, but this time it seemed to matter. *The tea ceremony, though; I could never do all that inching around.* That was Carol, inching toward Richard to demonstrate.

Two hours later, when people had left, Richard and Agnes were upstairs and I was in the kitchen washing teacups and glasses. Richard's voice cut through the running water: "It was six fucking years ago." A door slammed. "Seven years."

I had acid stomach. I didn't need my missed years of college to know that this was supposed to be like Mom and Dad having a fight, but there was something else. When Richard and Agnes worked for hours in the garden, or brewed tea like they were sending up the space shuttle, the end product was supposed to be a kind of equilibrium, and if they could have it, then others could too, but where was it now?

I almost slipped out before Richard got downstairs, but I had to rinse my hands. He said, "Henry, hey. Are you cleaning up? You don't have to clean up." He gestured upstairs, shook his head, and said, "It's fine."

I followed him into the living room and we sat down. "Is this weird for you?" he said.

"Is what weird?"

"All these people in and out of here. I realized, I haven't thought about it from your point of view." He picked up a glass I hadn't gotten to, examined the half-inch of amber liquid in it, and put it down. "Or just the way we do things here. That could easily be weird."

I reminded him about the other places I'd worked. "So, really, no place is weird for you," he said.

"I was going to say everyplace is."

He thought about that and said, "See you Monday?"

"Sure," I said.

The next morning I got up early, made a thermos of Genmaicha, and drove to Poughkeepsie. At Color Tile I bought caulk, Caulk-Be-Gone, mildew remover, a putty knife, a breathing mask, a spreader, and an instruction book. At Sherwin-Williams I got white paint, blue tape, turpentine, brushes, scrapers, stirrers, rollers, a pan, and a hat. At the Goodwill store I got rid of the books from the bookcase and bought a wooden plant stand like the one in Richard and Agnes's living room. Theirs had a ceramic urn on it, sitting on a piece of fringed fabric. I bought a blue pillowcase and a green glass canning jar.

On Sunday I put Caulk-Be-Gone on the nine ugly layers that worthless Herbert had applied in the golden days before Janice's restraining order. I let it soak for hours while I scraped paint off the walls, but the caulk wouldn't be gone. I bent under the slanting shower wall, hacking at it with the putty knife, and stuck myself twice. At 7:00 P.M. I got the last of it out, applied the mildew remover, spilled some of it where I'd stuck myself, screamed, washed it, went out for sandwich ingredients, and barked at the grocery cashier. When I put the new caulk on, my hands were shaking and my back was lit up with pain. My one layer looked worse than all of Herbert's and there was no reason to think it would leak any less. All I wanted was a shower, but I couldn't take one till the caulk dried at 4:00 A.M. I lay down for a minute and passed out till morning. When I got to work, Richard and Agnes were on the deck drinking Dragonwell and laughing.

• • •

One hot Saturday I washed my sheets in the bathroom sink and hung them on the clothesline in Janice's backyard. I started to go back upstairs but then turned around to stare at them. It was their least dingy moment of the week, but that wasn't what stopped me. They were a movie screen for the sunlight, pregnant with rest, making a sine wave out of the breeze from the river. By the time I stopped looking they were halfway dry.

I was making Rice-A-Roni on the hot plate one evening when Janice knocked on the door. "I was just curious to see what you've done up here," she said. "If it's a good time."

I said yes. She came in and shielded her eyes as though there were glare coming through the window, which was strange because the sun was on the other side of the sky. "That's bright," she said. "Do you mind if I close this?" She pulled the curtains, looked around, and said, "Wow, you've done a lot."

A car pulled up outside and its door slammed. Then there was pounding on Janice's front door and a guy's voice yelling, "Janice! Hey! Janice!"

"The white paint looks so much cleaner," she said.

"Open the fucking door, Janice!"

The pounding stopped, replaced by footsteps coming our way. She said, "Could I use your bathroom?"

"Uh, yeah," I said. "What should I—"

She grabbed my hand, looked me in the eye with apology and panic for a third of a second, went into the bathroom, and closed the door just as the footsteps reached the top of the stairs.

I opened the door. The guy was tall, in jeans and a green

canvas shirt. I said, "Hello?" trying to sound like I thought he was selling something.

"Is Janice here?"

"No, I'm sorry," I said. "This is the rental unit. I'm the tenant." You steal electricity. You beat up women. I mean, I once kind of *pushed* a woman a few times, and I've yelled, you know, but Jesus. And what's up with that shirt? Ranger McSquirrel? Folks, if we'll all be quiet for a minute, we can hear the mating cry of the Battering Throwback. It should sound like, 'Janice, Janice, I'm so sorry. Are you okay? I don't know what comes over me sometimes. I can't believe I would ever do something like that to you. I must have some crazy shit inside me.' *Crazy* is subjective, but *shit* I think we can all get together on.

"I can give her a message," I said.

"No, that's okay. I'll try back." You do that, Romeo. Try back sometime when I'm making Rice-A-Roni with the lights on and this whole illegal unit goes up like a Presto Log. He was turning to leave when there was a soft *clank* from the bathroom, Janice managing to bump into something.

He started toward it, but before I knew what I was doing I was blocking the doorway, meeting his eyes but trying to keep my expression plain. I wondered what my shoulder would feel like dislocated.

The weird thing was that I'd always been happy to quit my jobs at the first sign of conflict. The weirder thing was that, looking into Herbert's eyes, my second greatest desire was to talk to him, in a friendly way, about caulk. Yeah, I wanted to say, I tried putting some on there myself. It's the angle, isn't it? Getting yourself in there; and you're tall, so it must have been a real tiger cage. Wouldn't you think they could formulate it so you could control where it went, and how thick? If we can put a man on the moon, right?

I got my first greatest desire, which was him leaving. He slammed the door in my face and a few seconds later his car peeled out. After a minute Janice came out of the bathroom and said, "That's great what you did in there. The shower."

"Thanks," I said, and a special thank-you for leaving me out here with him and making that noise. Is that part of the arrangement as far as rent? Did you know that the Poughkeepsie Goodwill put half your books straight into the free box? The self-help and the Matt Helm novels? The Poughkeepsie Goodwill! It's a *punch line*, Janice. By the way, how were those self-help books? Any luck with that? On the road to a new life? Out of the shadows and into the self-assurance it takes to drag innocent bystanders into your domestic-disturbance theme park?

"I should pay for the materials," she said.

"No, that's okay," I said. It is, I thought. It's okay. I didn't mean what I was thinking before. I can see it, the yelling and hitting fifteen minutes before sex and then fifteen minutes after, the emergency room, Vicodin for your shoulder, Herbert stealing the Vicodin, a lawyer from a bus-bench ad, you getting the restraining order and then driving blind into traffic from the courthouse and the horns blowing, dumb *fucking* bitch.

"I should get back," she said. "This is nice, with the jar."

That weekend, in the crowd at Richard and Agnes's, there was a woman in expensive casual clothes—linen pants, a sweater in two subtle yellows, a blue velvet jacket—and a complex feathered haircut. She was talking to a guy with a shaved head and big black glasses, and she looked so sane and healthy I almost didn't recognize her. I went over and said, "Hi, I'm Henry Bay."

"Hi," she said. "Wendy Probst."

"I know," I said. "We met once before."

"Were you at the opening? I'm sorry, I get so—"

"No, it was a few years ago. I came to your house in Ohio. I was working for *Crochet Life* magazine. I came to take pictures of—"

"Oh my God. Yes. *Crochet Life*." She said to the shaved-head guy, "I used to make these throws with, you know, unicorns and Raggedy Anns and—"

"Ironically?"

"No, no. That was my work then. No one believes me about this. I used to sell them at crafts fairs. It was wonderful. There were women who made little people out of Ivory Snow bottles."

"That is wonderful."

"And this magazine that he was from was like a ladies' craft thing, which as far as I'm concerned is still what I do. The whole point of using this medium is that it's a quote ladies' craft, so it carries that whole—"

"No, absolutely," the guy said.

"People always put them on the wall," she said, "and I say, you know, they're *throws*. You can put them on your couch and get under them when you watch TV. Anyway, and—I'm sorry . . . ?"

"Henry."

"And Henry came and took pictures of these unicorns and things, that's . . ."

"Actually, I think it was the first ones you had people in."

"Oh. Yes. Oh, that poor lady, what was her . . . ?"

"Cerise Lander?"

"Cerise. Yes. She was nice. So that was when I was just starting to show."

I said, "To show?"

"In galleries. My first show was in Chicago. It must have been right around then."

The shaved-head guy said, "Have you seen her show that's up in New York now? It's amazing. It's called *Throes,* with an *e.* It's a great name."

"Do you think it's great?" Wendy said. "I don't know. They wanted . . . anyway." She turned to me. "So what are you doing now?"

"I work for Richard and Agnes. On their magazine."

"Oh, that's terrific." She smiled and lowered her voice. "I knew them before it was tea. I love it that they're these upstanding country people now."

Some new people came in. Half of them already knew Wendy and the rest were excited to meet her.

I wasn't surprised she'd forgotten me. I was feeling like I'd blundered in with a race of people who actually had something to offer, and sooner or later they'd wonder what I was doing there. As I edged to the back of the circle around her, Agnes came in and said, "Wendy!" They hugged, and then Agnes saw me and said, "Did you meet Henry?"

"Oh, Henry and I go way back," Wendy said. "Remind me to tell you. It's funny."

On Monday Richard asked me if I wanted to go to New York the next day. A tea importer named Randolph had bought an ad at the last minute and someone had to show him the layout, take a picture of his showroom, and bring it back that night to get it into the issue. "It's down on West Broadway," Agnes said.

"Okay," I said. I paused. "I haven't been there before. To New York."

"Wow," Agnes said.

"That's great," Richard said. "You should take the whole day. Go through Times Square. See a museum. Dance with a lamppost like Gene Kelly. Henry steps out."

Agnes called Randolph and made the appointment for 4:15 the next day. I went home at lunch, found Gerald's card, and left him a message. Two hours later, on the porch, Agnes answered the phone and handed it to me. Gerald said, "*Hey*, baby! Did that woman say, 'Cozy'?"

"Yeah," I said. "That's where I work. How are you?"

"*Cozy*! I would never leave the premises. But you are. You're coming tomorrow. I'm wall to wall tomorrow. I'm broadloom. I'm plump fat polyester. I tell you what, though. Take coffee with me." He did his Russian voice. "Palm Court of Plaza Hotel. Special hotel, Henry! Famous! Everyone love this! You can come to there at three ten?" I said yes.

In the morning I rushed to the train without making tea, and by the time I got to the station an invisible C clamp was squeezing my head like a melon. The Grab 'n' Go next to the station had supermarket teabags and hot water. I bought a cup and drank it on the platform, tasting sweepings from the tea-withering room—the sponsoring beverage of all-day bathrobes and cracked-linoleum kitchens—but with the first sip my jaw unclenched and my eye stopped jumping.

I hadn't realized how serious my habit was. I got on the train picturing the Manhattan of a made-for-cable movie, with the camera panning from a sidewalk full of hurrying extras to a doorway where I crouched sucking on a bag of Red Rose, its tag hanging from my mouth like a small animal's tail. I had a week's beard and a filthy overcoat that had gotten too big for me. A man in a spotless suit walked two steps past me, stopped, and turned around. We'd been business executives together. "Henry?" he said. "Henry Bay? Oh my God."

I sat on the west side of the train and stared out at the wide green river, sculls and sailboats, erector-set bridges, and trees massed on the high bank of the opposite shore. After an hour the river narrowed, the trees gave way to smokestacks and storage yards, and I saw a few long streets of brick and traffic before a tunnel swallowed us up.

The platform at Grand Central was gritty and stifling, but a few yards away was a marble concourse, cool and strangely clean for the foot traffic it was handling. Every beam on the ceiling was edged in cream filigree, every light bulb set in an inverted bowl of plaster foliage. Any one of those bowls could have been glass-cased in a Clayton museum, but there were hundreds here, dropping soft light on the food stalls and two-hundred-title newsstands while the conversations of hundreds of people, baffled by the high ceilings, made the sound of the continental switchboard in an old movie montage, and all this was before I even got upstairs.

Upstairs was much grander, as if to say, "You thought that was it? *Puh,* give us a break, something better is always coming. The ceiling up here is so far over your head we've painted constellations on it, and the windows are framed with ruinous man hours of bas-relief birds, branches, globes, and ship's wheels, because this is the compass everyone has to pass through, and the bustle of a thousand people is as calm as a mountainside because you're finally here, your ticket punched at last, although what kind of shadowy hick existence did you get yourself into that you've put it off this long?"

I pushed through a door into the wet air outside and was pressed into a sidewalk army that was ass-deep in purpose. Everyone, happy or miserable, well dressed or in Air Clown sneakers and sex-boast T-shirts, had the most know-where-they're-going faces I'd ever seen. All of them could tell you what was coming next and the five things after that, because on the most real and official of American streets that knowledge was the minimum. The rest of the country, people like me, were the dim relations these people kept having to break it down for, a nation of Henries holding a city of Barneys back. Even the mumbling schizophrenics here were the best in the country at what they did.

I went south on Madison Avenue, trying not to gawk but unable to resist the buildings' upward pull, the old ones climbing to gargoyles and gold ziggurats, the new ones so tall I pictured catapults instead of elevators. Soon I was passing Gerald's leafy side streets, with doormen, songbirds, and trees in wrought-iron cages with brass plaques that said THANK YOU FOR CARING TO CURB YOUR DOG.

Wendy Probst's art gallery shared a building on West Twenty-eighth Street with twelve others, all with white walls, track lighting, attractive women at big-screen Macintoshes, and shaved-head guys like Wendy's friend talking on phones. The throws in *Throes* were thirty thousand dollars and up. She'd branched out from the miseries of Belton, Ohio, to crochet couples falling from the World Trade Center and the stoning of Afghan adulteresses. She had all the material she could use now. The ratty horizon was on world tour.

I spent an hour there, then walked over to Fifth Avenue and north to the Plaza Hotel in a pedestrian traffic jam. People walked here like they drove elsewhere, cutting each other off with shoulders and using briefcases for bumpers. I felt the pressure. There was too much of everything, signs and faces racing at me, the subway's damp breath blowing from caves with stairs, and an untenable anarchy of fake vendors, flyer-thrusters, and marauding plaid school kids.

I wanted in. I wanted to be offhand, to lean on a building

with one foot up on the wall behind me and one hand at the small of my back, having a smoke and nodding half an inch at people I knew, in a muscle shirt, with muscles. I wasn't going to get it, though. New York put out the strongest could-I-live-here I'd ever felt, and the answer was no, not if I'd never once worked for a business that could afford the rent. Even if they could, who had the bulletproof morale to put out *Frisbee Golf* with *Sports Illustrated* three blocks away?

Half the sidewalk army was on cell phones. When I stopped for DON'T WALK signs I kept hearing guys Dad's age, with tired musical voices, saying things like *Don't let it get to you, I can't see the point, At a certain point it's not worth it, It's worth your life these days, Life is too short, Don't make yourself crazy, Okay take care of yourself, Okay it's good to talk to you, Okay.* I loved these guys. I felt like it was me they were talking to, their resigned sweetness my lullaby, but then the light would change and I'd lose them.

When I got to the Plaza at three they were serving Orchid Oolong in the lobby, but I went outside and waited while taxis and horse-drawn carriages dropped off everyone in the world but Gerald. By 3:40 I was embarrassed in front of the doormen. At 3:55 a black Crown Victoria pulled up and Gerald, in a blue blazer and gray pants, got out of the backseat, came toward me smiling, saw my face, looked contrite, and said, "Really sorry. Please." He waved me into the backseat, got in next to me, and told the driver, a foreign guy in a black suit and shades, "We need to get my man to . . ."

"West Broadway and Grand Street," I said.

"We don't have a lot of time," Gerald said. "Seventh Avenue might be good."

The driver said, "I take a try, my friend," as we pulled into traffic.

"Thanks," Gerald said, and turned to me. "That's a great thing here. If you don't know someone, you say 'my friend.' It's like, 'For purposes of this discussion, we grew up together, we went in the woods and smoked cigarettes, we enlisted the same day, we got laid on twin beds in a motel room that one time, and I lied to the FBI for you. You don't remember all that? No problem. Thirty-eight cents is your change, my friend.'" The car turned west. "Can you forgive me? My friend? At least tell me how you are."

"I'm okay," I said. "How are things going with the metals?"

"Yeah, that's a funny business," Gerald said, looking away for a second and then turning back to me. "It's good to see you."

"It's good to see you, too," I said. "I just have to do this thing for work."

"Hey, I understand. You got your mind on your money and your money on your mind. Same reason I'm late. I was talking to a guy, and then I was just listening to him talk, and then I was faking appendicitis to get out of there, but you know how people are these days."

We were ten minutes late downtown. Gerald asked if he should wait and I said, "No, come in with me. I have to go back after this." He sent the driver away.

The showroom was like Wendy Probst's gallery, but with spotlit mounds of tea leaves on stone columns instead of art. A short thin man in his thirties came out of the back, wearing the pants and vest of a pinstripe suit and a Julius Caesar haircut. "Good afternoon," he said. "Stephen Randolph."

"I'm Henry Bay," I said. "From *Cozy*."

"Oh. Okay, so not Richard. And you're?"

"Gerald."

"Hi, Gerald. Tea?"

We said yes and he put a kettle on. I read a price list, letterpress on deckled paper. Nothing cost less than seventy dollars a pound. Randolph said, "People say the prices are obscene, but in fact they're not. They're the price of having one thing in your life that isn't a compromise"—a sentence I never got tired of hearing from people who sold things to enthusiasts.

He swirled tea and water in a clear glass pot. "So Richard and Agnes are at the point where they're hiring people? That's nice. What do you think about what they're doing?"

"I think it's good," I said. "I mean—"

"Because I like them personally, but is it unfair to ask you that? It's like, here's a girl with doilies on her tits. Okay, but could we have something about tea for people who actually know about it?"

"I know what you mean about the doily thing," I said.

"She didn't have the tits for it, either. Not that it's my business." He served the tea. "This is the first Indian tea we did, and I'll keep importing it no matter how ridiculous it gets."

"How about that rupee?" Gerald said.

"Fuck me," Randolph said. "The year I've just had. What do you do?"

"Strategic metal trading."

"Oh, interesting. You trade for a company, or . . . ?"

"A few investors."

"Okay. Wow, so nerves of steel. Good for you."

Gerald tasted his tea and did an "Oh" of appreciation exactly like Richard's. "I get that a lot on this tea," Randolph said. He turned to me. "Your thoughts?"

"It's really good."

"I'm relieved to hear that, but what do you *think* of it?"

"Well, it seems like an Assam, from the . . . body, and—"

"You think so? You want to get back to me on that? It's

Satrupa Kama Black. Reasonably basic. See, this is what I'm talking about." He clapped his hands once. "Okay, can we get this picture taken?"

We walked north. "Clients," Gerald said.

I didn't answer.

He said, "What?"

"Nothing," I said. "It's fine."

"Are you pissed that I was talking to him? I was just trying to be the color guy."

"No, it's fine." We walked for a minute. "You know the thing you said to me when you came to Albany?"

"I don't know where I was this morning. What did I say in Albany?"

"You said, 'Living in shitty apartments and everything, that's what you should be doing, because you're—' "

"Okay, I definitely didn't say that."

"—because that went with what I was doing, so I—"

"Henry." He stopped walking. "What I *will* say is whatever you've got up your ass, I don't know what it is, and I don't know how it's going to get dislodged, but I've always had faith that it will be. I don't have that faith in too many people."

"I appreciate that."

"It's up there pretty far, though."

"Thanks. I have to catch a train now."

"You want to get a cab?" I shook my head. "Okay," he said. "I'll see you."

I took a last look at him. He wasn't the picture of good fortune he'd been in Albany, but it was too late to ask him about it now. I headed for the train station as late-afternoon light fell on the corners of the buildings and spilled down to the pavement, screwing me up worse than anything, because any one square of sidewalk was as beautiful as my clean wet sheets on the line.

I got off the train at 10:30 that night, drove to the *Cozy* house, and knocked softly on the door. When Richard came out onto the porch I gave him the ad layout and the digital camera. He looked at the pictures on the LCD and said, "Did he give you any trouble?"

"No, he was fine."

"How was New York?"

"It was great."

"Yeah, isn't that something?"

I nodded. "Do you want help with that?"

"Naah, I've got it. Thanks. I'll see you tomorrow."

He went back inside and I stood looking at the garden, the lighted paths like city streets. I wanted to go back to New York both immediately and never; I couldn't leave *Cozy* and couldn't stay. New York was one of the things that had been recommended to me over the years, along with big socks, *favela* music, Emulator sex, and celestial navigation. Here at *Cozy* the recommendations were certain alkaloids, compassion for our fellow fuckups, and self-immolating arts and crafts.

These things worked, I could see that. They did wonders for the ballerina, the song cycle guy, and even Tom Foley, and until that afternoon I'd been thinking they were doing something for me. I'd risked injury for someone I wasn't close to—my landlady, in fact—and I'd been going around noticing my surroundings, working outward from the treetops around the garage apartment. Weren't these signs that I'd advanced?

Right, I'd advanced enough to go to New York and blow off

my oldest friend. I was more Henry than ever, standing on the porch and denouncing myself to my onboard secret police. Maybe if I stayed longer, I thought, and Dobey said, "Sure, another two hundred years should do the trick." Three days later I was on a plane with one of Richard's old black suits in my luggage, headed for *Wakeboarding Monthly* in Imperial Beach, California.

8

It fell to me to be the public face of *Wakeboarding* at Hypergames VIII in Seal Beach. We had a writer and photographer there, but I still had to go to the wakeboard competitions and look wowed. The rest of the time I worked our expo table, giving fourteen-year-old enthusiasts logo key chains and questionable advice on mastering the hoochie glide.

The second day, I asked a woman in the O'Neill booth to watch my stuff while I went up to my hotel room for more ad rate cards. On my way back to the elevator there was a guy talking to a closed door, trying not to raise his voice.

"Misty, open the door, right now," he said. "I swear to God, open this door." Someone inside said something. "Because I need my jacket," the guy said. He was thirty-five and sunburned, in a B.U.M. EQUIPMENT T-shirt, cargo shorts, and sandals. "The hell am I giving you a reason for?"

I was five feet from him when a fifteen-year-old girl sprang out of the room holding a bunched-up silver windbreaker. She was an athlete, in Lycra bike shorts, a crop-top with the word HINDENBURG and a picture of a flaming BMX bike on it, bruise-colored makeup, and an eyebrow ring. She said, "Here's your fucking jacket," and hit him with it.

He got hold of the jacket and tried to take it away from her. "I'm your father," he said, grabbing for her wrist. "You don't close the door on me."

I dropped my rate cards and got between them. "Hey," I said. "Let's, okay. Hey."

She tried to hit him but got me instead, a solid shot to the chest. He reached around me on the other side, squeezing my shoulder. I said, "Okay, look, no, *hey*."

The elevator opened down the hall. A woman my age, in sweat shorts and a HINDENBURG T-shirt, came our way, neither hurrying nor wasting a second. "Hi, Misty. Hi, David," she said.

They let me go as she got closer. I guessed she was some kind of coach, not an athlete—her body wasn't chiseled like the kid's, but compact in the clinging sportswear. Her hips and auburn ponytail swayed slightly while everything else came straight toward us, full lips in the lead, followed by clear brown eyes under faintly dark lids. "How are we doing?" she said.

"Fucked," Misty said.

"Excuse me, what are you doing here?" the dad said.

"Misty called me a minute ago and asked me to come up." She turned to me. "Hi, I'm Patti. You're . . . ?"

"Henry." She waited. "I was just walking by."

She did a slightly impressed thing with her eyebrows. Her eyes said brains, while those dark lids were like half-lowered shades. It was a bracing combination. She turned back to the dad and daughter and said, "Is it something we can talk about?"

"No, thank you," the dad said. "I didn't let her go off with these people—"

"These people," Misty said. "Ooh ooh."

"—and get gang-raped or—"

"Oh fuck you," Misty said. "I wasn't going to get gang-raped. Jesus Christ."

"With who, with Daryl and those guys?" Patti said. Misty nodded. "Daryl's a good guy," Patti said to the dad. "As I know you are too." She had that here's-the-deal diction I'd kept hearing on my day in Manhattan. "We're all just trying to have a good weekend here."

"Oh, it's a wonderful weekend," the dad said. "I'm so glad her mother stuck me with this." He turned to Misty. "This is why I had to leave."

"Blow me," Misty said. She walked ten feet away and sat against the wall with her knees at her chest.

"Are you connected with all this?" the dad asked me.

"I'm with one of the magazines," I said.

"So you're promoting this too. To these kids."

"Are you *embarrassed*?" Misty called over to him. "Did I *embarrass* you?"

"You're not being in the thing tomorrow," he said to her. "That's for the disrespect. We're going home."

"That's completely up to you two," Patti said, miming hands-off, giving Misty a vote but slipping it in there.

The dad looked at Patti's clear eyes a second, turned to Misty, and said, "You know what? Do be in it. Break your neck, if possible. I'm good with that."

I picked up my rate cards, went to the elevator, pushed the button, and snuck a last look at Patti while I waited. Misty caught me at it and almost smiled, but she wasn't going to do that in front of her father.

Back at my booth I formed a plan to go to the next day's BMX competition and bump into Patti by chance, but she walked up to me as I was giving out my last key chain of the day.

"Thanks for that upstairs," she said.

"Oh," I said. "No, I was . . . are they okay?"

"In a sense," she said. "That's not that unusual. His kid finds something she can do so he goes movie of the week on her. I work for Hindenburg, obviously." She was still wearing the T-shirt but had changed into slacks. Hindenburg Heavy Industries made clothes, accessories, and watch caps for skateboarding and other X sports, and sponsored a few teams. "I'm the athlete coordinator. Theoretically I just make sure they show up on time, but that's theoretically. I personally don't care if she rides tomorrow. I mean, we need her, but let her skip it if it keeps them from killing each other. In case it looked like I was doing it for business."

"No, it didn't."

"Good. Anyway, you were the first responder, so I owe you a dinner," she said, and I looked at my watch.

We took a fifth-story pedestrian bridge from the hotel to the shopping mall and found a Japanese restaurant. Picking up her menu, Patti said, "Those people are making me have a drink. So is wakeboarding your life?"

"Just the part where you get swept under."

"That's so sad."

"No, I mean when I tried it. I've only been at the magazine a few weeks."

We started telling stories, comparing notes on a life of helping enthusiasts do things that thrilled their tiny fan bases and eluded the real world's notice. "They always get to be the baby," Patti said. "You never do."

"But you don't need to," I said.

"No, everyone needs to sometimes."

"No, that's right," I said, hearing myself start with "No" like her, trying to catch up.

"How'd you get into this?" she said. I told her, and around my ninth job we both started laughing.

"You're the restless kind," she said.

"I don't know," I said. "I wouldn't mind going somewhere and resting."

"Oh God, I know," she said, her wave dismissing the supposed romance of working too hard, which was big then. When she agreed with me my brain surprised me with homemade opiates, the warmth spreading out from the back of my neck. We concurred like that twice more that night, but we might not have, because her opinions fit no pattern. Only she knew what she thought, but she knew it solid. You had to bring your best game with her.

She said she'd grown up in New Jersey, the second of three kids, and after college she'd gone to work for a city youth program on the south side of Philadelphia. "Basically the program didn't exist. I think there was a kickball. But all the playgrounds were turf."

"Turf?"

"Of gangs. No, they were paved. They *should* have been turf. Anyway, a few of the kids had BMX bikes, and they could do like two tricks, so I said, 'Okay, here's something we can do, we'll have a bike rodeo. We'll build some ramps, or whatever you build, and we'll all learn how to do this.'

"By the second year, we closed off two blocks and the *paleta* guys came. The kids were doing seven-twenties and double tailwhips. A guy from Hindenburg came and signed up two of them for regional, and then he asked me. I wish I could say I had a crisis about it, but I was running from the bus to my building with my key out for three years because of the neighborhood."

We kept talking till they kicked us out. Patti was like a greatest hits of my life so far: she had special knowledge like Barney, she made fun of special knowledge like Gerald, and like those guys in New York saying, "Don't let it make you crazy," on their cell phones, she had hope that just edged out fatalism, the attitude it took to make the best of a factory-second world.

When we finally got back to the pedestrian bridge there was nobody on it but Misty. She was halfway across it, leaning out over the three-foot safety wall, pushing down on it with her hands like a gymnast about to vault. Her feet were six inches off the ground and her head was poised sixty feet over the wishing fountain—whether she was preparing to jump or just looking wasn't clear, but Patti didn't wait to find out. She kept walking but didn't speed up. Four feet from Misty, just short of spooking distance, she said, "Hi. You doing shoulders?"

Misty's feet quickly rose three more inches, but then stopped and slowly lowered to the floor. She turned toward us, her face a million miles away but coming back. "Yeah," she said.

Patti got next to her, turned her back to the safety wall, put the heels of her hands on it, did a few dips and said, "My back is so fucked up."

When she finished she stepped away from the wall, and

after a few seconds Misty did too. She put an arm around Patti's waist and Patti put an arm over her shoulders. Misty noticed me and said, "Hi. I'm sorry about my dad before." I said it was okay. Misty looked me over and said, "So, *Patti*."

"This is Henry," Patti said.

"Hi, Henry," Misty said. "Are you here for the thing?"

I nodded. "I'm from a magazine."

"Are you going to write about Patti? You should put in there that everyone loves Patti."

"It's a wakeboarding magazine," I said. "Otherwise I would."

"Good. See you tomorrow," she told Patti, and walked off toward the hotel.

Patti took my hand without taking her eyes off Misty. Her hand was sweating. After a few steps Misty turned around, pointed at our hands like a triumphant detective, and turned around again.

Patti's hotel room was like mine, full of strewn personal effects, piles of promo chum, and frantic lists on legal pads. We stood there holding each other for a minute, then kissed—seaweed, plum wine, relief—and made a hurried trail of clothes to the bathroom. In the shower she turned her back to me, lightly hitched a leg, reached back, and slipped my cock inside her before I knew what she was doing. We rocked that way for a minute before she slipped me out and turned to face me. Then I was on my knees, half-drowning, and then we were out of the shower, drying each other. In bed her moan had a laugh in it, for a while.

The phone woke us at six. She picked it up and said, "You know, I want to thank you. This has really been a wake-up call for me." She hung up and said, "They never laugh. You should go before my kids start coming."

We started kissing, though, and it was 6:40 before I walked out of the sleeping hotel onto a wide suburban street. The cars still had their headlights on, and I thought the headlights were beautiful and somehow witty. That afternoon Misty took second in the BMX finals, best on her team, and wouldn't let Patti get on the van to the airport until she kissed me hard in front of everyone.

Patti lived in Santa Cruz, 450 miles north of Imperial Beach, in the bottom half of a gray Victorian six blocks from the ocean. Every weekend I could afford the Fun Fare, I flew up to San Jose, where she picked me up in her Rabbit and drove us to her place over a winding mountain highway.

My life had been the same for so long that the changes now put me in a state of continuous surprise. I started seeing things from Patti's point of view, which made mine look like a squint. We talked all the time, and under the conversations we had out loud there was another one going on, with me saying, "You mean it's okay?" and her saying, "Yes, who told you it wasn't, and why were you waiting for someone to tell you it was?" Once, as we walked on a cliff road over the ocean, I said my work wasn't taking me anywhere. "Really?" she said. "It sounds like you go everywhere. What if you were one of those lawyers you were going to be? You'd be looking forward to casual Friday."

I didn't talk about the future, or what was happening between us. I wasn't worried about my independence. I'd had years of independence and never known what to do with it. Rent it out to married people? Make it into an end table? I just didn't want to push her.

But then *Wakeboarding* ran its course, and the only openings I could find were in Kentucky and Vermont, far from her. Suddenly I was looking at a commitment that would have been unthinkable a year earlier: Clean Page.

They'd been buying up magazines for five years. People at my jobs called them what people always call these things: the Death Star, the Evil Empire, the Brain Police. A Clean Page executive named Walter Denise had called me twice in three years, making jokes and trying to hire me. I'd said no both times, but their office was in San Jose, just over the hill from Santa Cruz.

Patti and I talked about it in a coffee shop where Highway 1 curled out of town, with fog blanking the windows. "I feel like I'm being a traitor," I said.

"Okay," she said, "but to what?"

I realized I had no answer to that. As the conversation went on I was moved, not by what we were talking about but by the fact that I had someone to talk to about it, being serious together the way people do, in a place where the waitresses patrolled with Silexes. "Did you like the guy on the phone?" Patti said. "What would you do there?" The harder I frowned and rubbed my temple, the happier part of me felt. This is how it's supposed to be, I thought, and asked her to marry me.

When she hesitated I thought, No kidding, I'm more surprised than you are, and there goes all the good I did with my four months of restraint, until she tilted her head and said, "You know what? Yeah."

I called Walter Denise, the Clean Page guy, the next day. He mentioned a salary a third higher than I was making at *Wakeboarding* and set a meeting for me and Tom Patrick, the founder and CEO. Walter and I agreed to meet beforehand at a Starbucks near their office.

He was waiting when I got there, a stocky bald guy in his thirties with an orange beard, drinking cappuccino and shaking his head over a copy of *Decoupage!*, which they'd just bought. We shook hands and I held out my résumé.

"What's this?" he said. "You don't need a résumé with us," but he took it and started to read. "Jesus," he said when he saw how long it was. "So do you know how to do all these things?"

"No, I tend to retain the wrong parts," I said. "Like the slang."

"No, the slang is the good part. What do you think we do for fun all day? 'Look out, you're going to *sam*.' 'No, I've got *slab hicks* on my *downtown plate*. Don't be such a *Clive of India*.'" He put the résumé down. "So have you figured out what actually drives these people?"

"I think it varies from—"

"They just *try* so hard. It's like the guy at the baseball game. He can't just wear the T-shirt with the team on it; he's got—like if it's the little demented Indian guy? He's got that on his socks, he's got it cut into his hair, he's got the tattoo. He's like, '*Boy*, am I a fan.'" He went back to the résumé. "Oh my God."

"What?"

"Dobey Publications. That's great. That's the press from the cereal boxes, right? It's that guy, Arthur Dobey."

"Arnold," I said.

"Yes. Arnold Dobey. Jesus. I saw him at a convention once. I think that's the guy in this business I most fear turning into. Although that's a crowded field."

He handed it back to me. "Here's the deal with Tom. Eight years ago he was going around in a Hyundai delivering Penny-Savers to liquor stores. He lived on Nabs. That's the guy you don't want to fuck with. The guy that had to wait. People call me up and go, 'Why does he yell and scream all the time?' That's why he yells and screams."

"Okay," I said. "That sounds a little scary."

"What?"

"That he yells and screams all the time."

"No, it's not scary if you're *here*." He finished his coffee. "It's scary if you're Arthur Dobey."

On the outside the Clean Page building reflected light like five stories of cop sunglasses. On the inside it had the kind of fluorescent lighting that puts a vampire in your motel mirror. Ten feet into the lobby the fresh air gave way to synthetic-fiber molecules defecting from the carpet. Walter and I took the elevator to the top floor and started past the receptionist, but she held up a finger and talked into her headset: "Walter plus one to see Tom."

"Henry Bay," Walter said.

"Do you have a visitor badge?"

"He can't have anything on his nipples," Walter said.

"Nobody likes you," she said. Walter nodded and led me down the hall past framed covers of *Spearfish*, *Skysurf*, and *Quick Raffia*.

Patrick's secretary said, "He's just wrapping up." We sat on a couch and listened through the closed door to Patrick yelling at someone. After ten minutes he opened the door, said, "Walter, yeah," and waved us in.

He was in his thirties, tall and trim, with short curly brown hair and ice-blue eyes. He wore a blue shirt, red tie, gray suit pants, and black socks, his wingtips parked in a corner. On the wall were floating-frame photos of a private plane, horses, and his family. He sat low in a chair and put his feet on a table so his body was a long flat line, and he passed an orange from hand to hand as he talked. It was a way of sitting that said he had the money a few times over and nothing more to prove but that he still came in, suffering everyone else's slower brains, so they would keep having a building to go to.

"That was Spalding," he said, nodding at his phone. "We have to cut these guys loose." He gestured to Walter to take care of it.

"Really. Okay," Walter said, and tried to get back to the tone he used for kidding about my nipples. "So here's Henry. *He* wasn't going to work here. Not Henry."

"Yeah," Patrick said. "Did you bring a résumé?" I handed it to him. He scanned the list of magazines. "Bought it, bought it, don't want it, bought it . . ." He put it down. "People hate us."

"I don't think—"

"*Hate* us. Because we came along and said 'What if this was a business?' We go to buy someone, the first thing they say is, 'Gee, do we have to leave North Dakota?' I say, 'No, because we want to preserve that unique character.' They say, 'Oh, that's great, because my brother Zeke is here, and my dog.' I don't want them *near* here. A square foot in North Dakota is free. But the product needs to meet minimal standards. So that's you. Anything you need, Walter is here."

I started to say something, but Walter clapped his hands on his knees, said, "And we're off," and stood up. In the hall he said, "That was good. So Monday," his hands wafting me onto the elevator.

There was a vending alcove off the parking garage. I wasn't a candy bar enthusiast but I started feeding dollars into a machine and didn't stop till I'd bought a Payday, a Hundred Grand, a Butterfingers, a Snickers, a NutRageous, and a Dark

Milky Way. I finally have a job with dental, I thought. I should use it. I ate the Snickers before I started the car but I couldn't touch the other ones. When I got to Santa Cruz I left them on top of a newspaper machine, figuring that with all the kids and homeless guys walking around, someone would end up eating them. No one said it had to be me.

part two

empty hand

9

Tom Patrick bought everything he saw, and no one could keep up. Before I knew it I was troubleshooting twelve troubled magazines, including *Hacky Sack World, Easy Felting, Handgun Shooter,* and *Spelunk*. At night Patti and I came home to a small wooden house with plumbing issues and a black-hole mortgage, in a San Jose neighborhood shuddering between two loud freeways that had slashed through it thirty years earlier. It was the kind of house, and the kind of job, that make you look around sometimes and wonder where you've misplaced the fat catalogue of possibilities you left home with. It was here a minute ago, I'd think, and then: I want to see Barney.

We'd seen him and his family a few times in the five years we'd been married, but we'd never been to their house in Kansas. I almost called him to ask if we could come, but I held off.

Sometimes, calling just to talk, I'd catch him at a bad time and get pauses and monosyllables, my brother the tough interview.

I decided to ask Patti to call Deirdre, but I had to wait a few days because it was possible now for me to catch Patti at a bad time too. In fairness, catching me at a bad time was no trouble at all.

Patti and I had started out speaking the same language, but these days our fluency was suffering. We had better and worse days, but the great ones, of late-night laughing and pet names for genitals, were going fast.

We were both overworked, with Clean Page piling more titles on me and Hindenburg dropping more kid athletes on her. They phoned her all the time, anguishing over their sprains and stepparents, and her method of dealing with them was efficiency itself. When a skateboarder called up freaking out, she'd listen sympathetically and then divert him with the discreetly disguised troubles of a motocross rider who'd called half an hour earlier. Then a Rollerblader would call up crying, and Patti would calm her down with the skateboarder's story, and so on. The cure for each one was the last one's nightmare. She was a better gossip than any therapist, and vice versa.

The only problem was that, wading deeper into their lives, she seemed to be wading away from ours. Or maybe it was just what she'd said in Seal Beach long ago: they always get to be the baby and you never do. I could live with that. It was when she gave me the stare she'd used on Misty's dad that I felt myself sinking.

I was more to blame than she was, though. We both traveled for work all the time, flying separately but having jet lag together, and I fell into a special logic in which everything—the house, our monthly nut, the existence of Clean Page—was her fault. She may have blamed me for Hindenburg the same way. Frequent flying gives you magic powers of reasoning. Sometimes I wanted to call Gerald and talk to him about all of it, but there was no good time for me to catch him, not since our day in New York.

I got Patti at a good time, she got Deirdre at one, Deirdre got Barney at one, and the trip was scheduled. Five days before we left, the editor of *Handgun Shooter* asked me to join him at a gun show in Dresser, Iowa, and meet advertisers.

I followed him around a baking Quonset hut as he shook hands and touched guns. Not everyone was buying guns, but everyone was touching them. The Glock tables were petting zoos. Along with the guns were blowguns, garrotes, and manuals on how to make silencers, convert semiautomatics to true machine guns, or drop out of sight forever.

In an alcove off the main floor there were tables selling conspiracy-theory pamphlets and a few novels, white-uprising stroke books with print quality worse than Dobey's. At one of the tables a mountain man was selling FREEBIRD T-shirts.

The drawing on the shirts was based on a police sketch of a guy who'd been seen leaving a package behind a climate research lab a year earlier. After examining the defused bomb's parts, the FBI was pretty sure the guy was Freebird. The sketch, showing a clean-shaven face with sunglasses and a hat pulled low, had produced no good leads, though he'd been sighted on the Appalachian Trail, in Hayden Lake, Idaho, and foraging in Dumpsters in Georgia, sometimes on the same day.

The T-shirts said FLY, FREEBIRD, FLY! and the artist was talented, a queasy fact in itself. In the drawing, a fierce bird with a face like the sketch soared over a map of the country, a stick of dynamite in one claw and a gun in the other. It was a caricature of a sketch of a disguise, and the silkscreen diluted it further, but the eyes spooked me anyway. When I looked up, the mountain man was grinning, daring me to object.

Back at the hotel I had seventeen phone calls to return. I started with Dick Donadio at *Monster Truck Tunin',* who said, "Have you heard anything?" as soon as he picked up.

I said I hadn't. Clean Page had been through a round of layoffs four months earlier and another one was rumored. All my phone calls started with "Have you heard anything?" and ended with "Anyway," a word that had risen from meaning "Please let me off the phone now" to become an asterisk attached to all of life: I can't sleep, history's off its meds, I'm one surprise urine test from eating government cheese, but anyway.

I returned calls for two more hours, picking yellowed laminate off the Hotel Dresser's phone information card. When I walked out of the hotel to go to the airport I stood looking at the street for a minute, wishing I had time for a walk. Sometime in the last few years I'd developed the closest thing I had to an enthusiasm of my own, collecting Claytons—towns that in the right light could stand in for the one in Illinois.

Nothing in my collection came up to the real Clayton, but I'd gotten less picky over time. The original was off-limits to me for reasons of both Jillian and Dobey, and there were a lot of honorable mentions out there. In a gracefully fading tertiary town I could find a trace of what I'd felt getting off that bus on spring break years ago, when just the river air made me happy.

Dresser showed promise. There were two old spangled movie houses, the Fox (FOR LEASE) and the Mexico (YOUTH CHOIR

RECITAL FRI.). The department store, with HENLEE's still inlaid on the entrance's marble apron, had become a nail salon, a cell phone store, and five vacancies.

In a good Clayton the ads for the old hotel say, "MEET ME UNDER THE BIG CLOCK" AT THE HOTEL SO-AND-SO. Sometimes the big clock has been stopped for years and the young business leaders have a fund drive going to fix it, with a thermometer sign in the park. In an outstanding Clayton there's a thousand-watt radio station, its announcers a little halting, on the hotel's mezzanine. In a lot of Claytons there are junk stores where you can page through old copies of *Life* and *Look* from a time when the job was to cover what interested everyone, before we split up into separate discussion groups for the closing session.

Some Claytons are college towns, and you know you're there when Senegalese pop music sifts onto your car radio after a few hundred miles of guys yelling that the UN is a pestilence down to its gift shop. In a few Claytons the conversation has moved on from "Back when the factory" and "Ever since the Wal-Mart" to "Some of us are trying to" and "Did you see what they're doing downtown," because that Clayton is getting its fifth or sixth wind and the people there feel useful instead of shunted off.

I drove to the airport with regret. I could have used an hour in the margins of a marginal town, walking past gravel-bed train tracks and the high school's stoner hill, the landscape that's left when the gold rush moves on.

When I got home that night Patti was on the phone, sitting up in bed in a HINDENBURG T-shirt with a picture of people on a ski lift pointing in horror at a burning snowboard in the sky. She waved at me but kept talking: "You have to put all that out of your head, and think about how big you can be."

I could tell who she was talking to. Kris Santangelo was in his late twenties, from La Puente, and Hindenburg saw him as the kind of skateboard star who could have his poster in a few million kids' bedrooms and his motions captured for choppy replication on the Xbox. He had the talent, the look, and enough attitude for the whole team.

A few months after signing with Hindenburg he'd moved to San Francisco. On the night he arrived, Patti got home at 11:30, saying she'd had to get him settled in his apartment and find him some warm clothes. A week later, as she told me a story about some duneboarder's sister's parents having her kidnapped to an unregulated teenage boot camp in Utah, I started to feel like my face was going to slide off my head if she didn't stop talking. It was the first time I'd ever felt that way, and I realized that I thought she and Santangelo might be sleeping together. I almost asked her a few times but I wasn't sure we'd bounce back from that one, even if I was wrong.

"You can be international now," she said on the phone. "You can be huge." I went to take a shower. When I got into bed she was asleep, or wanted to be.

I went to work at six the next morning, trying to get ahead so I'd be free on our weekend at Barney's. I ghostwrote the editor's columns for three magazines, making them adjustable so that a piece for *Spearhunting* could be adapted for use in *Quilting Basket*: *I look at these young guys/gals with their fancy gear, who've never had to thread/kickstart/program/cast/whittle a J-37, and I have to smile. They are me. They are all of us.*

Walter Denise walked in at 10:30 twisting a rolled-up magazine in his hands and asking how the gun show had been. When I told him about the FREEBIRD T-shirts he said, "Did you get me one?"

"Why would you want one?"

"I love things like that. They confirm all my worst shit about people."

"Did you talk to Tom?" I had asked to be relieved of a few magazines before I drove into an abutment some night.

"I did," Walter said. "Here's where we are." He unrolled the magazine he was holding. It was *Inside Trout*, not one of mine, with a hooked fish in a death lurch filling the cover. "He needs you to ream this out."

I took off my glasses and rubbed my eyes. "Walter—"

"I brought the other thing up with him but I caught him at a bad time. We're going into some cutbacks."

He handed me the magazine as Tom Patrick opened the door. "Walter, the exhaust kit people," he said. "We'll do ten percent off the card for nine months. That's it."

"Right," Walter said. "That's a little different from what we—"

"I don't need the minutes of the meeting, I just need you to—"

"No, I—"

"—pick up the phone. Fucking nuisance, the whole thing."

"Yeah. No, it is," Walter said. "We've been more than—"

"Am I *clearing* it with you?"

"No," Walter said.

Tom looked at me, said, "How are you?" and left.

"He's very happy with what you've been doing, by the way," Walter said. After a few months on the job I'd realized that Walter lived for Tom's abuse. "You want to have lunch?"

"I have to go to Sacramento," I said. "*Kustom Chopper*'s having a rally against the helmet law."

"Good. Who thought up *that* bill? 'Mister Chairman, we're losing precious members of the Nazi Jokers.' "

When he left I pushed a stack of papers aside so I could go through *Inside Trout*. My office was a mess, the furniture hidden under piles of manuscripts, memos, back issues, spec sheets, and press releases. Somewhere in one of the piles was a book about how to organize your paperwork and optimize your life. I hadn't read it but it was supposed to be one of the better ones, and had been a big seller. It was by Dad.

10

Patti and I walked out of the Kansas City airport into hot soaking air, rented a Spectra, and drove to Barney and Deirdre's yellow house and vegetable garden on a half acre at the edge of Lawrence. Beside their front door was a long row of hiking shoes, gum boots, galoshes, cross-trainers, clogs, and sandals. I remembered this folkway from the other college towns I'd been in: the number of shoes outside the door, and the activities they were muddy from, signaled the family's wealth in the next world. When we added Patti's clean lime Hindenburgs and my black Rockports to the lineup, they looked like the mean developer at the town meeting in a movie with sass and heart.

Barney answered the door in a brown flannel shirt, oatmeal jersey, gray cords, and brown socks, a dirt rainbow. Deirdre came up behind him in a gray sweatshirt and one of her mossy long skirts. Barney looked like he hadn't been sleeping, and an activist's despairing smile had settled on Deirdre's face.

In the hugs Patti got elbow clutch and brief cheek contact from Barney, I got a three-count nose-to-ear off Deirdre, Patti and Deirdre gave each other full waist-up, and Barney and I shook hands. Over his shoulder I saw the living room: futons, paper-lantern lights, and a few hundred books on each of whose twenty-sixth pages I would have bogged down for good.

The kids ran in, yelling, "Hello!" and wearing most of the color in the house. Michael was eight, Pearl ten. After their hugs they grinned curiously at us, wondering what treats we might have brought from California: grosser candy, thunkier music, or rubbery black-and-yellow clothes like Aunt Patti was wearing. They were right: our duffel bags were too big for overnight. We put our stuff in the guest room upstairs, and when we came down everyone was in the pale yellow kitchen making dinner.

We offered to help, but Barney, oiling a wok, said, "No, the kids like to do it. Michael, please get me twelve grams of dried mushrooms. Pearl, let me have half a liter of quinoa, please." The kitchen counters were lined with jars of dry foods, their names in calligraphy on old, red-bordered filing labels—MILLET, BUCKWHEAT, ADZUKI BEANS—with a lab scale beside them. Deirdre chopped vegetables that Barney stir-fried in sesame oil. She weighed the portions before putting them on plates.

When we sat down Michael said, "Aunt Patti, do you have guys that skateboard where you work?"

"Guys and gals," Patti said. "Yes. They're going to the X Games in a few weeks."

Pearl said, "What are the X Games?"

Deirdre, looking pleased, said, "You could be speaking Mandarin to these two."

"It's a big contest for skateboarding and BMX bikes and stuff," Patti said.

"Because we saw some guys that skateboard," Michael said. "They went up on the curved thing and then they went off it? We thought they were going to crash."

"Sometimes people crash, but they usually don't," Patti said. "It's centrifugal force."

"I know what centrifugal force is," Pearl said.

"It's not centrifugal force," Barney said.

"Oh," Patti said. "I thought it was."

"What magazine are you working at now?" Deirdre said.

"I work on a few different ones," I said. "One of them's about boogie boarding."

"Damien does that when they go to Florida. You go in the water and hold on to it," Pearl said, giving Deirdre an I-know-Mandarin look.

After dinner we had a free hour before Deirdre was to take Patti and me to a madrigal concert at the university. We went up to our room to wrap the presents we'd brought the kids, big-wheeled mountain boards and Hindenburg clothes. The door opened a crack when we were almost finished. Michael peeked in and then ran down the hall yelling, "Pearl!"

A minute later both kids came in, with Deirdre behind them. "Hi," she said. "Could I see what we're doing here, please?"

Patti pulled the paper aside, exposing a mountain board. The kids lunged for it, but Deirdre said, "Leave that there, please. Michael? Leave that there." She turned to us. "This is nice of you, but I wish you'd asked us first."

"I'm sorry," I said. "We—"

"We don't want them having skateboards."

"They're not skateboards," Patti said. "They're mountain boards."

"What's a mountain board?" Deirdre said. "I'm sorry, I don't know what a mountain board is."

"It's for grass and dirt," Patti said. "They could use it in the yard. It's—"

"No," Deirdre said. She looked at the clothes. "None of this. I'm sorry—"

Barney came in and said, "What's going on?"

I said, "We brought some presents."

"Why not?" Michael said.

"Could you take Pearl and Michael downstairs, please?" Deirdre said to Barney. He was looking at the clothes. There was a black-and-yellow tank top for Pearl, a red hoodie for Michael, and T-shirts with a burning skull eating the Hindenburg logo. "How come the skulls are on fire?" Barney said. "Is that about the Hindenburg disaster?"

Deirdre said, "Could you . . . ?"

"I heard you," Barney said. "I'm asking a question."

"It's more of a joke," Patti said. "It's like—"

"I'm sorry," Deirdre said. "I know this is your work, but we don't want this for them. It's not just the safety. Every time they go out the door they get assaulted by this culture." She held up the tank top. "All this fake sex and—"

"No, it's so you can move around," Patti said. "When you see the women who do sports in—"

"I have seen them, with the things that say 'Nike,' with sweatshops, all over their—"

"All our sewing is—"

"Why *not*?" Michael yelled.

Deirdre's look at Barney said, "See?"

"Let's go downstairs," Barney said, in Dad's old voice of seething calm. The kids followed him away.

"You know, we're living through an emergency these days," Deirdre said. I nodded, although I hadn't been following the news closely and wasn't sure which emergency she meant. "They have backpacks. Anywhere they go, they've got flashlights, drinking water, first aid kits and emergency meals. We have them too. I need them to be focused."

"Because of . . . ?"

"Because of how the world is now."

That emergency. "I'm sorry," I said.

"It's okay," Deirdre said. "We should get going."

She went downstairs. Patti said, "*Fuck* her."

While Patti got dressed I went out to Deirdre's Volvo, which had lifesaving hammers bracketed to the doors and a library of scolding bumper stickers on the back. Barney was in the driver's seat. I got in next to him and said, "I'm sorry about the presents."

"That's okay," he said. "It's just that now they want them and they don't understand why they can't have them."

"I don't understand, either," I said.

"I kind of understand," he said, almost telling me something, a lifelong habit.

He blew the car horn. "I have to get to work," he said. "We're trying to get money renewed and we're not getting a lot of results right now." I nodded sympathetically, making an effort, although I was wondering why you couldn't just be related to people without making an effort. Barney hit the horn again, harder. A minute later the others came out.

The plan was for Barney and the kids to get off at his lab, where he'd work and they'd do homework, while the rest of us went to the concert. Deirdre was cheerful on the drive, chatting about the excellence of the Lawrence Madrigal Singers as if the mountain board argument had been her after-work martini. Barney drove silently, Patti looked stony, and the kids seemed to tune out.

We pulled up in front of Barney's lab, a three-story concrete building. In a second, seven people came out of the dusk and surrounded the car, too fast for Barney to drive away. They joined hands, forming a circle around us.

"Goddamn it," Deirdre said.

"I didn't see the van," Barney said. It was across the way, an Econoline with blown-up sonogram pictures taped to its panels.

The people in the circle stared at us through the windows. Pearl put a hand on Michael's shoulder as Barney and I got out of the car.

"Dr. Bay, we're here to ask you and your colleagues to stop doing this Frankenstein science," a fortyish lady in a windbreaker said. "The embryos can't talk, so we're here to talk for them."

"Yeah, I remember all this," Barney said.

"You remember it but you're still doing it," a guy in a FUNDAMENT HOUSE T-shirt said. "That's why we're here again."

"We don't have time for this today," Barney said.

I looked around the circle. There were some college-age kids, but most of the people were older. With their sloganed clothes and ad hoc friendships they could have been any of the enthusiast clumps I'd covered, rock hounds or Yahtzee fiends.

A guy in a T-shirt that read THERE'S NO FIRST AMENDMENT TO THE TEN COMMANDMENTS broke out of the circle and lay down on the hood of the car. Three women lifted their paired hands and started singing that they weren't afraid. A few students slowed down to watch, but most of them seemed to have seen it before.

Barney speed-dialed his cell phone. "This is Dr. Bay," he said. "I've got someone on my car in front of Crofter. We're in kind of a hurry. Thank you." He hung up and talked to the guy on the car. "He's going to be here in a minute. Do you think you could leave now?"

"This isn't for your convenience, Dr. Bay," the guy on the car said.

"No kidding," Barney said. "How come you get to be on the car today? Where's Derek?"

"Derek's on retreat."

The circle had closed in, the faces close to ours now. One of the young singing women decided I could be swayed, or even saved. She leaned close to me, coffee and doughnuts from the van ride on her breath, her gaze marching into mine in a blitz of sanctioned intimacy. All the love on earth was mine for the asking. Quit it, I thought.

A tall, edgy-looking guy with bushy hair and a beard said, "I'd like to talk to the children." He bent close to Pearl's window. "Pearl? Michael?"

Deirdre threw her door open, got out, and faced him across the car roof. "Get away from the car," she said. "Right now."

The guy ignored her and talked to the kids through the window. "Can I just talk to you guys for a minute? Is that okay?"

"Leave them alone," Barney said. His anger made his face geological, with ledges over his eyes and ridges beside them.

"What are you afraid of?" the guy asked Barney.

Barney turned to the windbreaker lady. "Make him move," he said.

"What are you afraid of?" the guy said again.

The lady hesitated, then put a hand on the guy's arm and said, "Martin—"

Patti was out of the car now, moving in quickly on the guy. "She told you to get away from the car," she said.

"It's okay," the windbreaker lady told Patti, and tugged on the tall guy's shoulder. "Martin, let's go over here for a minute," she said. The guy stood up from the window but didn't move away.

A campus cop, young and mustached, rolled up on a mountain bike. "I need you folks to get away from the car," he said. "And I will have to cite you."

The guy at Pearl's window backed away. "I'm sorry about the thing with the kids," the guy on the hood said softly to Barney as he stood up. "Martin's new." The women kept singing as they moved toward their van.

Deirdre asked the kids if they were okay. Pearl nodded, then Michael. "You notice he knew their names," Deirdre said. "They love that kind of thing."

"You should get to your concert," Barney said. "Let's go," he told the kids. "Straight ahead." They got out of the car and walked with him to the lab.

When they were inside, Deirdre started the car and we drove in silence to the concert. By the time we got there I was sick of everyone, and I wasn't clear on what madrigals were but I didn't expect to like them.

Six women in white blouses and long velvet skirts sang to a half-full lecture hall. The songs turned out to be mostly religious, and after what we'd just come from I considered walking right out. In honor of her childhood, Mom called religion "Halloween on speed," and Dad liked to say we were "decent, church-fearing Americans." I'd thought of them fondly on the drive over. But there was a look people got on their faces when they listened to that kind of music, head tilted and a fifth of a smile, hearing the promise of home. Somewhere in the first few songs I caught that look on Deirdre, and a trace of it on Patti, and then I felt it on myself.

In the morning Barney and Deirdre weighed out six portions of trail mix and put them in their emergency backpacks, and we all went for a walk on a muddy road around a lake. Barney had us tuck our pants into our socks in case of ticks, while Deirdre passed out sunblock and bug spray.

As we started walking she asked what everyone thought we should do with the Hindenburg gifts. When there were no suggestions she said, "Do you know any kids in California whose parents would think those things were appropriate?"

"Lots," Patti said.

"I think that might be nice," Deirdre said, "because then they could be a gift to those kids from Michael and Pearl. What do you guys think?"

"Okay," Pearl said.

"Michael?" Deirdre said.

"Yeah."

"First deer," Pearl said, as a whitetail froze beside the path and then ran into the woods.

"Okay," Deirdre said. "Why don't we get out the crafts stuff when we get back, and maybe Henry and Patti would help you guys make gift cards for those kids, and that would be Henry and Patti's present to you. What do you think about that?"

"I think it's great," Patti said, and I knew that by "it" she meant the moment when she'd be on the plane with earbuds and a drink.

Barney had dropped back by himself. I slowed down to join him. "That was weird, with those people last night," I said. The protestors had been gone when we got to the lab after the concert, and no one had mentioned them since.

"It was going on when I got here," Barney said. "You can't not do the work."

"Right, no," I said.

"It's like those shirts you guys brought, with the burning skulls," he said. "You know what I think that's about? It's how your head would feel if you wanted to think but you didn't have the resources for it. It's like, 'Is it just me, or is it hot in here?' We should sell those shirts to everyone that has that problem. We could all quit what we're doing." He sped up to catch the others, leaving me behind.

Back at the house Patti and I sat on the living room floor with the kids, cutting gift cards out of construction paper, gluing yarn and noodles to them, and sticking them on the mountain boards. No one scored hugs when we left except for a quickie Patti got off Pearl, and Barney's mumbled goodbye left me with as big a phantom limb as ever. A week later, in San Jose, I took one of the mountain boards for a novice ride in the park. When I saw a kid watching me the way I'd watched Don on his kite buggy, I handed it over.

11

I got a call at work from Pete Levitan, the editor of *Model Kit World* in Learned, Pennsylvania, one of the titles I oversaw. "I've got a Dane Fredericks problem," he said. "He's two weeks late with a story on burnishing. I think he's going through some kind of, I don't know what. We were having a conversation about gloss creep and he just went off on me. I was wondering if you could take him for coffee or something."

I said okay and called Fredericks late that afternoon, when he'd be home from his job dispatching BART trains in San Francisco. He was one of *Model Kit*'s star freelancers and I'd met him once, at a no-host coffee Clean Page gave for its local writers. He was a radio, capable of talking about fuselage decals for forty minutes, but that was typical.

"Dane?" I said. "It's Henry Bay at Clean Page."

There was a pause, and then he said, "Hi," in a guilty exhalation, as if he'd been moving from state to state for years but always knew they'd get him on the overdue burnishing story. "I'm really sorry about this," he said. "That they had to call you in on it."

"They didn't call me in," I said. "I was just talking to Pete and he thought maybe we should get together."

"I'm sorry I yelled at him. I've got a situation going on here."

"What are you doing Saturday?"

"Saturday." He sighed. "That's kind of the crux. Saturday is KitFest. I mean, I'll go, but it's not going to be pleasant."

"Okay," I said. "We can do it another day."

"I mean, if you wanted to go over there together, that would be great. Rather than me walking in there by myself."

I was running behind and had to get off the phone, so I said I'd go with him. When Saturday morning came I was still running behind, with three shirts taking too long in the dryer. I checked on them in the middle of shaving, triaged two of them onto hangers and let the third one ride, remembered my car needed gas, realized I had only enough time to go to the gas station that had the problem panhandler, and heard Patti, on the phone, say, "God. Let me—hold on a second."

She caught me by the dryer. "I've got an emergency with one of my Rollerbladers," she said. "Can you take Kris and Strother to their in-store?"

"Kris" was Santangelo, the one she might be sleeping with, although the way she said his name revealed nothing. "I'm taking that guy to the model kit thing," I said. "I'm picking him up at ten thirty."

"So they're all in San Francisco and the in-store's at one in Pacifica. Cici can bring them back."

"No, but I'm taking him to the airport Hilton," I said. "He wants me to go in with him." The shaving cream was doing something chemical on my skin. "Can't they take a bus?"

"It's in their deal to get driven."

"Okay."

"It wouldn't be one bus. It's like three separate bus districts. They'd have to be gone two hours ago."

"Okay."

"Strother knew the kid that got shot on the bus."

"Okay," I said, punching the *kay* more than I should have, and rushed past her to finish shaving. The shirt in the dryer felt almost dry until I put it on. I hadn't eaten breakfast and my stomach made a noise like the word *diurnal*.

I said, "I need their addresses," and went looking for my keys, annoying myself by trying a few places more than once. I looked twice on a table where a newspaper was open to the headline THE PARKS ARE IN HIS BLOOD. I'd been walking past that phrase for three days and it was starting to strobe. I found the keys on a chair the second time I looked there.

Patti came back from her computer and gave me a piece of paper with the addresses and phone numbers of the skateboarders, the store where they were appearing, and the restaurant near home where we were meeting people for dinner. She was on the phone when I left, saying, "What's the probation officer's name? No, the mother's officer."

When I sat back in my car the shirt wasn't dry by any standard, and I leaned forward till Palo Alto. It wasn't raining for once, but the sky was black. We were having a long rainy season, with ants, mildew, wet cuffs, darkness at lunch, and lost-dog flyers washing off phone poles in smeared shreds, a world gone bad in the refrigerator.

Dane Fredericks, the *Model Kit World* writer, lived in a

stucco cottage in the Excelsior district of San Francisco. A woman in her forties was working in the yard, which was covered in lumps of white rock instead of grass. She was putting the sootier lumps in a bucket and replacing them with new ones from a Lowe's sack. She wore gardening gloves and waterproof clogs despite the lack of water involved. I said, "Hi. I'm Henry Bay."

She stood up. "Yes. You're Dane's publisher." We shook hands. "I'm Candice."

"That looks nice," I said, pointing to the rocks. She thanked me, opened the front door, yelled "Dane," and left me in the doorway.

I went in. Every level surface in the house was covered with plastic models: cars, planes, blimps, castles, ad mascots, and Kodiak bears, all in the same half-melted realism, interspersed with piles of styrene, balsa, molding wax, and airbrush nozzles. In the kitchen the models had overrun the stove, but the microwave, with Mary Martin and the firing on Fort Sumter on top of it, still looked functional.

Dane came in wearing sweatpants, a GLUE KEEPS ME TOGETHER T-shirt, and a BART windbreaker on a walrus body. "Henry," he said glumly, and picked up a three-foot-long black carrying case. He shook his head and sighed. "I guess we should do this."

We went outside. He told Candice he'd be back by six, and they kissed as she handed him some money. When he started to put the model case in the backseat I said, "Can that go in the trunk? We have to pick a couple of guys up."

"What guys?"

I told him about the skateboarders.

"Oh, God," he said, "is that really necessary?" He wedged into the front seat with the case standing up between his knees.

"They're my wife's guys," I said. "I'm helping her out."

"I wish you would have given me some kind of warning," he said. "I hate those kids. They come into a public transit system that people are trying to use, and that's their playground. They're told over and over, 'Carry your skateboard, carry your skateboard,' so what do they not do? They literally go down the stair railings on them. God, that pisses me off."

"No, I can imagine," I said. "These guys probably don't use the system that much, though. They get driven as part of their deal."

"Oh, that's a nice deal," he said. "Not to have to lower yourself down with regular people."

We drove in silence to Noe Valley, where I double-parked at Strother's house and beeped. He came out right away, seventeen and skinny in faded jeans, sky-blue Hindenburg shoes, and a short-sleeve plaid shirt in the L.A. beach style of 1962. His hair was from then too, a pomaded shelf shading his forehead. He tripped down the steps like a gyroscope and landed in the Echo's backseat with his skateboard on his knees, wheels up. The artwork on the board's underside was a street scene that leveraged the aesthetics of Japanese schoolgirls, Mexican graffiti taggers, and fifties Futurists. As we pulled out he said, "All right. Patti's husband."

"Yeah, hi. I'm Henry Bay. This is Dane Fredericks."

"Dane. That's a great name. I'm Strother." He turned to me. "So how sick is Patti?"

"Yeah, she's great," I said. Dane looked confused. Don't worry, I thought, I'm the Switchblade Priest. I can talk to the young.

"Like in Hong Kong?" Strother said. "These local guys took us to a hotel with these great railings, and the hotel guy instantly comes out and goes, 'You can't be here! I only tell you once!' So Patti goes up to him and says, 'Hi, what a beautiful structure you have here,' and she's saying how the greatest thing the local kids could ever dream of is for us to be there, and she's like, 'You could be a hero to all the vast kids of Hong Kong,' and the kids start cheering for the guy, so he goes, 'Okay. Ten minutes,' and Kris ollied this huge railing, so then it actually *was* the greatest thing for them. But Hong Kong was pretty cool, because Singapore is perverted. You skate where they don't want you to in Singapore, they *whip* you. Literally. It's like pirates. The guy should have a parrot. But Patti, yeah."

"I didn't know you guys went to Singapore," I said.

"No, that was orchestra. American Youth Orchestra? I had jet lag and I just got a new oboe. I was pulling notes out of my butt completely. But Singapore was worse than here, and this is pretty bad as far as people getting pissed at you for skating. Not just yelling, but people will literally aim their car at you so they just miss. I swear. But yeah, oboe. Do you play music at all?" I shook my head. "Dane?"

Dane shook his head, glowering out the window and tapping on his black case. I didn't know what bothered him most, the skateboard nationalism, the free travel, or the implicit cello girls, with their load-bearing thighs and their journals full of violet-inked entries about Strother.

Kris Santangelo lived in a condo complex near Stern Grove, where he opened the door wearing nothing but blue bikini underpants. He was trim. He said "Wait a minute" to someone on his cordless phone and "What?" to me. Before I could answer, he saw Strother in the Echo, said, "Oh," and waved me inside.

The bedroom blinds were drawn, the bed a mess, and there was a smell of recent sex, like air let out of a beach toy. He continued his phone call, his hair flapping in his eyes. "Yeah, well, now it's definitely coming to a, you know, a culmination, because the guy is here to take me down there and I don't know if I'm going. A guy. I don't know. Hold on. Who are you?"

"I'm Henry Bay. I'm Patti's husband."

"Oh yeah? You're getting that?" He grinned in a way that could have meant anything from "Why would she want to sleep with you?" to "Who would want to sleep with either one of you?" to "That's funny, I was just sleeping with her two weeks ago in the hospitality suite in Austin." It beat me. I wasn't the Switchblade Priest.

"It's Patti's husband," he said on the phone. "I don't know, but he's here. Well, yeah, I'm getting in the car if this is resolved. I'm not getting in the car otherwise." He parted the blinds, looked out at the car again, and saw Dane. "God, look at *that* guy. Hold on." He put the phone down and slipped on a coral-colored T-shirt that showed Lucy from *Peanuts* with her head thrown back in porn-star ecstasy. She was reaching down on herself, her hand just out of the picture and wiggle lines around her wrist. The back of the shirt said, I'M COMING, YOU BLOCKHEAD.

"No, I did voice it," he said on the phone. "I voiced it to Patti and she said she was voicing it to you." He snapped the bikini's elastic. "Because I'm out there exemplifying you guys' shoes, and I'm supposed to have X number of stickers that are mine to sell, and—No, no way, because I give of myself out there, and do you see me going around with the thing where they measure your foot? In the shoe store? Because I'm not a shoe salesman, I'm—no, the metal thing, with the—okay, forget that, that's not the point." He pointed at a pair of jeans in the closet. I handed them to him. "This has nothing to do with your and my's sex relationship. I'm trying to keep this separate from that. What? I don't know." He put the pants on. "She's some cunt. I can't speak for that. I have to go. What? Yeah, no, I'm going. Yeah, the business thing is fine. I don't care. What? Oh, fuck off."

He pushed End and threw the phone on the bed. I followed him out to the parking berms, where he got his skateboard out of a Passport with off-road lights. The artwork on his board showed bleeding hands gripping a crown of thorns. In the car he said to Strother, "She's torturing me to the fucking death, man. Hey, can we go?"

They started discussing kick-flips and seemed to be ignoring Dane and me. "The story you're doing for Pete," I said to Dane. "Is there something about it that's kind of stopping you?"

"The five most common burnishing mistakes?" Dane said. "No, I could do that in my sleep. It's like I said on the phone, there's this other thing going on." He glanced at the rearview. "I have a club with some guys where we get together and model every week. It's always at my house, and I always have to get the snacks. It's supposed to be BYO snacks, but isn't it just the strangest thing how some people forget? 'Oh, I remembered to bring my 1:72 Mercury that I keep screwing up the foiling on and I have to ask you to help me, but somehow I can't remember to bring taco chips.' Then they enter these things in competition and people go, 'Wow, that looks good.' Yeah, I wonder how *that* happened.

"So this one guy, Craig Decker. I call him Craig *Dicker* now. I mean, not to other people, but that's my name for him. He's a good modeler. Or in certain ways he's good. He's good with brass. So, but Craig's big thing now is making his own decals on the computer. He got a printer that does decals. So two weeks ago, everyone's there, and he holds up these decals and he says, '*These* insignia can go on a *life*-scale car,' and they're city parking stickers. An Area A sticker and an Area C. And these guys are going, '*Wow*, Craig, that's *great*.' And I got"—his voice tightened—"so fucking angry."

Kris and Strother had stopped talking, but Dane didn't notice. He said, "But I didn't—I just waited for the merriment to die down, and I said, 'I don't want that in my house.' Just calmly, I said, 'Craig? I don't want that here.' And he says, 'Why, what's the problem?' I said, 'The problem is it's illegal, A, and it's selfish, Craig,' and he goes, 'Oh, give me a break,' like I'm being unreasonable. I said, 'You make those in your computer, and all your friends' names and phone numbers are in that computer, and when this gets discovered and your computer gets confiscated, everyone here that thinks this is so wonderful is going to have to go down and lose I don't know how much time off of work, and be fingerprinted, and then you're permanently in the database, and for all I know you have porno on there,' and this guy Terry jumps up and goes, 'Okay, calm down, Dane. Just calm down.' "

"Nobody should ever tell anybody to calm down," Kris said. "That's the worst fucking thing you can say to someone."

There was a moment of silence as Dane realized they were listening to him, and then he said, "I didn't need to be told to calm down. I was making a rational point."

"Yeah, but either way," Kris said. "It's like, 'Calm down? Oh, *thank* you, man. I didn't know I was, like, showing signs of *life* there. God, think what could have happened.' "

"People with cars are out of control," Strother said.

"Well, this was like let's see if we can break the infrastructure completely," Dane said. "I said, 'Craig, at least concede to me that it's unfair to the poor slobs that pay for stickers and you take their parking space because they don't possess your skills for making decals at the level of Revell in about 1981.' And everyone goes—" He gasped. "Like 'What a terrible thing you did!' Not at Craig, at me."

"Yeah, because you broke his shit down," Kris said.

"I said, 'If I had that kit,' the kit he's been making, I said, 'I would have scratch-built everything but the wheels or I wouldn't have even bothered.' Because he makes a few brass parts and we're all supposed to go over there today and say this is the best One-forty-three Jeep of the year? *Bull*shit."

"Go *ahead,* caller," Kris said.

"Some people really are named Dicker, though," Strother said. "I knew a guy that was named that."

Dane said, "So now everybody is saying stuff. Things that have nothing to do with modeling. I said, 'Everybody out.'"

"Hell, yes," Kris said. "It's your house and your snacks."

"So he's going to be where we're going now?" Strother said. "Craig?"

"We all have a table together," Dane said.

"You think something's gonna go down?" Kris said.

"What do you mean?" Dane said.

"I'm going to go in with Dane," I said. "I'll just be a few minutes."

"What, we don't get to go in?" Kris said.

"We have to get you to your event."

"But this is a public thing, though, right?" Kris said.

"If it's in a hotel, yeah," Strother said. "It's for everyone with the money to get in."

"Strother has the money for us both to get in," Kris said.

"No," Strother said.

"Patti's husband, come on," Kris said. "You're being the guy from the company. You're like, 'You guys just shut up and perform.' You're like, 'I just want my thirty pieces of flesh.' Hey, guy?"

"Dane," Strother said.

"Dane. That's great," Kris said. "Dane, do you mind if we go in?"

"I don't know. Do you know what the event is?"

"I know what it *should* be," Kris said. "It should be a salute to excellence. To those who have shaken off the false thing of, you know, glue huffing."

"The stereotype," Strother said.

"The stereotype, and they've stepped forth into excellence," Kris said.

"The glue thing is such ancient history," Dane said. "Anyone that would level that at us. That's not even a consideration."

"Dane," Kris said, "have Strother and myself had some shit leveled at us? I would say we have."

We walked down the center aisle of the show, Dane staring straight ahead as if he were integrating a high school, Kris and Strother walking a step behind us like muscle in the movies. We stopped where four guys sat on folding chairs behind a table with a dozen models on it, including a minutely detailed Vietnam-era Jeep.

The four of them stood up to face the four of us. People nearby grew quieter, as if expecting someone to slap leather. One modeler was consumptively thin, one was fat, one had a thick beard, and one wore a striped short-sleeve business shirt with a tie and no jacket, the Controlled Dynamics look.

I introduced myself, but no one answered. I said, "This Jeep is great. Who did the Jeep?"

"I did," the thin guy said. Kris's eyes did a Secret Service flicker.

"I work for the company that publishes the magazine Dane writes for," I said.

"Did you know Dane writes for a magazine?" the bearded guy said.

"No, he never mentioned that," the fat guy said. There was some dry laughter.

"Guys, I'd like to display my model so it's entered," Dane said.

"How about these guys?" Craig said. "Would they like to display some things too?"

"No," Kris said. "We're just here to improve on our model-making skills."

"You guys aren't modelers," Craig said.

"I wouldn't be saying that to me," Kris said. "I made a model of the Stonestown mall out of Fudgsicle sticks and Vaseline. It wasn't that scale shit, either. Everything in it was a different size. The muffin thing was three times as big as the parking lot. It was great."

"Oh, these guys are cute," the bearded guy said.

"I don't think that shirt is cute," Craig said, pointing at Lucy jerking off. "I think it's disgusting." He turned to Dane. "What do you think of that?"

"What?" Dane said, and focused on the shirt for the first time. Kris obligingly turned around to show him I'M COMING, YOU BLOCKHEAD. They'd done a nice job on the *Peanuts* font.

Craig said, "How come that's okay and what I did isn't okay?"

"That's not okay with me," Dane said. "I think it's disgusting too."

"No, but wait," Strother said. "Look at what kids go through. All the time you're a kid, everyone's telling you what to do, and then you finally find something that's yours."

"Yeah, and maybe it isn't baseball," Kris said. "Maybe it's your pussy."

"This is unbelievable," the thin guy said.

"Look," I said. "Excuse me. I'm just giving these guys a ride,

ing something as good as that." Kris smirked and put Craig's Jeep on the table.

"We have to go," I said.

"Yeah," Dane said. "Thanks a whole lot, Henry."

I said, "Not now, Dane."

"Oh, *sorry*." He turned to Craig. "Anybody got working steam engines?"

Craig hesitated and then said, "Yeah, Harry's showing one." Dane went behind the table and opened his model case.

I headed for the exit with Kris and Strother following me, and called Deirdre as I walked. "Is Barney there?" I said.

"No. He's at a conference in Idaho."

"Do you know where he's staying there? I just had a question."

"It's the Westin something."

I got the number from her, tried it, and left him another message. Strother called shotgun. As I drove onto the freeway I called Information and got connected to *Ice Climbing*. No one I knew still worked there. I asked the woman who answered the phone where Haystack Peak was.

"Idaho," she said. "Caribou National Forest."

I called 411 again and got through to park headquarters. "I want to report someone trying to climb Haystack Peak," I said. "I'm concerned about his safety."

"Okay, sir," the ranger said. "Is he in distress? Has he contacted you that he's in distress?"

"No. I just don't think he knows what he's doing."

"Does he have appropriate gear?"

"Yes. I think so."

"We can't tell him not to go up. That's not in our purview."

"Can you go by and see if he's okay?"

"I can mention it to the next ranger going out in that area, yes." I thanked him and rang off.

Kris said, "Patti's husband is like a guardian angel of some kind." I glared at him in the rearview mirror, heard Strother yell, "Look out!" and saw a Presto Rooter van cut in front of me. I hit the brakes, fishtailed for an epic second, barely missed the van, careened onto the shoulder, and stopped. Strother, ashen, said, "Should I drive?"

"No," I said. "I just need you guys to shut up."

"Patti's husband, come on," Kris said. "Didn't you like it when that guy was friends with his friends again? I loved that part."

"I'm going to drop you down there and someone named Cici is taking you home," I said.

"I'm gonna skate some great shit today," Kris said. "I can feel it."

In the lot next to the skateboard store in Pacifica were a few hundred waiting kids, a two-story ramp, and a Swag Van from the heavy metal radio station with the grow-light sponsors. I decided to call Patti from a pay phone so my cell wouldn't be busy if Barney called, and found one in a restaurant over the beach. When she answered I said, "Barney called me. He said he was going ice climbing in Idaho. He—"

"*Who* called you?"

"Barney."

"I don't understand."

"I know."

"Did he sound upset, or . . . ?"

"No, he sounded happy. He's supposed to call me back."

"That's so weird. How did it go with Kris and Strother and the guy?"

"That was fine," I said.

Walking down to the beach, I heard cheers a block away, looked over, and saw Kris Santangelo shoot over the lip of the ramp. He was an arc of pure energy against the sky and so forth. I paced on the sand, trying not to worry about Barney, till it was time to go.

Dinner was at a modern Italian restaurant at the top of our price range, with Kristin, who designed shirts for Hindenburg; her husband, Jon, a graphic artist who did a lot of regional perishable foods packaging but was trying to get some more challenging things going; their friend Ed, who sold bulk telephony minutes; and his wife, Belinda, who customized RV interiors. I got there last. Patti said, "Did he call?"

"Not yet," I said.

"Patti was just telling us," Belinda said. "Your brother is mountain climbing?"

"Ice climbing," I said. "I think it's okay."

"But he's never been up before?" Kristin said. "That's pretty technical if you haven't done it. It's like these huge icicles hanging off—"

"Let's get you a drink," Ed said.

"*Ice* climbing," Jon said.

"Is he an older brother or younger?" Belinda said.

"I think it's okay," I said again. My phone rang. I walked to the bathroom hallway as I answered. "Henry?" The wind noise was still there, but softer.

"Barney? Where are you?"

"I just got down. It was amazing."

"Where are you now?"

"I'm going back to the hotel." A car door closed and the wind cut out.

"How long are you staying there?"

"Two more days. Hey, you want to come out here?"

"Okay," I said. "Sure."

"That'd be great. There's some other stuff I want to try here. You could do some with me."

"But Barney? Why are you doing this?"

"I know. I know," he said. "What makes us do this? If you've done it, I don't have to say a word. If you haven't done it, nothing I can say will explain it to you."

On my way back to the table I realized I'd read those sentences somewhere—*Motocross X-treme* or maybe *Bodyboard Shreddin'*, someplace where I'd helped compile the codex of the risk monkeys. The world had tilted. I asked Patti to order for me and went back to the hallway to book my plane.

12

I landed in Idaho in blowing snow and rented a Forester, the cheapest thing that would stay on the roads. The rental clerk's directions got me stuck for twenty minutes in a gridlocked business district where you could buy a hundred paintings of snug chalets but no milk. The milk would be in a parallel downtown, where the rental clerks lived and traffic was light.

Barney's Westin was six wooden trapezoids wedged into a hillside between ski runs. The conference schedule in the lobby said a panel on blastomere cleavage was just starting. There was security, as Barney had said, a big guy in a suit and earpiece at the door to the Conestoga Room. He let me look inside, but Barney wasn't there.

I called his cell. "Great, you're here," he said. "I'm at Snow Angel. Come over, okay? I've got to suit up."

I detoured around the downtown to Snow Angel, a funkier

resort whose guests looked like Patti's snowboarders. I didn't see Barney on the slopes, and was about to call him again when I saw the luge run.

It was modeled after the Olympic ones, a wooden trough lined with smooth ice, running down the mountain in a series of sharp banked turns. In the start house at the top a guy in a red neoprene suit and pointed booties lay down on his sled, face up and feet first. He put his gloved hands on the ice, rocked the sled back and forth a few times, and shoved off, pawing the ice twice more for speed and then putting his hands in the sled as gravity took over.

He hit the first turn hard but shifted his weight, banked through it, and came out level. A crowd of fifty cheered him on, while I braced myself every time he bumped the side of the trough. He straightened out just in time for the steep final straightaway and the braking uphill stretch that ended the run. When he stood up, yelling and shaking off snow, I saw his face. He wasn't Barney. Barney was carrying his sled into the start house.

I ran up the hill through the snow, but he was already taking off. We reached the first turn at the same time, so I was only a few feet from him when his troubles began.

He slammed his sled into the corner of the turn and came out of it on the wall of the run, trying to get the sled's runners back down. The next turn was worse, putting him so far up the wall that only one runner was on the ice. The crowd was yelling, "Aah, no, God," and I heard myself shout "Barney!" It looked like he'd either crash in the snow or flip over and be facedown on the ice at sixty miles an hour, but finally he dropped back into the trough, crashed through the rest of the turns, and wobbled into the finish.

People ran to see if he was okay. The snow on his face was

red from his scrapes but he stood up from the sled, high-fived the kid who handed him a towel, and yelled, "Yes!" as if he'd just broken the course record. The crowd laughed and applauded. He took off his gloves, wiped his face, saw me, yelled, "Henry!" came over, and hugged me.

"Are you okay?" I said.

"I'm great." He saw blood on the towel, scooped up some snow, and rubbed it on his face as he started walking toward the parking lot. "That third turn, boy. You should never anticipate. What'd you rent?"

"A Forester. Barney—"

"Perfect. Let's get something to eat."

He led me to a bicycle rack by the parking lot and unlocked a mountain bike whose tires were studded with steel bolts for riding on ice. "They rent these in town," he said. "We can get you one later."

There were clothes bungeed to the bike's rear rack. He opened the car door and stood behind it to change, replacing the luge suit with ski pants, a down parka, lobster gloves, and hiking boots. Then he threw the bike in the back of the Forester and smiled at me. "Sometimes," he said, "you really need to get away."

He had me drive to a restaurant in the milk district, a big room smelling of wet clothes and coffee. We got a booth and Barney ordered the Posthole Digger, which was four eggs, four pancakes, sausage, hash browns, cream gravy, and biscuits. I ordered the Slimmer, which was the same thing with cottage cheese instead of gravy.

"So," Barney said, "how's Patti?"

"She's fine."

"I bet. Her teams are winning everything." In place of his usual scrutiny he looked at me affably, like he wasn't trying to solve anything. It made me nervous.

"Barney? Could you tell me what's going on here?"

"Yeah. Where to start?" he said, and drained his coffee in two sips. "Well. When you moved to Illinois, I was pretty annoyed at you. I don't know if you remember that."

"Of course I remember. I thought you were still annoyed."

"No, but I was then."

"I wanted to stay at college and help that lawyer—"

"No," he said, still cheerful. "By definition, what we *do* is what we want. We might not like the *reasons* we want to, we might not do what we *wish* we wanted to, but if we didn't want to we wouldn't do it.

"Anyway, you remember that time you showed me a copy of *Ice Climbing*, and I said it seemed like people need a lot of stimulus? I kept thinking about that. I didn't understand those people and I didn't understand what you were doing there. I mean, you were obviously attracted to it. The places you were living—we were always so impatient to get out of Rancho Cahuenga, but you were calling me from places that made Rancho Cahuenga look like Renaissance Florence. Silica, Missouri? It's two speed traps and a Superfund site. I checked."

The food came. Barney put his hash browns on top of his pancakes, put a fried egg on top of that, sliced the egg into runny checks, poured maple syrup and gravy over the whole thing, cut a layer-cake wedge of it and started to eat.

"I wanted to know why you liked it so much," he said, "because when you were growing up, and you didn't know what you wanted to do? I was always watching you and thinking, 'I want something really good to come get him.'" Just like that, I had two hot tears behind my eyelids.

"So I went to this bookstore in Lawrence where they have hundreds of magazines," Barney said. "A wall of them. It made me dizzy at first. Quilting. Souping up cars. All these areas where people are keeping up with the literature every month." He was putting the Posthole Digger away fast, though he was as thin as he'd been in Kansas.

"After a while I was spending a lot of time in that bookstore. I would lie to Deirdre about where I was, because I didn't think it would make sense to her. That was scary, initially, the lying. I felt like one of these guys who sleep with their students. But I would make up an errand, and it was shocking how easy it was. The steering's pulling to the left, Tagaki wants to show me some gene expressions, pretty much anything and you're out the door. I think those guys might enjoy that as much as the sex. Or not, you know. Put that aside."

"Why didn't you tell me you were reading them?" I said.

"I am telling you. Was there a deadline?" He shrugged, still smiling. "I was reading an issue of *Ultra Running*. I kept following it after you worked there. They had these pictures of people doing hundred-mile foot races in the desert, with those close-ups of the heat rash and the scorpion bites, and I said, 'What's going on with these people? No one's making them do this.'" He mopped up gravy with a pancake. "They're conditioning themselves as harshly as anything since foot-binding, and they're putting themselves in situations that the conditioning might get them out of but it might not. It's uncertain. And the uncertainty seems to be part of what they're doing it for."

He finished his food and looked at mine. I pushed it over to him. "I had this conference coming up in Santa Fe, on new nuclear-transfer technologies, and I'd seen something in *Ultra Running* about an all-night event in New Mexico where the racers were weeping and seeing Indian spirits and so on. I'd been going to the field house, but that was stuff like Pilates for Busy People, which is designed to let you go back to work without taking a shower. Whereas sweat is a factor in this, right? Just like pain is a factor. Elevated pulse. Endorphins. All factors.

"So I stepped it up. I got out there on the farm roads. Again, I didn't tell Deirdre. But after a while I was *gliding*. You remember when we rode our bikes on Transformer Way right after they paved it? That's what it was like, but without the bicycle.

"So the first night of the conference, I snuck off to the desert and ran all night. By the time the sun came up I was an Indian hunter, you know, 'I'm a shadow flying over the rocks. Something just thought it saw me, but then it looked again and I was gone.' I went back to the hotel and ran into some guys from the conference. I told them I'd been jogging around in the parking lot for half an hour. They said, 'Good for you, I should really do that.'

"The next conference, ovasomagenesis in Delaware, I rented roller skis. I'd never been skiing before. They told me to go to some park where I could fool around without getting hurt, but I drove six miles up a mountain road instead. I start skiing down this narrow, winding road; the descents are like ten degrees, and there's a sheer drop with no guardrail.

"It was so *fast*, Henry. And so cold. I was using ninety-eight percent of my brain to steer, and all that was left was the lizard brain, so I was thinking 'Cold too cold why cold cold?' you know? There certainly wasn't room to think about the things I was dealing with at home. Which there were a lot of."

"I had a sense," I said.

"So now I knew what the attraction was. But then a car comes around a curve. I'm an inch from their mirror and an inch from the side of the road, and then I'm off the road, I can feel the pebbles under my wheels, and just past the pebbles is the drop, it's like fifty feet. I'm correcting my course about five times a second.

"When I made it down I thought, 'Okay, that was stupid. Never again.' Then I started walking back up to my car, and within ten minutes I knew I was going to do it again. I was going to do it all day."

"Barney—"

"So you and the groups you've worked with over the years, you've really done something for people," he said. "For me, definitely."

"It sounds great," I said. I was suddenly starring in the life of the guy who'd always starred in mine. I had no idea how that might play out. "I'm just concerned about the safety part."

His face clouded for the first time. "You're not going to tell Deirdre, are you? She thinks I'm weighing my food here."

"No. I'm just concerned."

He nodded. "The uncertainty. But you know what, Henry? The uncertainty's always there anyway. It's been there all along. I just wasn't *using* it before. It's like having this wonderful saxophone that you never play."

When we got back to the Westin, the panel discussion had ended and scientists were milling in the lobby. On our way to the elevator, people came up to Barney to ask him questions or compliment him on papers he'd written. Upstairs he changed into his bike clothes, an old-school woollen jersey with block letters saying IL GRANDE CICLISMO, tights with a chamois crotch liner, cleated shoes, and fingerless gloves. I stuck with my jeans and sweater.

The bike store was in the chalet-painting district, and it

took us fifteen minutes to park. I rented a bike with studded tires like Barney's and signed a waiver that absolved the store of ever having gone into business.

As we rode out of town Barney sought out the ugliest patches of black ice to ride over, showing me how the bolts on the tires kept us upright. It was fun, although the seam of my jeans was already shredding my perineum.

After half an hour we turned onto a dirt fire road that climbed for two miles to a tree-lined ridge. I was in no shape to ride uphill, and Barney pulled away from the start. The studded tires broke the thin ice that covered the mud, which sucked my wheels to a crawl. I stood up on the pedals, rocking the bike sloppily and gasping for air that was too cold to breathe. Barney kept turning and smiling at me from farther and farther away.

He waited for me at the top. When we'd been up there for a minute, looking down at a valley of fir trees while I caught my breath, he said, "Do you remember when you called me up and said nothing was working out but it was okay?"

"When?"

"A long time ago. You said it had to be okay because that was what was happening. You were losing your job."

"Oh. Yeah."

"Where were you?"

"Ohio." I hugged myself, trying to stop my teeth from chattering. "I was there to see a woman who made crochets."

"Was that the woman you weren't getting anywhere with?"

"What?"

"When you called, you said, 'There's a woman I'm not getting anywhere with, either.'"

"Oh. No. That was a business trip. I was working for *Crochet Life.*"

"I think I missed that one."

"I was only there three days."

"Wow. Was that the shortest?"

I nodded.

"Who was the woman you weren't getting anywhere with?"

"She worked at *Kite Buggy*. Why?"

"I don't know. It sounded bad. What was her name?"

"Jillian." He nodded and looked sympathetic. It was like being back on the science fair balcony, except that I was afraid he'd jump off this time. "Should we go back?" I said.

"Yeah. I was thinking down there." He pointed down the rocky hillside, where there was no trail.

"I don't think we should do that," I said.

"Are you sure? The suspension on these is pretty good. You guys gave it three sprockets."

He started down, bouncing over rocks and tree roots, before I could answer. I tried to go slowly, but the hill was steep, my vision blurred as the cold made my eyes tear, and the scree kept catching my front wheel and steering me toward rocks and trees. When it aimed me at a car-size outcropping I panicked, hit the brakes, locked the front wheel, fell over with the bike, and slid six feet into a tree. The bike's frame slammed into my crotch but at least I'd stopped moving. Barney, at the bottom, yelled, "Are you okay?"

I croaked back that I was. He pedaled a slow schoolyard pirouette, his ass hovering over the seat, as he waited for me.

I got out from under the bike and stood up, my mouth full of a copper adrenaline taste I couldn't spit out, and walked the bike down to where he was. He said, "Wasn't that great?" with a fifteen-year-old's oblivious smile. I couldn't remember him smiling it even once when he was fifteen, but he was smiling the hell out of it now.

• • •

I rode back to the hotel behind him, scraped and wet but on mercifully paved roads. We returned the bikes and went to a drugstore to get alcohol and bandages "for your road rash," Barney said. It was a depressingly chipper phrase, and I knew exactly where he'd gotten it.

The cold had anesthetized me but the pain blossomed in the shower while I thought, Is Barney crazy? Too long at the science fair? Or just happy for once? Even with the roller skiing he's no crazier than the people I've been working with all these years, and what a helpful gauge that is.

It's like he likes me now," I said to Patti when I got back to San Jose.

"Of course he likes you." She'd paused the DVD she was watching on a guy coughing blood in an alley while two guys kicked him. She was in a gritty-crime-drama cycle.

"Not of course," I said. "I'm worried that he's trying to hurt himself."

"Why would he want to hurt himself?"

"I don't know," I said, "but he's going down a mountain sixty miles an hour on a sled and he doesn't know how."

"You could glue noodles on his sled and give it to another child," she said.

"Look," I said.

"No, you saw how it is there. He has to do *some*thing."

"You and Deirdre always got along before," I said.

"Getting along with people gets less exciting," Patti said, and started the movie again.

• • •

The next day I called Barney in Idaho and told him I'd had a good time. "Yeah, I'm sorry you had to leave," he said. "There's whitewater here. I'll call you next time I go someplace."

I said that sounded good and hung up. The Barney-is-happy and Barney-is-crazy theories took turns in my head, like parallel universes vibrating five minutes apart, and I remembered something Gerald had said in college. "When automation started happening, all these movies came out that had robots in them. They'd have this scene where the scientists were testing the new robot they invented. It was like, 'Gentlemen, the robot is a creature of pure logic. Everything has to add up. Observe.' And they'd tell the robot, 'The sky is blue,' and then they'd tell it, 'The sky is green.' So the robot would start turning its head back and forth, trying to reconcile that, and then smoke would come out of its ears and a few springs would burst out of its head, and then it would just flop over. They had that in a few different movies. You know, variations on it. People loved it. They thought it was hilarious. They thought it was about robots."

13

We just bought this," Walter Denise said, handing me a magazine called *Exotic Pets.* "Tom wants you to go tomorrow."

The cover photo showed a woman's hand with long pink fingernails and six rings, scratching the head of a monkey-like animal whose amber eyes asked what it had done to get itself into this situation. The main line was LEMURS AS PETS? THE CONTROVERSY CONTINUES!

"I can't take another one," I said.

"I realize," Walter said, and pointed at the magazine. "It's in Montana. They have like seventy animals at their office. You're not one of those people that pass out from methane, are you?"

When he left I called Ingrid Saperstein, the editor of *Exotic*

Pets, to introduce myself and tell her I was coming. "We'll be so happy to meet you," she said. "Everybody's going to be on their best behavior. *You're* going to be on your best behavior, aren't you?" I started to answer but realized she was talking to someone on her end. "Yes, you are," she said. There was cawing.

We hung up and I flipped through the issue, past photos of pythons on sofas and ferrets dressed up as Houston Astros. If nothing else, there had to be a better name for the editor's column than "Off the Beaten Pet."

In the morning I flew to Bozeman, rented a Focus, and drove to the small town nearest the magazine. I was hoping for a "Meet Me Under the Big Clock" hotel, but there were only chains. I checked into one, drove another hour, and turned onto a long dirt driveway with a damp zoo smell. At the end of it were two doorless garages, dark inside, with twenty pairs of green and yellow eyes looking out. Outside were long tables of labeled cages full of wallabies, rat snakes, and bush babies.

I entered the main building through a door with a NO DOGS sign and almost stepped on a foot-long turtle. It snapped at me and I backed into the art director, who pointed out Ingrid. She was thirty and short, with frizzy brown hair and a film of hairs and feathers on her clothes. "It's so good to meet you," she said. "Henry, this is Edward. Edward's a fennec fox."

The panting animal on her wrist looked as fake as a jackalope on a gag postcard, but it was real, with a bat's face, a Chihuahua's body, and ears so big I couldn't see how it held its head up. "Edward comes from the desert," Ingrid said. "These big old ears keep him cool. Yes they do. And this is Frankie. Frankie is a kinkajou." This one, its own worst enemy with a cat's body and a rodent's head, sat on Ingrid's shoulder with its tail curled up in her hair. "Frankie has a little problem with peeing on my desk blotter, don't you? Shake hands with Henry, Frankie."

At the staff meeting the people sat in chairs while the animals roamed the layout table, scattering sunflower seeds and defending territory. The photo editor pitched a feature on Nile monitor lizards. "They're amazing looking," he said. "They get up to seven feet."

"There are problems when they get that big, though," the reptile editor said. "You buy it as a hatchling, and they don't tell you it can take your cat's head off one day. You can get one without a temper, but you have to go to Gerald Hauser."

"I don't think it's a feature," Ingrid said. "I think it's a Spotlight. Do you think it's a Spotlight?" she asked the prairie dog at her breast. "Yes, you do."

I wondered if the Gerald Hauser they were talking about could possibly be the one I knew. We hadn't spoken since I'd been a jerk to him in New York six years earlier. Could he have gone from strategic metals to exotic pets? He could talk to anyone, but did that include seven-foot lizards? It was too weird an image not to check.

When the meeting was over I asked the reptile editor what his Gerald looked like. "We had a picture of him a few months ago," he said, and opened a back issue to "Petting Parties," a spread of small photos taken at pet shows and zoo openings. There was Gerald, with a woman and a jerboa at a convention booth. He was talking with the avidity I remembered, his floor-trader hands in the air.

"I think that's the only thing we have on him," the reptile editor said. "He's very low profile. You'll see him at something like Species Showcase next month, but he doesn't do most of the shows. He's got the calmest animals I've ever seen, though. The red porcupine boom? That was him."

• • •

I was nervous about seeing Gerald again, but what he'd said in New York about me having something up my ass seemed like a dare now, and I got on a plane. Species Showcase, in Anaheim, was my thousandth trade show, a noisy small town of booths under a convention center's vaulting struts. I found Gerald's location on the program map and worked my way there past bikers with fat snakes on their shoulders and tween girls buying possum milk substitute.

His booth was the classiest one, its partitions faced in smooth ceramic instead of acoustic cheese. A beautiful young woman at a desk in the middle of the space watched Gerald talk to a couple in their twenties next to a wire-mesh enclosure eight feet long.

He'd put on an extra ten pounds, mostly swallowed up by his height, and gone back to the 1947 shirt and pants but had kept the New York blazer. When he saw me coming he held his hands up in mock surrender and said, "I don't want any trouble. Unless it's *interesting* trouble. Some way of doing trouble we haven't seen before." He laughed and put an arm around me. "*My* man. This is Henry Bay. A very old friend of mine. You look wonderful. Can I show you something in a mandrill? Something with a big purple ass?" The couple laughed and introduced themselves.

"This is Leonard," Gerald said to me, pointing into the wire enclosure. "Leonard's an ornate Nile monitor. These guys are thinking about having Leonard move in with them."

"Wow," I said.

"I know," the woman said, "it's pretty major. But look at him."

Leonard was six feet long, with bands of yellow spots circling his fat green body. His house, open on top, had heat lamps, a humidifier, and a rock bridge for him to lie on. He looked up at me with cautious black eyes as his tongue, a bright pink reed, shot eight inches out of his mouth. "That's Henry, Leonard," Gerald said. "Henry's with me. Leonard's smelling you with his tongue."

He leaned down and put his arm into the enclosure. Leonard climbed on to it and rested his head on Gerald's shoulder as Gerald stood up. The young couple sighed, and people passing by stopped to watch.

"You don't want to do this unless Leonard knows you very well," Gerald said. "You might not want to do it at all. Certainly not without protective clothing." He knelt, and Leonard slid back in to the enclosure and on to the rock bridge. "We're going to do some basking now," Gerald said.

The young guy handed Gerald some snapshots of a big yard with banana trees and a pond. "This is our backyard," he said. "He could pretty much go around out there."

"Watched at all times," Gerald said.

"Definitely," the woman said.

"Because if he climbs this tree he'll fall and break his head," Gerald said. "They're good climbers but they're even better fallers."

He held the photos up to the lizard's face. "Look at that nice backyard, Leonard. Do you think you'd like to live there?" He turned to the couple. "Leonard has no idea what he's looking at or what I'm talking about. Whatever you do here today, don't let anyone run that kind of shit on you." The couple nodded. He gave the pictures back.

"Now, I can't sell you guys Leonard," Gerald said. They looked stricken. "What I *can* sell you is the time I've spent with him that's made him feel like no one's about to make him into cowboy boots."

"Right," the guy said. "That would be great."

"Why don't you walk around and think about it?" Gerald said. "I think you and he are good together, but you should take your time."

The couple nodded solemnly, thanked Gerald several times, and left. Gerald showed me around his booth, introducing me to a sugar glider, a redheaded iguana, and the woman at the desk. "Henry, this is Katie. Henry and I are going to the disgusting café. Would you like a spoiled brownie wrapped in vinyl?" She said no thanks and we started walking.

"I'm sorry about New York," I said.

"You think *you're* sorry about New York," he said. "I thought New York was going to come through for me. I thought New York and I were going to grow old together."

It took us fifteen minutes to cross the hall, with people stopping Gerald to praise his animals or say they'd been wanting to meet him. A guy in a loud sweater, with a little monkey on his shoulder, came toward us. Gerald spoke under his breath: "Look at this fool. Look at the sweater. He looks like one of those guys who fuck with Batman."

"That's a great monitor you're showing," the guy said. "Did I see him go up on your shoulder? That's amazing."

"Leonard constantly surprises me and I constantly disappoint Leonard," Gerald said. "That's our deal."

"That's great," the guy said. "Have you met Justine?" He pointed the monkey at Gerald.

"Hi, Justine," Gerald said, and nodded goodbye. When the guy was out of earshot he said, "A colorful fact about the playful marmoset is that people who take them out of their habitat and sell them ought to be shot."

The café was a stockade of partitions with wilted chef's salads for $11.50. We bought coffee and sat at a table. "How'd you locate me?" Gerald said.

"I work for the company that publishes *Exotic Pets*."

"Clean Page," Gerald said, shaking his head like when he'd said, "Controlled Dynamics," the day I met him. "We don't dig the brother Tom Patrick, but he doesn't need us to. I like that editor, though. Ingrid. She's a little 'Whose nose is it,' but all these people are. They talk baby talk to animals that could disembowel them. You live there? San Jose?"

I nodded. "How about you?"

"Not far. Mill Valley."

A fancy Marin County suburb. "Can you get propane there?"

"Sure. Health propane."

"Did you get tired of the metals?" I said.

"Not tired, no, but . . . when I saw you was after jihad, right? But we didn't talk about it." I shook my head.

"The idea of jihad is that it sweeps away everything in its path," he said. "It certainly did that with me. I ran thirty blocks uptown with that cloud coming after me, and of course I had no idea what I might have been running *toward*. I didn't know what they might have going in Times Square. I just ran. That was the fucked-up Pamplona out there. It was the fucked-up Mardi Gras."

"I'm sorry," I said. "I should have asked you about it."

"I don't see why. I didn't have anything to say that you haven't heard a dozen times. The wet handkerchief over the face? The school gym in New Jersey? I couldn't reach my girlfriend for two days? You've heard all that."

"Was she okay?"

"Chloe?" He nodded and showed me his ring. "We're wed. You still need to meet her." He pointed to my hand. "There's a Mrs. Henry as well."

"Patti."

"With an *i*?" I nodded. He closed his eyes, smiled, and

opened them. "You know what they say all the time in strategic metals? They sit at their trading screens and say"—he put his hand by his mouth and sprang his fingers apart, as if teaching me a phrase of Italian—"'I'm getting fucking killed here.' And now people *were* getting fucking killed there. It came true. And yet it was a miracle, how fast they got our screens back up. I think we were all kind of awed by that. If they'd gotten me back up as fast as my screen, it would have been spectacular."

He poured two sugars into his last inch of coffee. "But there was still that smell. The smell wasn't going anywhere. You could go five hundred miles from home, buy all new clothes there, pour salt water through your nose, it didn't make any difference. All the perfumes of Arabia, Henry. Well. City people. Complain, complain.

"So that time I saw you, I was already on my way out of metals. I was wondering what I could do that might mean a little more to people. I don't mean I had no self-interest. I'm a commercial traveler. I come to the Quality Inn with my sample case and fall asleep with my shoes on. I take some steam with a man who has six stores and whose order I hope to write."

"I think you're doing better than that," I said, nodding toward his double booth.

He waved it off. "People kept saying that people would feel better if they could go back to familiar things. The comfort food. The Spaldeens. I had my doubts. I wasn't sure the familiar was really there to go back to.

"Chloe and I went to Yellowstone. She revitalized the main street of Kalispell and then we drove down. Have you been there?" I shook my head. "If you walk for a day you can still get off by yourself. We slept by a stream. I get up in the morning, I go to get wood, and I'm just going into the trees when this buffalo walks up to me.

"We both stop, like five feet apart. The buffalo's the size of a station wagon. It's got the beard, the big shoulders, the serape feature on the side. But what I can't take my eyes off are the eyes." He showed me the buffalo's clear stare. "And his breathing is slow. I'm scared, but my breathing slows down anyway, to match. My face gets the same as his. My shoulders. Five minutes. Eight minutes.

"Finally the buffalo walks away. It shuffles off to Buffalo. People are shuffling off this mortal buffalo all over the place, but for once I'm not thinking about that. I go to get the wood but my steps feel different. It's like I'm pressing down on the ground with five hundred pounds per leg.

"I go back to where we slept, and I'm thinking it really doesn't matter how much of the familiar I put in place, because the strange is coming over to kill me later anyway. The strange believes in things I couldn't even dream about. There's drunk with God and then there's mean drunk with God. But I said, 'What if I could be friends with the strange? Just with a piece of it, just for a while? Would that help?' "

He saw he was leaning over the table, and sat back. "So I started learning about animals. I'd already eaten vegetables and sold minerals, so why not?"

"I always wondered what you meant when I saw you that time," I said. "When you said the metals were a funny business."

He thought for a minute, considering how much to tell me. "Actually?" he said. "There were certain difficulties even before the eleventh. I came up against some regulatory issues. And of course the difficulties I ran into weren't just mine, they were my investors'. People said some strongly worded things about me. I said a few about myself." He stood up. "I like the buffalo story better, though. It's true too, as far as it goes."

When we got back to his booth the young couple was waiting to say yes. Gerald suggested skipping some of the usual paperwork. They hesitated, then looked at Leonard and agreed. In college I'd thought Gerald would go around shaming the modern day into behaving itself, but that was college. He closed the deal, throwing in some frozen food balls and a few anecdotes.

See, I said to myself, it's not that hard to change what you do. You run into a buffalo or walk into a Franklin Covey store, crochet crooked or just lie down on a luge sled, paw the ice, and go. Everyone's doing it. When I was leaving, Gerald said we'd have to get together for dinner soon, "and bring the wives." I waited for him to ask me if I hated it when people said that, but he never did.

14

I'm going to Colorado to see Dad on tour," Barney said on the phone. "You want to go?"

"On tour?"

"Yeah, it's twelve cities. Mom isn't doing all of it but she's going to this one. It's called The Big Meeting. They have six or seven speakers. The Colorado one is near Pikes Peak. We could do some bouldering. Let me give you the phone number."

I asked Patti if she wanted to go to Colorado and she said yes. We were having a good day, and she liked seeing Mom.

I mail-ordered the tickets, which came tucked into a glossy program with soaring eagles on the cover. The speakers included an ex–vice president of the United States, a two-time carpeting saleswoman of the year, Dad, and a football player whose career had been ended by knee injuries three weeks into his first pro season and who'd written an inspirational bestseller called *I Can Still Pray on Them*.

Dad got off the plane in Colorado bulging with energy. Everyone else, including Mom, looked suitably wrecked from the flight and the long delay before it, but Dad bounced out of the Jetway like a bullet list of travel tips, hydrated and aisle-stretched, inhaling the noxious mix of contrail and Cinnabon like it was an ocean breeze. Even with his hair getting gray he looked younger, fit and tan in a straw-colored suit and cocoa Mephistos. Mom wore her work outfit, with an upgrade from flip-flops to Huaraches. They both hugged us, customary for Mom but new for Dad, who got two-count chest and cheek off Patti.

I asked if we were meeting Barney. "No, he's getting in tomorrow," Dad said. "We have to stop at baggage claim up here. They made me check my chair."

The cardboard box Dad took off the carousel was four feet square and six inches thick. We lashed it to the roof of his rented Land Cruiser with bungee cords from his carryon.

The fifteen-minute drive to the hotel took us through sunshine, a blinding thunderstorm, and then rainbows. The office parks and shopping centers here were like everywhere else, but the landscape and weather kept staging over-the-top parables, with cloudbanks straining the sun into searchlights and snowcapped Pikes Peak glaring down at gray walls of sky forked with lightning. It was known as a religious area, and I felt that if I lived there I'd be devout about something inside of two weeks.

The hotel lobby was huge, with mounted caribou heads looking down on triumphal coffee urns, but our room was tiny. Patti got some vodka and a bag of shellacked Japanese crackers from the minibar, lay down with both pillows behind her, flipped through the movies on TV, and found a domestic drama where people had loud arguments and drank milk from the carton.

Mom and Dad had a dinner date with a guy who was publishing a day planner featuring the take-away points from Dad's books, and Patti said the minibar food had been dinner for her. I went to the bar off the lobby for wings and ranch. When I got back she was asleep in her HINDENBURG T-shirt, the blanket at her waist. Looking at her, I forgot our problems momentarily and felt a surge of love, the old chest panic. If I'd tried to wear that shirt I'd have been a vampire sucking on youth, but on Patti it was as if all the kid brio from Burning Man to Phuket had settled on her breasts, which were being flattened an optimum half inch by the stretched black fabric.

I got into bed with her but couldn't sleep. Previews of the bouldering expedition with Barney played in my mind, using two miserable weekends from my job at *Rappel* for source material. I saw the new Barney on top of a rock formation, watching the sun rise with one perfect tear of joy on his cheek, like Gerald's monk. All these years he'd had three times the brains I did, and now he was going to beat me at having none.

When I finished worrying about Barney I started worrying that Patti would tell Mom about our problems while I was off trying to boulder. There were no sides to take, but Mom would take Patti's. She'd know I'd built the rut we were in, that I was a natural rut-builder like Dad, except that Dad had walked out of the family rut business in his two-hundred-dollar walking shoes, leaving me in charge.

In the morning I rented bouldering shoes and a harness at a climbing store, got dressed for Dad's speech, and met Barney in the hotel lobby. His tweed sport coat had a pale rectangle over the pocket from a hundred conferences' worth of HELLO stickers. "Dad went on ahead with the vice president guy," he said. "They have a warm-up routine they do together."

Patti and Mom came off the elevator in twice-a-year dresses, stockings, and makeup. Barney hadn't seen Patti since he'd said goodbye to us in Lawrence with no eye or body contact, but he gave her extended temple-press now.

We went in the Land Cruiser, Mom driving. "You must be getting a kick out of Dad doing this," Barney said to her.

"Uh-huh," Mom said.

The event was in a covered arena, a big silver disc with twelve pairs of glass doors. Long tables in the lobby were piled with salesmanship books and motivational CDs. The salespeople at the tables over-enunciated their pitches and focused on the browsers' eyes, and the browsers focused and enunciated right back at them, a closed loop of technique learned from the previous year's CDs.

Half the four thousand seats had sold. There were lots of people in suits, but also youth groups, Air Force Academy cadets, Sedona types, and knit-hat chemo klatches. Behind the podium a giant video screen showed a repeating montage of wheat, flags, fireworks, the Grand Canyon, and kids playing in hydrant spray on a ghetto street. The music repeated too, a stirring-esque synthesizer melody that hurled itself up the scale every twenty seconds.

The first speaker was the quota-smashing carpet saleswoman, who said, "You see, women have an advantage, because women have been going to the supermarket all these years, and a lot of what happens in business is just like going to the supermarket. You put your foot down and doors open up for you."

"We should be writing this down," Patti deadpanned to Mom.

When the saleswoman finished, the emcee introduced Dad, who came onstage carrying the web chair he'd sat in for the summer he got laid off. Barney smiled and nudged me.

Dad unfolded the chair, put it down beside the podium, went to the mic, and said, "Back in the 1980s, I lost my job." His speaking voice was different, full of breath and portent. "The company I thought I was going to work for till I was sixty-five went out of business and took my pension with it. Sad story, but it's not unusual. It gets a little less unusual every time you turn on the news."

He took the wireless mic off the podium and walked around. "So I did what the people at programs like this one are always telling you to do. I created my own job. I created a job sitting in that chair and looking out at the street. That's the hardest job I ever had, because you don't get a lot of feedback from your boss when your boss is an eight-dollar chair from the drugstore.

"After a while I got a job at a salad bar. I went from managing forty people to slicing forty pounds of cucumbers. But it turns out there's a satisfaction you get from doing something real like that, seeing people eat those cucumbers. I started feeling better."

I looked at Barney. He was smiling proudly, a kid watching his father in a local theatrical, loving the glue-on beard and the laboring accent. Barney, I thought, are you really buying this? Can we speak the true samba here? Dad is the office expert who hasn't been in an office for fifteen years, and he hated the salad bar.

Dad held up a business card. "My card," he said. "It's a flimsy little item. It's nothing. But it's everything, because it says what I do. It says I *have* something to do. You take this away from people, they dry up and blow away." Barney, did you know you can have the business card and flutter down the street like a gum wrapper anyway? Can we talk behind Dad's back again, just once for old time's sake? I know I haven't said anything either, but why don't you start?

After Dad they brought on the ex–vice president, who looked like the sandy-haired dad in a family movie, his blow-torch smile betrayed by nervous eyes as if he were bracing for his kids' next prank. During his one term in office he'd called India a key part of Europe and said that *Sesame Street* "subjects America's children to a threateningly run-down urban environment, where living in a garbage can is held up as being a badge of honor." The president had dumped him from the ticket the next time but lost anyway.

"I had the honor of serving with a great president and meeting with heads of state from all over the world," he told the crowd, "but it's every bit as great of an honor to be talking to your organization today. Or to this gathering, rather. To this group. I mean that."

He was followed by Brent Targill, the football player who'd been retired by knee injuries. He hobbled out of the wings, stiff and grimacing, then stopped halfway to the podium, pointed at the audience like "Gotcha!" and grinned, walking almost normally the rest of the way. He was in his late thirties, with the sly smile of a coach kidding his players on awards night.

He recounted "hearing that crunch" at the bottom of a midfield pileup and knowing it was over. After two years of moping, he said, he'd realized he could serve a higher purpose with youth counseling and a prison ministry, because "it turned out

I still had a coach. I had a coach that was willing to die, just to give me a victory. He—boy, you folks are quick. I say that in New York, they think I'm talking about Jimmy Johnson. True story. But that's not who I mean."

I looked at Barney again. His stare of concentration was suddenly back, fiercer than ever, as if Targill's homily of the fractures held the mysteries of nature. The more religious Targill got in the five minutes that followed, the harder Barney focused.

"Hey, you folks have been awesome," Targill finally said into the hush he'd made. He reached into the back of the podium, pulled out a football, yelled "Deep!" and threw it into the audience as he walked off. Everyone, including Barney, cheered for a lady in a pantsuit who caught it.

In the dressing room the speakers were eating grapes and wiping off makeup. We all told Dad he'd been great, except Mom, who hugged him but didn't say anything. Dad introduced us to Targill and said, "Why don't we all get something to eat?"

"Absolutely," Targill said. "Hey, Veepster?"

"You're on," the ex-VP said, but Patti and Mom said they were tired from traveling. "Okay, just the guys, then," the ex-VP said. "It could get wild. I'm kidding."

We went in the ex-VP's rented Impala to an Australian-themed restaurant built to look like a desolate sheepherding outpost, but fun. "We can go around back," Targill said.

"I'm way ahead of you," the ex-VP said, and parked by the rear entrance. As we walked to the door he put a hand on my shoulder and quietly said, "Brent thinks he's the one that gets recognized."

Dad went first, a non-celebrity scout, and got us a table near the kitchen. By the time the food came the ex-vice was on his third bourbon and asking Barney what he did for a living.

"Biology," Barney said. "Stem cells."

"That's an exciting area, okay? We just think that's something where the most vibrant solution is for private industry to step up." He turned to me. "What kind of work do you do . . ."

"Henry," I said. "I'm in magazine publishing."

"That's good too, okay," he said, "but I'd like to know why they think they can write these things where they distort people. No one will give me an answer on this."

Dad said, "Henry doesn't—"

"I don't mean him. But when they twist how someone gets portrayed so they look foolish and so on. I don't mean Henry here at all."

"He's at the company that does *Maximum Snorkel,*" Barney said. "Clean Page."

The ex-VP's face changed. "Oh. Clean—that's Tom Patrick. I didn't realize. No, he's terrific. He's one of the people that stood up for me when there weren't that many, I'll tell you. That's a great company. You know what he told me? That people were making money with magazines about tattoos and the thing where they pierce themselves, but he wasn't going to touch it because kids are hanging on by a fingernail already. Would you tell him hi for me?"

I said I would. Dad put a hand on my shoulder and smiled at Barney. "Both my guys are doing great," he said.

The ex-VP had two more bourbons and a brandy before we went out to the car. He wanted to drive, but Targill, who'd had only half a beer, asked him for the keys.

"It's my rental," the ex-VP said. "My name is on it."

"Veepster, you're drunk, okay?" Targill said.

"Don't call me that. I never should have gone on this thing."

"I won't call you that," Targill said. "Sorry. I'd just like to go back and get some sleep."

"Why? What do you have, a prayer breakfast tomorrow?"

"Yes, actually."

"That's great. With the local movers and shakers. Jesus."

"I'll walk back if I have to," Targill said. "Knees and everything."

"Fuck your knees," the ex-vice said, taking a wobbling step toward Targill as a family with a ten-year-old boy and a seven-year-old girl came out of the restaurant. The kids looked over at us as the parents tried to keep them moving toward their car. Dad waved at them. Everything after the salad bar was heaven.

"See, this could get in the media," Targill said.

"Oh, they'd love that," the ex-vice said. "That would be their big story of all time." He gave Targill the keys.

Back at the hotel Dad and I walked the former vice through the parking lot, keeping him upright and away from Targill, who walked ahead of us with Barney.

"Prayer breakfast," the ex-VP said. "I went to fucking Davos."

"Steady as she goes," Dad said.

"You just hand it all off to Him," Targill was saying to Barney. "Everything you've been carrying on your back all this time."

"He was hitting on the carpet lady," the ex-VP said. "It's always the holy ones."

Targill put his hand on Barney's shoulder. "You might want

to fall by this breakfast thing in the morning," he said. "Just to give you a feel for it."

"I'd like to," Barney said, "but I promised my brother we'd go rock-climbing."

In the room Patti was watching a DMX movie. She said, "Hi, are you drunk?"

I said, "No, but the *Sesame Street* guy is."

"He's my favorite."

"Yeah. How was it with my mom?"

"Okay," she said. "A little sad, though. She said she was thinking of leaving your dad for a while."

"When? When he got laid off?"

"No, when he started doing this stuff. Because it's so weird. But then she decided it was like he was getting paid back by the guys that wrecked his old company. She decided it's all the same guys."

"Wow." I paused. "How did that come up?"

"What do you mean?"

"No, I just, were you just on the general subject of marriage, or . . . ?"

"Oh, for God's sake. Yeah, I told her all our problems. She's going to *yell* at you."

"That's not what I—"

"Give me the benefit."

"I do."

"Then please press or say what your fucking problem is." It sounded like Kris Santangelo. *She* was the Switchblade Priest. I said I didn't have a problem. She said, "That's good," and turned off the TV and the lights.

• • •

At five in the morning I met Barney downstairs, saying hello in a hushed voice as if there were someone in the two-acre lobby I could wake up. He was studying a climbing map he'd cut out of *Rappel*, which Tom Patrick was about to buy after cutting off its oxygen by giving away ads in *Ascend*. Barney was in climbing shoes, his emergency backpack stuffed with ropes.

We drove a few miles up Pikes Peak and parked his rented CR-V at a trailhead. It was a half hour till sunrise, with grudging violet light leaking into the sky.

The trail climbed past red rock formations with pubic fringes of pines and scrub at their bases. There were huge stacked flanges of rock, frozen ocean waves of it, and walls that looked like whole mountain ranges condensed into a hundred yards. When the trail narrowed to single track, Barney got ahead of me, and I lost sight of his bouncing backpack the first time I stopped to catch my breath.

Soon it was light enough for me to see the dirt underfoot, red as Mars in a movie, and the surfaces of the rock formations. In the craggy friezes I saw horse heads, elephant tusks, men in the moon, and Indians on nickels, and holes like navels, pockmarks, sourdough tunnels, and toe prints in wet sand. Then it occurred to me that I wasn't supposed to be seeing all those things, that the idea was to see the rocks as just rocks. I had no idea whose idea that was. It just seemed purer.

Half an hour later I saw Barney up ahead. He'd stopped to watch the sunrise, and I stopped too. The light spread out across the canyon wall so fast it scared me, as if I was nocturnal and had to find cover. It was a sunrise that made me colder. I didn't know what I was doing there: Patti was mad, Dad was weird, and the rented shoes were killing me. When Barney turned and looked at me his expression was nothing like the tear of joy I'd pictured. He looked as bad as I felt. He started walking again before I could reach him.

In an hour we were in a meadow that looked like pictures of the Alps, with tall grass, shimmering aspens, and moss-covered rocks. The air was thin but sweet, as if sunlight had replaced the oxygen. We were high now but the summit, a jagged black crown striped with snow, was so much higher it looked like five mountains away instead of the same one we were on.

The rocks Barney wanted to climb were smoothed vertical boulders that covered a hillside. The biggest one, a sand-colored obelisk fifty feet tall, had a crack running nearly all the way up it, ranging in width from a fingertip to almost a foot.

We put on climbing harnesses, leather waistbands attached to loops around our thighs. Barney took a long nylon rope from his backpack, secured it around a tree, tied it to our harnesses, and loaded his belt with cams, carabiners, and rope runners.

He chalked his hands and started climbing as I paid out rope. When he was ten feet up he placed his first anchor, wedging a nut into the crack and tying it to the climbing rope. He yelled, "On belay?" I yelled, "Belay on!" He yelled, "Climbing!" I yelled, "Climb!" and he continued up, using wrinkles in the rock as stair steps and handholds.

I'd seen people do this well. They moved fluidly, doing the climbing with their legs and always knowing where their feet were going next before they moved them. Barney's moves were choppy and he put his weight on his hands, but he had enthusiasm, and after half an hour he'd climbed thirty-five feet and put three anchors in the rock. I moved around to watch him so I could copy his holds when my turn came. He was sixty feet up when he fell.

This was supposed to be routine. Climbers fell onto the rope all the time. When Barney lost his balance and yelled, "Falling!" I should have been standing braced so I could bend the rope across my harness and keep him from dropping any farther. If I did it right he'd fall only a few feet before his last anchor stopped him.

I'd moved out of line with the climbing rope, though, and put slack between myself and the anchoring tree. The force of his fall yanked me back into line, toward the boulders. I tripped over my feet and stumbled straight at the rock face until the line from the tree went taut. The rope tore from my hands, burning them, and I fell to the ground, catching an upside-down glimpse of Barney plunging and yelling, "Henry!"

I scrambled up on to one knee, grabbed the rope, and wrenched it across my harness. He finally stopped falling, bounced hard on the rope, and said, "Jesus!" I stood up, panting, and yelled that I was sorry.

He'd stopped at one of his anchors and was hanging sideways on the rope. He flailed himself upright, climbed the rope a few feet, got back on the rock, and yelled, "On belay?" with an edge in his voice.

I went to where I should have been all along and yelled, "Belay on," the burn on my hands throbbing as I held the rope tight. He climbed more cautiously now, and it was forty minutes before he hoisted himself to the top of the big boulder. He anchored the rope there, and I started up.

Barney pulled in rope as I climbed, so any fall I took would be short. I followed his chalk marks but kept missing the footholds, my legs dangling as my eyes filled with sweat.

I was supposed to remove the anchors he'd left in the rock. The first few were easy, but twenty feet from Barney, as I stood on bad holds and banged on a taper nut, my left leg started shaking violently. In *Rappel* it was called sewing-machine leg. I'd edited a box on ten ways to avoid it.

"Relax!" Barney yelled. That had been first on the list. I closed my eyes, put my weight on my good leg, leaned toward the rock, and breathed deeply till the thin air made me dizzy. The shaking slowed down.

I left the anchor in the rock and kept climbing. When I finally reached him he gave me a hand up and I almost fell on him, all my limbs shaking now. "Are you okay?" he said.

"Yeah," I said. "I'm really sorry."

"It's okay. Let's wait a minute and we'll go down. I guess we shouldn't try to rappel."

I didn't say anything, and we walked down the rope. You were supposed to lean back but I bent toward the rock, stubbing my feet on every step. When I dropped to the ground at the bottom he asked again if I was okay.

"Yeah," I said. "I always do this, pretty much."

"Do what?"

My calf cramped. "Every place I work, they take me out to do whatever the thing is, and this is how I do."

"How come?"

"I don't know. Because I'm not good at it." He handed me a water bottle. My starring in his life hadn't lasted long. He sat down next to me.

"How are things with Patti?" he said.

"Medium," I said.

"Yeah, they seem medium. Is that because of Jillian?"

"What? No," I said. I know I almost dropped you on your head just now, but Jesus. For the first time I could remember, I didn't really care if he liked me or not. It was an alien feeling, but I checked and it was still there. "I haven't talked to Jillian in years," I said. He helped me stand, and we gathered up the rope.

• • •

Off the hotel lobby was a business center, a day spa for my kind, where you could fax and compute behind a tinted glass door, bathing in dejuvenating electromagnetic fields and acrylic smells, walking out with a fresh cubicle tan and enhanced eye bags. I went in there when we got back, logged onto my office computer, and put in twenty minutes on the "Kicked in the Sack!" page of next month's *Hacky Sack World*.

When I got out and headed for the elevators I saw Barney sitting on a bench in a courtyard off the lobby, his back to me. I decided to say goodbye now and save time, but when I got out there I saw he was talking on his cell phone.

"Honey, that's not true," he said. "No. I would never do that. It's not true, sweetheart. Please. I've told you that. No, honey. You know that's not how it is."

He hadn't seen me. I slipped back inside and got on the elevator, hoping that my fight with Patti had expired while I was away. It had. She gave me hotel lotion for my rope burns and said, "So what's with Barney today?"

"I can't answer that," I said. "I don't know what's with any of them. They're just these people I'm related to."

"No, I know," Patti said. "I mean, I like your mom. I like all of them."

"No, I *like* them," I said. "I just don't want to *think* about them all the time," thinking, Watch this, Barney. It's not that hard. It's just you and your wife against all outside parties. I thought you and Deirdre had that, monitoring Pearl and Michael's cultural intake and all that, but from that phone call you were having it sounds like things are only medium there.

"Well, God, look at my family," Patti said. "Look at Stewart and Stephanie."

"Stewart's okay," I said. "Stephanie's okay." Are you getting this, Barney, the fair-mindedness to the point of science fiction that says Patti's sister and brother-in-law, matching New Jersey shark lawyers, are in any sense okay?

"This place," Patti said, looking out the window. "This gradient we're in here."

"No, it's weird," I said. She started telling me about a phone call she'd had that morning, about some snowboarder's mother's sister, and I got engrossed on purpose, thinking, Check this out, Barney, it's not rocket science. Maybe that's your problem. Just listen, be interested in what you're not interested in, take out a five-minute mortgage on your patience and then the patience floods in for real.

I said goodbye to Barney by voice mail, and we did quick hugs at Mom and Dad's room because the day-planner guy was there for coffee. My peace with Patti lasted all the way home, and on the plane she told me that Misty, the BMX girl we'd maybe saved from going off the pedestrian bridge, was in college now, studying clinical psychology. She said she'd heard that a few months ago. She'd been meaning to tell me.

15

a week later Barney called and said, "I'm going to a conference in Illinois next weekend. It's in the woods, down near St. Louis. I was wondering if you'd want to meet me there."

"I don't think so," I said. I knew the area from my Clayton days but I wasn't ready for another visit like the one we'd just had in Colorado.

"Okay," he said, but then paused. "There was some stuff I wanted to tell you about."

"What kind of stuff?"

He paused again. "About Pearl."

I landed in St. Louis on Saturday morning, rented a Cobalt, and drove across the Mississippi to the big farms and small towns of southern Illinois. An hour from the airport I was far enough out in the country that the graffiti were legible and spoke of love.

The conference center was in the hills, its back against the forest. I parked by the main building, a screen-windowed hexagon, and got out. The guest rooms were cabins connected by gravel paths through thinned-out woods. It was eighty-five degrees and humid, with bugs humming like bad wiring.

The lodge-style lobby was full of waxed wood, Indian blankets, and the smell of cinnamon coffee. I tried Barney's room on the house phone and got no answer, but a guy with a conference nametag heard me and said, "I think he's in the forest. There's a path that starts back there."

The trailhead at the back of the property had a SHAWNEE NATIONAL FOREST sign, with a placard tacked to it that said, SNAKE MIGRATION IN PROGRESS—DO NOT DISTURB OR COLLECT SNAKES. I walked in. The trail was overgrown, the forest sloping steeply down from it on either side. Trees and grasses grew from every depth to every height, making a green mosaic that blocked out everything but a few islands of hot sky. The ground was a carpet of dust and leaf fragments that took detailed footprints. After twenty minutes I came around a turn and saw Barney a quarter mile away, flying through the air.

He was zip-lining, an enthusiasm I knew about because Clean Page had just bought *Zip-Line World*, a monthly in Lumley, South Dakota. He'd strung a hundred-foot steel cable between two trees, like a tightrope over the gorge beside the trail. Holding a handle that hooked onto the cable, his body in an *L* like a human tramway car, he sailed between the trees at what looked like thirty miles an hour. Two feet from the tree on the far side, he squeezed the handbrake and stopped.

He caught sight of me as he returned to the tree on my side.

When he stopped he grabbed the trunk with his legs, held on to a branch, unclipped the handle from the cable, and climbed down.

"Hey," he said, catching his breath. "You just get in?"

I nodded. He didn't have a safety harness for the zip line, just the handle. He'd mastered the saxophone of uncertainty.

"I'm glad you came," he said, sitting down on a rock. "So. This stuff about Pearl."

I sat on a rock across from his. He looked at the ground for a minute and then said, "About a year ago? It was after you guys came to visit. One Saturday, I was supposed to take her to math team, and I knocked on her door and she wouldn't come out. She said, 'No, thank you, I don't want to go,' but she sounded like she was crying. I said, 'That's okay, you don't have to go, but what's wrong? Can I come in?' She didn't say anything. Deirdre came over and she wouldn't open the door for her, either."

"So we're both saying, 'It's okay, Pearl, just tell us what's wrong,' and she says, 'Nothing's wrong, I just want to be by myself.' I said, 'Okay, I'm going away, and if you want to talk, just tell me.' I start to leave and the door opens, and she says, 'I'm crying because of the babies that never grow up.'

"I said, 'Pearl, you know that's not true. You know that's not what we're doing.'"

"Those people talked to her?" I said.

"I don't know," Barney said. "I asked her, but she wouldn't say. It could be kids. It could be a friend of hers. I said, 'Sweetie, you know this, you've been to the lab. You know that's not what we're doing, or I wouldn't be doing it,' and she starts crying and closes the door again.

"And then that's how it was for a long time. She'd sit there at dinner, not eating and not talking. Deirdre would say, 'Okay, you have to eat something,' and she'd eat something. She'd be polite and that's it, or she'd talk to Michael but not us. Michael was okay at first, but then it started scaring him."

"I'm sorry," I said.

"It's a little better now. It's kind of normal. Although sometimes she wakes up crying and she stops eating again, and then I'm constantly saying, 'No, sweetie, that's not what I do. There aren't any babies. It's some cells, it's cells from people who were trying to get some help having a baby but there wasn't any baby, and the lab they went to was going to throw the cells away, and . . .'" He shook his head. "I thought if I understood the religious thing better. I was talking to that football guy in Colorado, trying to get a sense of it."

It was quiet for a minute. "Was that when you started luging and stuff?" I said.

He considered. "That was part of it." He looked the way he'd looked during that cold sunrise in Colorado, and I turned away for a minute. The breeze drew a singing note from the zip line. No one was starring in anyone's life now, and the bugs were getting worse. He held the handle out to me. "You want to try this?"

"Thanks," I said. "No, I think I'll go check in and get a shower. Are you okay here if I go back?"

"Sure. I'm just going to do this another few minutes. We can have breakfast. Save me a seat, okay?"

I said I would and started back. The trees' shadows were shortening, the heat closing in. In ten minutes I sweated through my shirt.

I was half a mile away from Barney and a mile from the conference center when a guy with a beard, in hiking clothes and a daypack, came toward me on the path. I'd seen him before somewhere. He's probably here for the conference, I decided, and I must have seen him at the one in Idaho, where Barney was talking to the other scientists before our bike ride.

Then he got closer and I knew where I'd actually seen him, not in Idaho but outside Barney's lab in Kansas, bending down to Pearl's car window and saying he wanted to talk to the kids.

He was passing me. He turned his eyes away but I saw them for a second, and it came to me that I'd seen his face even before Kansas. It was on the FREEBIRD T-shirt at the gun show.

I turned around. He had a hand in one pocket and was walking fast toward where Barney was zip-lining. I ran after him.

I might have been wrong but I didn't think so. The clean-cut police sketch didn't look like the guy at Barney's lab but the face on the T-shirt did, its mess of feathers filling in for the hair and beard.

I ran up behind him and yelled, "Freebird!" like a guy with five brain cells holding up his lighter at a mud festival. He turned around, his hand coming out of his pocket with a gun in it.

Time didn't slow down, the way people talk about. Everything has led up to this, my public interest work starts now—those were some of the things that didn't go through my mind. Time kept running, leaving me none to think in, which was ideal. The lizard brain saw sun on metal and I flailed at his arm, catching hold of his wrist with one hand and pushing him with the other.

His heel caught on a thick root that crossed the trail and he lost his balance. I fell with him, fighting to point the gun away from me, my hand going white against its knurled butt as I looked at his furious eyes and bared teeth.

I yelled Barney's name as Freebird twisted under me in the dirt, getting his weight behind his hand and turning the barrel back toward me. I jumped off him, dived off the trail and ran down the hillside, hoping my knowing who he was would make me a more pressing problem than Barney was.

It did. The gun went off behind me as I ran down the hill under a racket of terrified birds, twisting my ankle. There was a second shot. I ran faster. My wind had never been good and my side hurt already, but I crashed deeper into green, tripped over it and scraped my face on it, hid behind a tree to catch my breath and rub my ankle, looked back up the hillside and saw nothing moving. I slipped my phone from my pocket and read NO SERVICE. When I started out again I heard the crackle my steps made, took my shoes off, and let the brush tear my feet as I ran.

I got to the bottom of the hill, crossed a dry streambed, and went up the other side, my brain a bird whose cry was *Where's Barney? Where's Barney?* I put my shoes back on, and when I couldn't run anymore I walked.

I walked all day. By afternoon, as I walked on flat ground under high stone bluffs, my clothes had dried salty and my throat was half closed by thirst. I heard water and followed the sound, but it wasn't flowing, just stirred by a breeze. I was on the spongy bank of a swamp, black water under a thick rind of yellow algae. Tangles of vines and broken trees choked the landscape, as if the earth could corrupt itself just fine with no help from people. It seemed weird that there were no dinosaurs there to eat it all.

I started back toward the bluffs, stepping on a branch that felt wrong under my foot and that turned out to be a snake two feet long. I jumped back, tripping and falling, as its head reared up in the air, jaws open wide, its white fangs hideous against the white skin inside its mouth. I braced for its strike but it shot past me, down the bank and into the yellow-skinned water.

I stood up slowly and started walking again, one eye checking the branches underfoot and the other watching for Freebird. Half an hour later I sat down on a bank of dead leaves, took my glasses off, and put them down while I rubbed my eyes. When I opened them, my glasses were gone.

They were rimless, hidden somewhere in the blur of leaves around me. I started searching on my hands and knees, staring at the leaves from an inch away, but lowering my head made me so dizzy I almost passed out. It was the thirst. I fell back on the leaves with my hands on my face. When I took them off, my left eye was too swollen to open. Then I realized the other half of my face was swollen too, along with most of my neck and both arms. It could have been poison oak, poison ivy, or, given the Shawnee's location in the middle of the country and how bad the itching was, both.

I scratched at the emerging blisters with the heel of my hand, then with my nails, and then as if I were trying to take my skin off. I'd be dead soon anyway. I was running from a motivated psycho with an excellent track record and I was going to die without ever getting the joke, finding a home, or dislodging the obstruction Gerald said was in my ass. I hadn't been sharp enough to recognize the guy from the T-shirt at Barney's lab, and here we were.

Barney's ambition was to repair all of life from the inside out. Had I even had an ambition? Stay fed and stay out of trouble, and how was I doing on those? I saw a fixed trajectory from Rancho Cahuenga, where everything made sense until childhood ended and life turned baffling for good, to San Jose, where dental made cowards of us all, to a national swamp where I'd die of hunger if the motivated psycho didn't shoot me first.

I started looking for my glasses again, sifting through leaves and making a mound of those I'd searched, until my blistered fingers touched a lens. I put them on and looked around. This is it, I thought, the rough ground we crossed to settle the country, a new land whose fabled streets were paved with good intentions.

I looked at the hundred shapes of leaves—teardrops, dog paws, spades, diamonds, hearts, clover, gum-wrapper mint, cereal-box grain tassels, and a tangle of weeds like a nine-dollar California salad. Thad Anderson at *Country Ways* had tried to teach me edible plants but I'd barely paid attention. I deserved to starve now.

Then I saw a plant with umbrella-shaped leaves and thought I remembered Thad's scarred hands lifting them to show me some little fruits underneath. I bent over and pulled the leaves back, and there they were, berries shaped like apples. There were a few more growing nearby. The berries were nothing to eat, and they started the stomach juices, so I was hungrier than before, but there was water in them.

I sat still. I'd remembered a plant. It was possible that not all my useless knowledge was useless, that maybe I hadn't really wasted every minute, or at least it was too soon to say so until the end, though that could be any second now. I wanted Jillian's woodlore, but what I needed was Patti's attitude. In Kansas she'd been ready to bite the guy who was chasing me now. We should have let her, I thought. She'd be worried about me. I stood up and started walking again.

Thad had said to pick a direction so you didn't walk in circles, and he'd shown me how to take bearings with a watch face. My watch was digital but I could draw a clock face that showed the time. I had no paper but I scratched the clock on a leaf with a twig, put it down, and stuck the twig in the dirt to make a shadow. My guess was that I wanted northwest, and I set out that way. Once I had a destination the cadence of walking was a mild tranquilizer, like half a beer or a cup of Richard and Agnes's green tea, and the itching began to cool.

After a while I started praying: "Please get Barney out of this, and then me, and if you could check on Deirdre, Michael, Pearl, and Patti, but right now the thing is Barney. Also, thanks for my ten seconds of being able to do something violent, and I'm ready to stop seeing the replay of that anytime now, but that's not key." I didn't bother with the "Okay, I know you might not exist" preamble that I'd used a handful of times before. I just did it, for the usual reason, which was what could it hurt that hadn't already been beaten senseless?

At 4:00 P.M. I was at the base of a tall hill. I'd avoided trails so far, but the switchback up the hill was screened by trees and I needed the view from the top. I climbed as fast as I could, and at the summit I saw what I'd hoped to, the Mississippi in the distance and the towns and farms on the near shore.

I found where I wanted to go, drew a watch face on another leaf, and lined up the direction. As I started down the hill my exhausted mind decided that switchback trails were one of mankind's greatest inventions. If you tried to go straight up a hill this steep you'd fall back down, but if you sneaked up on your destination sideways, never facing it, you got closer all the time.

An hour later I was at the edge of a clearing. An old VW van was parked fifty yards away from me and ten yards from the weedy jeep trail it had come in on. On the door side of the van, a tarp was fastened to the roofline and staked to the ground, making half a tent. Clothes were drying on a rope between two trees, and a woman was heating something over a fire. I started to go back into the woods, but she saw me and yelled, "Hi." I waved. She put a hand over her eyes to look at me and shouted, "Are you okay?"

"Yes," I yelled. Two girls, six and eleven, came out of the van, followed by a man who waved me over.

The adults were in their thirties, the woman thin in blue jeans, a red denim jacket, and a plaid shirt. The saucepan she was heating was on a round grill from a backyard Weber, suspended over the fire on two piles of rocks. The man was balding and stocky, in cords and an old Henley shirt. The girls wore jeans, the younger one a VEGGIE TALES sweatshirt, the older one a HIGH SCHOOL MUSICAL T-shirt and a plastic hoop over her hair. She held a Discman in both hands, her name on it in thick marker letters.

"Are you all right?" the dad said. "Looks like you've got some poison oak there." I said I was okay. "I'm Howard," he said. "This is Dianne."

"I've got some lotion inside," Dianne said, and introduced the kids, the older one Angela and the younger Corinne. "Would you like some dinner?"

"Thank you. Yeah." I looked back at the woods. "Maybe I should get some of that lotion from you."

"Sure," Dianne said, and picked up the saucepan.

The van's backseats were on the ground under the tarp. Inside, their place had been taken by a card table and milk crate chairs. Sleeping bags were piled in the front seat. The lotion Dianne gave me was hand cream, but it helped.

The table was set with bowls, two plastic and two paper. Angela set a place for me and Dianne served miso soup and flatbread crackers. I ate my few ounces of soup as slowly as I could, felt it bloom into gas in my empty stomach, and damped it with crackers. A gunshot went off in the woods and I jumped.

"There's a lot of hunters out now," Howard said. "Turkey season. I'm hoping to get one myself."

"We lived at the campground before," Angela said, holding the Discman in one hand as she ate. "We're not really official here."

"He can see that, honey," Howard said.

"We had a downturn," Angela said. "We're sitting it out for a while."

"Angela, that isn't something we go ahead and say to people," Dianne said.

"I know."

"Well, but you just did, though."

"I'm sorry."

"That's okay."

"That was good soup," Howard said as the kids cleared the table. "Thank you, honey. Who wants to sing?"

"Me!" Corinne shouted, the first word she'd said since I'd gotten there. Howard started singing a folk song with a tick-tock melody, about an immigrant who'd come to his new land without any money,

But the land was sweet and good,
I did what I could.

Angela looked embarrassed but still sang, and Dianne sang with her eyes far away. The guy in the song got a shack, a cow, a horse, and a series of other animals, all failures. Howard sang, "I called my shack," and the others sang, "Break my back." He sang, "I called my duck," and they sang, "Out of luck." It seemed like an insane choice, the "Old McDonald's Farm" of ruin, but Corinne loved it. Howard gestured at me to join in, but when we got to "I did what I could," my voice broke like it was changing, and I had to stop.

A few songs later it was dusk. Howard turned on a battery lantern, reached under the table, and brought out a board that held a half-finished jigsaw puzzle of Paris.

"I should get going," I said. "Thank you."

"Good luck on the rest of your trip," Howard said.

"You'll get that looked at," Dianne said, touching her face where mine was messed up, and I said I would.

Outside I stopped by the clothesline and checked to see that no one was watching from the van. I had eighty dollars in my wallet. I put sixty in the pocket of what looked like Dianne's jeans and took off. Going back into the woods, I had the feeling that goes with helping, half virtue and half ricocheting embarrassment. Then I realized that my most recent brush with helping anyone had been when Patti and I ran into Misty on the pedestrian bridge, and then I remembered what happened after that, and for the next hour all I could think about was sex.

I walked in the dark, using what I hoped was the North Star to take bearings the way Thad had shown me. The night was loud with baying and bird screeches, animals or Freebird crashing around, and the constant buzz of insects. My brain was the loudest of all: *He's right behind you, too slow, vine, next tree, you'll start hearing the shot but then nothing, where's Barney?* When I walked into trees a few times, I decided I had to take a chance and sleep a while. I slipped under a bank of dead leaves. You did do what you could, I thought. You're not Barney but you're not worthless Herbert, either. Lie down and think you're on your boyhood bicycle, ride past the gates of a big old place, be nine, ride all day.

I woke before dawn and started walking again, weak and slow. At first light, a sick monochrome on rocks and branches, I sped up. The bumps on my skin oozed a clear fluid now and still itched. I was making a clock face on another leaf when there was a gunshot to my right, somewhere close.

A hundred yards to my left the earth ended in midair on top of limestone bluffs. I ran there and looked over the edge. Fifty yards below me was another swamp, covered with algae and maybe full of snakes like the one I'd seen slither into the water before. I started climbing down, but the stone edge crumbled under my feet.

Falling took longer than I would have thought, but I still forgot to hold my breath and had only half a lungful when I plunged through the scum into a foul syrup of cold water and decomposed plants. I pictured the splash I'd made, a flare going up to guide Freebird.

My shoes and velocity dragged me under. I flailed with my arms, finally stopped sinking and struggled upward, my head bursting from no air. When I surfaced, gasping, the greasy water ran into my mouth. I went back under and swam blindly away from the bluffs, finally coming to shore at the side of a dirt road.

I put a hand on the bank, looked back at the bluffs, saw no one, dragged myself up on to the road and ran, stumbling in my wet clothes and bracing for the gunshot. Up ahead, on the other side of the road, was a clear river inlet with islands of water lilies.

I took my shoes off, waded in fast, and swam underwater with a shoe in each hand. I saw the water lilies' long stems waving in the current, swam around a cluster of them, stood on the soft bottom, and came up for air, hiding my head behind a shantytown of jammed-in leaves. The water looked fresh enough to drink and I gulped some, went back under and swam, stopping for air at each cluster of lilies till I reached the inlet's far shore.

When I came up on the bank I was in the woods again, but I could hear a train whistle now, and the thin roar of cars on a highway. I put my shoes on and stumbled toward the sounds. In twenty minutes I was on the shoulder of a two-lane road, not far from where I'd been aiming. I ran across the road and got down in the drainage ditch, keeping an eye on the woods.

The ditch went past big houses set back from the road. I came to one where three days' newspapers lay in the driveway, the owners still away for the weekend. The St. Louis Sunday paper's plastic bag had a bubble on it, labeled FREE SAMPLE! NEW WISEGRAINS PLUS!

I tore it open and took out a foil packet with a picture of breakfast divots tumbling into a bowl with sliced peaches and splashing milk. I stayed low in the ditch and poured all three ounces into my mouth, closed my eyes, and chewed silage mixed with corn syrup and vitamins, crunchy workforce Ritalin, the taste of all our hometowns. I dropped the bag and moved on, imagining the annoyance of the people I'd robbed. I was a homeowner myself. Crouching ditch weasel was just a sideline.

The road widened to four lanes as it came into town. I passed a Montessori school and a nude furniture outlet, both after my time, and ran the last two blocks with people staring at me.

The lobby directory still said DOBEY PUBLICATIONS 2ND FL. He'd said never to show my face again, and look at it now. I climbed the stairs, barged through the OWNER door, and said, "I'm sorry about this. I need some help. I've been in the woods."

"I can see that," the owner said. She came out from behind her desk and steered me to the sofa. "Henry 'Hank,' you need to sit down."

Dobey had sold Jillian the business three years earlier and retired to Alabama. I had a personal demon who couldn't find Florida.

She looked only a little different, no bangs and some faint lines by her eyes. When I picked up her phone and started dialing she went out the door, mouthing, "I'll be right back." I caught myself wondering if I'd made any points with her by having been in the woods. Dobey, live from Mobile, shook his head and said I was incapable of personal development.

Patti answered her cell phone in half a ring and said, "Where are you?" When I told her I was okay she said, "Oh, God" and started to cry. Jillian came in with bananas, graham crackers, and Gatorade thinned with water, and went out again.

"Are you home?" I said.

"No, I'm in Illinois," Patti said. "I'm at the hospital where Barney is. In Edmundstown. He's okay. He's not conscious but they think he's okay. They don't know."

I started to put my face in my hand but it hurt. "He was shot?" I said.

"No, he fell. He hit his head. Where are you?"

"I'm in Illinois too. I'm where I used to work. A guy was chasing me. Freebird. I thought he was going to shoot Barney. He was the guy who hassled us in the car with Barney and the kids that time."

"I know," she said. "They caught him. The forest rangers. The ones that were looking for you."

Jillian called Jeff, arranged for me to shower and change at his house, and told the receptionist to cancel her day. In her car she said Freebird's arrest had been leading the news. When I told her about Barney she said, "God, I'm sorry. Do you want to go straight there?"

"No, I should get cleaned up," I said.

She filled me in on the years since I'd seen her. *Nine-Hole Golfer* and *Tropical Fish Owner* had folded soon after *Kite Buggy*. Dobey had tried magazines about home brewing, home security, satellite-dish TV, flag football, prop airplane building, mopeds, and tai chi, none successfully.

Jillian had bought the business for a dollar and the assumption of debts, sold the cereal-box press for scrap, found a printer in St. Louis, and started titles about bluegrass music and family camping. They were doing okay, but the mainstay all these years had been *Crochet Life*. Cerise Lander had found a woman in Vermont who did terrific angels and Hobbits, and signed her to an eight-year exclusive. Jillian had married Jack, the adult-ed bookbinding teacher, who was also a state hydrologist and played dobro on jam nights at Riddenhauer's. They had a three-year-old daughter.

Jeff's small house was on a riverside street, with a green fiberglass carport sheltering his Galaxie and two kayaks. When he saw me he said, "Henry, wow. Give your child the Outward Bound experience and he will come home to you like this."

"Henry's brother's in the hospital in Edmundstown," Jillian said.

"Whoa, sorry. Is he okay?"

"They think so," I said. "They don't know."

"We should get over there," Jeff said. He gave me a towel and some clean clothes. When I undressed, the smell of sweat and swamp water filled the tin shower stall. I washed the mud off with poison oak scrub and watched chips of gravel go down the drain.

Jeff's house was full of drying kayak clothes, murky green light, and books disintegrating in the river air. He was at the other end of the dial from the enthusiasts I'd been keeping apprised of the latest models all these years. Everything he touched turned discontinued, and the Pendleton he lent me had the bald patches of a museum tapestry. It seemed like a brilliant way to live.

The hospital was five stories of brick with a long plain portico extending from the entrance into the parking lot. A sixty-year-old guy sat under it on a bench, wearing a patient's gown, smoking a cigarette, and clutching the upright of his wheeled IV stanchion. We smiled at him, but his smiling obligation had expired.

Inside, the lady at the desk looked at my face and asked if I was looking for the emergency room. I told her we were there for Barney. "He's in neurology, on three," she said, "but you still want to get that looked at."

The waiting room was across from the elevator, and Patti saw us come off and ran to meet me. We held each other, taking turns saying it was okay. When we let go I said, "This is Jeff. This is Jillian. This is my wife Patti." Something weightless fell into place.

Jillian squeezed Patti's hand and said, "I'm sorry we're meeting like this. We'll have to do it over." Patti nodded. "We should get going," Jillian said. "Let me know what happens."

I pulled Patti aside on the way to the waiting room and asked if she'd told anyone about Freebird chasing me. She said she hadn't, and I told her we should keep it that way. I could picture a chat room's worth of Freebird enthusiasts hearing that Barney was the target and coming to finish the job.

Mom, Dad, and Barney's son, Michael, were in the waiting room, along with two other patients' families. Mom and Dad looked composed, but Mom's left hand was squeezing a Kleenex into diamonds. Michael looked terrified and stuck close to Mom.

They asked if I was okay and I said yes. My story was that I'd arrived at the conference center, gone looking for Barney, and immediately gotten lost. I was a little annoyed at how readily everyone believed it.

"Deirdre's in with him now, and then you can go in if you want," Dad said. "They said it's helpful to talk to him."

A guy in a BULLS T-shirt, from one of the other families, leaned toward us and said, "It's definitely helpful. They think they're taking everything in. They said to talk to them positively."

I asked where Pearl was. "Pearl stays in there," Michael said.

"Do they know what happened?" I said.

"He fell off the thing he was using," Dad said. "A zip liner?" I saw it: Barney hearing the noises, twisting toward them, letting go of the handle, and falling into the gorge.

Deirdre came to the doorway and said, "Henry, hi. Could I talk to you?"

I followed her into the corridor, where nurses were walking around exhausted and the hospital smells of steamed rice and Lysol fought it out. "What happened?" she said. "Were you there?"

I shook my head. "I was looking for him but I got lost."

"But why was he up on that thing? He doesn't do things like that."

"I don't know," I said. "How's Pearl?"

She did an "okay, considering" thing with her head and led me to Barney's room. "Pearl, Uncle Henry's here," she said as we went in.

It was a semi-private room but Barney was the only patient, his bed near the window, his eyes closed and mouth slightly open. Both legs and one arm were in inflatable casts and his head was half covered in bandages. A swarm of wires connected him to monitors flashing numbers and sawtooths. Pearl sat in a chair by the bed, crying softly as if she'd cried loudly for a day or two first. She looked up at me for only a second before her eyes went back to Barney. Deirdre squeezed her as if that had been going on for a few days too, then left us.

I went over to the bed. "Barney, hey," I said. "It's Henry. Hi. Barney, it's Henry. You look great. I was worried, because you're in the hospital, but you look great. You're doing really well." I paused, heard the machines hiss and Pearl sobbing, and started again. "Mom and Dad are here, and Deirdre and Patti, and Michael, and Pearl's right here. We're all here to see you when you wake up. We're in Illinois. You were at a conference here and you had an accident, but you're fine now. When you wake up you'll be fine."

One of the monitors beeped and I jumped, but its lights stayed green and it didn't do it again. "You're doing great, Barney. The thing is for you to just rest and not worry about anything, because everything's fine." I was terrible at this. "We're all right here."

I went back to the waiting room, borrowed Patti's phone, and called my office from the corridor. "Jesus, where are you?" Walter said. "Tom's really pissed. *Copter Hunting* is completely fucked up."

I told him about Barney being in the hospital and then, with my voice lowered, about Freebird chasing me. "Fuck. Okay, that's amazing," he said. "Let me tell Tom that." I made him promise not to. "Okay, if you're sure," he said. "I'll give him the family emergency, but I'd love to have this too."

Patti and I picked up my rental car at the conference center and returned it in town. On the way back to the hospital I told her what Barney had told me about Pearl. "God," she said. "Poor Pearl now."

I went to the emergency room, showed my Clean Page health card, and got steroid cream and Prednisone. In the lobby I bought a *St. Louis Post-Dispatch* and took it back to the waiting room. The follow-up coverage of Freebird's capture included a backgrounder on his "strange odyssey" to the moody loner hall of fame. He'd been identified as "Martin," who'd been with Fundament House in Lawrence for two months, but the group said they'd had no knowledge of his true identity or his violent actions. They were praying for him and his victims, retaining a lawyer just in case, and suspending demonstrations at the lab for two weeks as a good-faith gesture to the community.

There was also a boxed story on the two park rangers who'd caught him:

> *By a unique turn of events, it was the snake migration, a twice-annual event in the Shawnee Forest, that led Rangers Dugan and Micetti to capture a fugitive who had eluded federal law enforcement for years.*
>
> *Since 1972, rangers have closed a forest road to auto traffic for two months in spring and again in autumn, so that cottonmouths, moccasins, and more than thirty other species of snake can migrate between cliff caves and swampland without being hit by cars. Because the collecting of snakes is prohibited, park regulations forbid*

the carrying of snake hooks, snake bags, pillowcases, or even Ziploc bags.

"This individual was holding a Ziploc bag and behaving in a furtive manner," Micetti said. "That turned out to be something he was eating out of, but we took a look in his pack for snake paraphernalia and we found some other stuff"—a handgun, as well as homemade detonator tubes, explosive hematite powder, and other potential bomb-making materials. "At that point, we constrained him there." The rangers turned the suspect over to county sheriff's deputies, and were back at their visitor center in time to give a slide show on mushroom identification that afternoon.

The next day Barney was still in a coma. Patti got Pearl to take a walk with her, the first time she'd left his room. I went in and talked to him three times, doing the same material as before and some childhood anecdotes that never came to a point. In between, I worked on my laptop in the waiting room and made phone calls under the portico outside, exchanging unsmiling looks with the IV guy while he smoked.

The following day Barney was the same, and I went to a coffee place with Wi-Fi to answer e-mail and edit copy. *The Four Seasons* was starting on their stereo for the third time when Patti called to say Barney's eyes were open.

When I got there everyone was standing around Barney's bed but Michael, who stood back by the wall looking scared. Deirdre was holding one of Barney's hands, Pearl the other. His eyes were open but not looking at anyone, his lips fluttering around an oval of teeth. A doctor came in, leaned over him, and said, "Dr. Bay? Barney? Hey, it's Dr. Milgrim, and your family's all here as well. How are you doing?"

For a second Barney followed the doctor's eyes. Then a soft thready noise came from his throat, the first sound he'd made since the injury, and I had to steady myself on the bed-rail. "This is good stuff, folks," the doctor said. "Very promising stuff."

Deirdre held Barney's hand to her chest and started to cry. When the doctor left we waited for Barney to make the sound again, but he fell asleep.

Patti and I had a room at the Major Edmunds Hotel, where a sign in the lobby advertised dancing till 9:30 in the fourth-floor Skyline Room. Our room had forty-year footpaths in the carpet and cigarette burns on the furniture, faded Clayton glory a few towns from the real thing. I lay down on the bumpy bedspread and Patti got next to me.

"I should have known who the guy was," I said. "I should have gotten Barney out of the woods. I should have helped him more."

"You helped him a lot," she said. "For years. It's like me and Kris Santangelo."

I turned to look at her. "How do you mean?"

"You know. They have their little specialty, but they need us to even get out the door."

We kissed, then started slipping out of our clothes and kicking them off the bed. A few kisses later she paused. "We can go out the door too," she said. "No one's stopping us."

Two days later Barney was making eye contact with all of us, and Pearl was sure she understood the sounds he made even though no one else did. "That was 'Deirdre'! Mom, he said, 'Deirdre'! That was either 'hi' or 'fine.' He said, 'love'! Grandma, did you hear it?"

The next day Mom, Dad, and Patti flew home to work. When I walked into Barney's room three days later he looked at me and said, "*Eh*-ree," too clearly to be anyone's imagination. Michael gasped, Pearl yelled "Yes!" and Deirdre asked a nurse to get the doctor.

Barney slurred out our names some more and looked baffled by our thrilled reactions. The doctor came in and said, "Barney, I'm Stu Milgrim. I'm your doctor here in Edmundstown. Edmundstown, Illinois."

"Noy?"

"Illinois. Yes. You had an accident. You hit your head. You're in the hospital, okay?"

"Okay."

"You were unconscious for a while but you're doing really well now. You're recognizing people and talking and it's all good quality stuff. We just need you to keep resting and going along the way you're going, okay?"

Barney nodded, looked around the room, frowned, and said, "Hotel?"

His speech got clearer every day, but he couldn't retain what had happened or where he was. He knew where he lived, but not what year it was or who was president.

Deirdre called someone she knew at the hospital in Lawrence, and two days later a neurologist came from St. Louis. He had the high-end doctor look that says, "I went into this because I'm immensely compassionate, but you'll have to take my word for that because I only sleep three hours a night and

I'm going to smack the next person who asks me something stupid."

He let Deirdre and me come into Barney's room with him. When he asked Barney what kind of work he did, Barney thought for a minute and said, "Lemma?"

"Science. Yes. You're a cell biologist."

"Yeah," Barney said, a child's trusting "Yeah" that was all wrong for him.

"You lost some neural cells in an accident. Your scan is showing me low activity in the diencephalon and the medial frontal cortex. You know where the diencephalon is?" Barney waved his good arm at his head. "Good. Okay. I'll be back to see you soon."

In the hall the neurologist said that short-term memory loss often happened with concussion, that Barney had a lot of old memories available but that new ones were melting like snowflakes, and that a patient's brain, hating not to know things, would jump into the gaps with guesses, dream material, or memories from eight or eighteen years ago. Sometimes people recovered.

I stayed two more days, till I couldn't put off Walter any longer and booked a flight home. The day I left, the neurologist told Deirdre about a rehab place in Houston that got good results. I went into Barney's room and said, "I have to go back to California now, Barney, okay?"

"Okay."

"I'll come see you in a couple weeks. You might be in a different place then, where they'll help you get better. Barney, don't pull on that, okay? That's part of the equipment."

"Okay."

"You'll be better soon. You can run in the desert."

"Desert areas."

"That's right. I'll call you tomorrow, okay?"

"Give me a call," he said.

"I will. Don't pull on that, okay? There you go."

"There you go," he said. I picked up his hand and told him how great he was doing till I missed my plane.

The one I took got in late, and Patti met me at the airport. We hugged in the same boarding area where we'd hugged hello and goodbye every weekend of our Fun Fare courtship, two airport remodels ago. The hugging then had been all horny naiveté, but this was romance too, the idea that something as haywire as love would get us through this.

I called Barney every morning, first in Edmundstown and then Houston, and listened to his lax new voice say things like "We're at the hotel in Canada" or "I have to go to the lab now. There's a meeting." When I hung up and went to the office I was almost normal, except for a continuous stomachache and a tendency to ask people how they were too often, because I now expected the bottom to drop out of everyone and everything.

The day before I went to Houston, Walter and I met with Tom Patrick to go over our plans for *Zip-Line World*. When we were wrapping up, Walter said, "Tell Tom what happened to you. With the guy." I said no but he insisted, and I told Patrick how I'd gotten away from Freebird.

"That's impressive," Patrick said. "Have you talked to any media?"

"No. I'm kind of trying to be quiet about it."

"Nice," Patrick said, although his expression suggested

I was an idiot. "Walter said you've got someone who's brain-damaged?"

"Head-injured," I said.

"Right. You know who that happened to?" he said to Walter. "Bob DeBonis. I don't think they've made any progress with him. I hope yours works out, though."

"Thanks," I said, and stood up to go. "I met someone who said to say hello to you."

I gave him the ex–vice president's regards. Patrick rolled his eyes. "Him and the mad bomber," he said. "Boy, can you pick 'em."

16

I flew overnight to Houston, rented an Accent, and drove to the Starling Center for Rehabilitation, a tan hacienda in a medical complex shaded by carob trees whose dry pods crackled underfoot. I'd worried about finding a locked ward, but the lobby looked like the conversation area of a savings and loan. There were ten patients there, one talking to himself in a speeding whisper and another tearing page after page from a magazine, but most of them quietly watching TV. A few were paired with staff people. The uniform was a peach polo shirt with a picture of a starling poised for flight.

I was almost at the desk when a woman in her sixties rushed up to me, grabbed my arm, and thrust her baffled face close to mine. Terrible breath poured from her mouth as she said, *"Where's my Ted?"*

A polo-shirt woman came over, eased my forearm free, and said, "I don't think he knows that, Grace. I'll tell you what, let's have a seat over here with Frances." As she led Grace away she gave me a smile that said, "You know how it is." I wanted to have no idea how it was. I told the guy at the desk I was there to see Barney, and he said to try the patio.

He was out there, whispering to himself in a wheelchair under a pepper tree, in a floppy tennis hat, shorts, and a T-shirt from the dads' club of Pearl and Michael's school. His hands were on his knees, palms up and fingers fluttering. There were older patients on either side of him, snoozing in the sun. When he saw me he smiled, said, "Henry!" rose halfway out of the wheelchair, and fell back in. His fractures were healing but the brain injury had screwed up his balance and he was relearning how to walk. "Is sister here?"

"Patti? No, she had to work. But Dad is coming."

He beamed at me. "That's wonderful."

A polo-shirt guy came out and said it was time for lunch. I wheeled Barney into a dining room of round Formica tables, with patients' shaky artwork on the walls. Over tomato soup the patient across from us asked if we were brothers. "I can always tell if people are brothers," she said, "but I need to see them both."

"Dad!" Barney said. I looked up and saw my father walking toward us in another perfect suit, this one blue. "That's terrific," Barney said, "that we're all staying here."

"I know," Dad said, squeezing Barney's shoulder. "It worked out great."

After lunch we took Barney to physical therapy, left him with the trainer, and sat down outside. "I brought him this," Dad said. "I think it might help."

He handed me a spiral-bound datebook with a smiling

picture of himself on the cover and a time-management tip from him on every page. I looked from the picture to the real dad in front of me, and was about to ask him why he would give a schedule book to someone whose schedule had been obliterated, when he misread my look and said, "Oh, I brought one for you too. It's in the car."

We took Barney to his room, where the furniture was white and the walls powder blue. Every day an attendant pinned up a flyer with Barney's name and age, the date, where he was, what had happened to him, and seasonal clip art of people throwing footballs and raking leaves.

Dad and Barney sat at the desk with the datebook open in front of them. "Okay," Dad said, "what's something you might have to do this afternoon?"

"Go to a meeting," Barney said.

"Okay. So you write that in there."

Barney scrawled *meeting* in the 3:00 P.M. slot. "We're going to have a country," he said. "We have some farmers coming, and some horseshoe guys."

"Blacksmiths?" Dad said.

"Yes," Barney said. "So we get liberty. And we wear wigs in the room." Next to *meeting* he started a jagged drawing of a standing man. "We have people coming in boats from their old countries, because God is too strict. God is scaring the kids. That's one of the things, for our meeting."

"To take up," Dad said.

"Yeah."

"So we make that a bullet item."

Dad pointed to where the bullet items went. Barney nodded but kept drawing the man, who was holding a sledgehammer now. "It doesn't matter how late we stay up," he said. "We have to finish. And then we'll all stand in line and sign it. Then we'll take questions, if anyone has questions."

A polo-shirt woman came to the door. "Barney," she said, "it's almost three o'clock. Time for that meeting."

The meeting was a memory class. Barney's fellow students were a guy who'd gone through a windshield, a woman who'd been without oxygen to her brain for ten minutes after a heart attack, a guy who'd crashed his motorcycle, a guy who'd confused his wife's once-a-day pills with his three-a-days, and a woman who'd almost drowned.

"Who had 'meeting' in their book for today?" the teacher asked.

Barney and the half-drowned woman held their datebooks up. The motorcycle guy giggled, clapped, and said, "All right, Barney! All right, Celeste!"

Paula looked at Barney's book. "'Meeting,' good, and that's a nice drawing," she said. "Who is that?"

Barney stared at the drawing. Dad whispered, "Blacksmith."

"Sshh," Barney said to Dad. "He's the village smithy," he told Paula. "His funding required him to hammer all day. His arms were so big from using the hammer that he didn't even need the hammer anymore. He said, 'Get that hammer out of here. That hammer's gonna be the death of me.'"

"All *right*, Barney!" the motorcycle guy said.

Dad and I had dinner at his hotel, a fancy one near Herrman Park. We didn't talk about Barney. I told him about the strange animals at Species Showcase and he told me about helping a brass quintet in Seattle set long-term goals. In the morning we ate toaster waffles and banana chunks with Barney, and then Dad said, "I'd better get going. I have a thing in Minnesota."

We wheeled Barney to the lobby. "This is all good, what's happening," Dad said.

"Yeah?" Barney said.

"Definitely. You're making a lot of progress."

"Sometimes there's nothing for a while," Barney said, "and we'll attack it another way."

"Sure," Dad said. "You need to approach it freshly."

"You used to give people extensions for that," Barney said. "Like for the ailerons."

"I did when I could," Dad said. "See, you remember that. Your memory's good."

"Yeah," Barney said.

Dad leaned down to hug him and said, "You can have all the extensions you need. You just take your time."

"Okay. Thank you very much," Barney said.

Dad stood up, clapped my shoulder, and went out the door. Barney watched him walk to his car and said, "I think he's got a lot weighing on him now."

The relatives talked on the phone all the time. What did the specialist say, no, his exact words, where are we on activities of daily living, did the physical therapy lady look happy? The specialist's exact words were "You know those weird thoughts you have just before you fall asleep, a whole situation you think is real, and then you realize it isn't as you're going under? That's where your brother is all the time."

I could see that when I sat with Barney, his bewilderment

forcing his eyes a little farther back into his face each time I visited. I couldn't take it for long, and a half-hour errand was a luxury vacation—gum and underwear at Target, a hospital cafeteria with salt-flavored gravy on everything—but then I'd hurry back to him, and when the visit was over I couldn't stand to leave. I split the difference by crying in the rent-a-car before driving to the airport, my shoulders shaking limp in a broad cross-section of the American rental fleet as the months went by. I'd come back as soon as I could, and when Barney was at music therapy I'd make business calls from the William P. Starling Courtyard, where people who didn't know where they were would draw close to me and nod at what I was saying to Walter Denise, just to have something to agree with.

The flyers in Barney's room were illustrated with snowmen now, and he'd lost another five pounds he couldn't spare. As I wheeled him out of memory class he talked to me from the side of his mouth, conspiring: "I'll give you five bucks if you get me out of here."

I said, "Barney, you're joking."

"Yeah, you don't have to get me out of here. It's okay."

"No, I mean you're making jokes now. I think that's good."

"It makes Michael less nervous," he said. "It makes Henry less nervous."

When we got to his room the mail was there, drawings from Pearl and Michael and a sixteen-page article, "Neurotrophic Improvement of Synaptic Transmission," by Barnard Bay, University of Kansas, and Parmalit Singh, Johns Hopkins, with a handwritten note that said, "Barney, here's our offprint, as promised. I enjoyed our phone call. I can tell you're knitting cells together in the hippocampus a mile a minute. I'm sure we will be yelling at one another about quantifying data before the snows melt. Fondest regards, Pat."

Barney flipped through the article, whispering over the charts and tables. When he finished he wheeled himself to the door and said, "I have to go downstairs now. We're presenting this."

"Wait," I said. "That's not what we're doing now."

"I have to go," he said, trying to wheel past me.

"We're in Houston, Barney," I said, jumping to block the wheelchair. He had a nice Paralympics feint going. "We're at the rehab place." I jumped too hard and knocked into the doorjamb.

A polo-shirt guy, one of the bigger ones, came in and said, "How are we doing here?"

"People are waiting!" Barney said, standing out of the wheelchair and grabbing my arm.

"Okay, you know what, that's not appropriate," the polo-shirt guy said. "Let's get you settled down here." He tried to ease Barney into the wheelchair, but Barney pushed him away, knocking over a jar of jellybeans from a well-wisher at Stanford. When a second polo-shirt guy came in, Barney gave up and fell into the wheelchair, out of breath.

"How we doing, big guy?" the second one said. "Little better?"

"Yeah," Barney said.

The first one waved me into the hall and closed the door to the room. "This isn't that unusual of a thing," he said. "They might need to dial his medication a little. Probably the best thing is if you come in tomorrow."

"I have to go home tonight," I said. I had a Fun Fare.

I got in the car and drove toward the airport, but a few blocks before I got there I pulled into the parking lot of a liquor store. It was dusk, the air full of neon, jet fumes, and rippling heat waves.

I'd promised Patti, Mom, and Deirdre that I'd call them, but I called Information instead and asked for Parmalit Singh in Baltimore. When he answered I introduced myself and thanked him for sending the article. "It meant a lot to him," I said.

"No, of course," he said, in a mild accent, South Asia giving way to Eastern Shore. "He should see his work. He should reap the fruits. How is he responding?"

"Really well," I said. "I think he'll be out of there soon."

"That's terrific. Please say hello for me, will you?"

"Sure. Okay. I won't keep you."

"No, that's fine," he said. "It's good to get the news."

I pressed the phone harder to my ear. I could hear the sounds of his house in the background, a string quartet on the stereo and a little kid laughing. It was the opposite of where I was: warm light on wooden floors in some University Park or Hill or Commons. I could even hear the sounds outside his window, a rough-engined car downshifting and college kids laughing on their way somewhere.

Actually, I couldn't hear any of that. I'd heard only his voice, and the silence after his polite goodnight. My brain, like my brother's, leapt to fill in the spaces.

In February Barney went home to Lawrence. He'd been there three weeks when I visited, landing late in the morning and renting a Fit. The sun glared like camera flashes on six inches of snow, and a fresh blizzard was expected that night.

Deirdre let me in and gave me limited neck and shoulder. She looked okay, but her forbearing smile was worn to nothing.

Barney was in the living room, sitting on the couch in his

grays and browns. He'd gained a few pounds back and replaced the wheelchair with a walking stick. Just after I got there the kids came home from school, hugged me, and then sat on the couch with Barney, who pulled them close and said, "What are you working on?"

"Atoms," Michael said, opening his binder to show Barney his homework.

"That's very good," Barney said. "Henry, look at this." He held up Michael's drawing of an "Our Friend the Atom" atom, with particles making hood-ornament ovals around the nucleus.

"I was in the desert for this," Barney told Michael. "In New Mexico. I couldn't tell you and Pearl what I was doing there. I apologize for that. They said, 'Go to the hotel in Santa Fe and someone will get in touch with you, but don't tell anyone what you're doing. Tell them you're there for your health. For the desert air.'

"I waited for three days and then a Jeep came for me. The driver said, 'What are you guys doing out there?' I told him we were from the USO. I said we were writing music for the soldiers. The driver said"—Barney's face lit up—"'You passed, buddy! You passed the test!'

"But now we're out there and we never stop working. The president keeps calling up to ask how it's going. People say we're killing people but we're not. We're saving them. It's called Little Boy but it's not a real little boy, so don't worry, okay? Pearl?"

"Okay," Pearl said.

He kissed her head and pulled them both closer. The kids were nervous now, stuck on the couch with the broken national memory, but in the months since his injury they'd turned the humoring skills of children everywhere into superpowers.

"When we go out there, I'm with a guy next to me," Barney said. "I go, 'We're playing God here. We're playing Trinity.' He goes, 'Yeah, and Trinity's unbeaten.' He's always kidding. And then we watched it with sunglasses. We said, 'We're like Shiva, because we have all the arms now.'" He pointed across the room. "There."

He watched the explosion, the cloud rising and the glare speeding over the sand. The dread on his face, a forecast of lifelong haunting, was everything it would have been.

Deirdre, in the doorway, said, "Barney?"

He looked up at her, New Mexico gone. The bomb had never happened. Decades of history relaxed. "Do you want to help with dinner?" she said.

"Sure."

Deirdre ran the cooking the way Barney had before, asking him and the kids to measure tofu and barley. She and Pearl steered him away from knives and the stove. They'd stopped weighing the portions.

The next morning Barney had a visit from his lab colleague Ralph Dreher, a stubby guy in his fifties with giant eyebrows. He handed Barney a scientific paper and said, "This is pretty interesting, the alloantigen stuff. I'll come back with Dick in a few days and we'll talk about it."

The doorbell rang again that afternoon, when Deirdre and Michael were at the store, Pearl was doing homework in the kitchen, and Barney was listening to a samba CD Dad had sent him. I opened the door to find a guy in his thirties holding an airport thriller and a book of crossword puzzles.

"Hi," he said. "I just brought some things by for Dr. Bay to pass the time with. I thought I might say hi to him if it's a good time. Did I meet you before?"

"Yes," I said. "Kind of." He held the books out. I hesitated, then took them. I said, "This might not be a—"

"Who's here?" Barney said, coming up behind me with his cane.

"Hey, Dr. Bay. How are you doing?"

"I'm fine. How are you?"

"I'm good. Thank you. I don't know if you remember me. Last time we saw each other we had quite a discussion. I was lying down on your car. We were waiting for the security folks to come haul me out of there. They were busy with a dog problem right then, so you and I had a little time to talk."

"I remember the dog," Barney said. "It was a short-haired dog."

"I don't think you saw it then. But you could have seen it another time. That could have easily happened."

"Were you sick?"

"When? Oh, as far as the lying down. No, that was something where we had a difference of opinion. We don't need to talk about that now. I just wanted to say I hope you're feeling better. We're sorry about what happened. We've got people praying over you." Barney looked up. "I mean—"

"Thank you for coming," Pearl said from the doorway. "We have to ask you to leave now. My dad is tired."

I came back in April with Patti. The day we got there Deirdre said we could all go for a walk when the kids got home. "Barney can go half a mile now."

"We could take a walk on Higuera Street," Barney said. He still sat on the couch most of the day, but his voice was stronger and his fingers didn't twitch.

"That's in California, sweetie," Deirdre said. "That's where you went to college. We're in Lawrence now."

"Yeah."

The radio was on low, tuned to the day's bad news. Patti said, "Can I turn this off?"

"Yes," Barney said. "It's more depressing than a big dance number."

Deirdre said, "Okay, sweetie, but a big dance number wouldn't be depressing."

"Yes, it would," Patti said. "They're completely depressing."

"Sister's right," Barney said.

"What's her name?" Deirdre said.

"Patti."

"Good," Deirdre said.

Barney picked up the TV remote, turned it on, and found an adventure show where people were rock-climbing. He said, "Henry and I did that, in Colorado. He almost dropped me but then he caught me."

Deirdre, keeping her voice light, said, "Did you guys really do that, Henry?"

I looked at Barney. He shrugged. "Yes," I said.

Deirdre said, "Jesus, Henry," and walked out of the room.

Barney said, "What did Henry do?"

I followed her into the hall. She said, "I asked you this at the hospital. You said, 'Gee, I don't know, Deirdre, Barney doesn't do things like that.' " Her eyes teared up.

I said, "Could we go back in there?"

In the living room I turned the TV off and said, "Barney, Deirdre wants to hear about the sports you did. Is that okay?"

"Yeah."

I told them about his ice-climbing, desert-running, white-water rafting and roller-skiing, the mountain-biking and bouldering we did together, my meeting with Freebird, the websites, the Ernie guy—everything I knew. When I finished Barney said, "Wow."

Deirdre sat next to him on the couch and said, "Did you really do all those things?"

"I think so," he said.

She put her arms around him. "You could have hurt yourself."

"No, I *did* hurt myself."

"Do you remember hurting yourself?"

He thought for a minute. "I think so."

"That's good," she said.

When I went back in June, Barney was withdrawn, sitting on the couch, scowling at dust in a sunbeam, and rarely talking. "The neurologist says it's a normal phase," Deirdre said.

I sat with him in silence most of the day. The party I wished to speak to wasn't available, and when he had been available I hadn't said a number of things I should have.

That night I called Gerald, whom I hadn't talked to since Species Showcase, and told him about Barney.

"God, I'm sorry," he said. "How's he doing?"

"They think better. It's hard to tell right now."

"Do you stay there or go back and forth?"

"Back and forth," I said. "I'll be home tomorrow night."

"Good. I'd like to see you. We're getting ready to move back to New York."

"How come?"

"I miss my guys there. I think my coffee guy here disapproves of coffee."

In the morning Barney still wasn't talking, but at noon, when Ralph Dreher came by with Dick Tagaki, another guy from the lab, Barney waved them in and said, "We can spread our stuff out here."

They covered the coffee table with notes and printouts. "Dick's got a new angle on this motor neuron business," Dreher said.

"I don't know if it's really an angle," Tagaki said, handing Barney some papers. He was thirty, with a madras shirt and a brush cut. "This is with neuroepithelials from BG02."

Barney read the papers, his lips moving over the phrases. When he finished he looked up and said, "This should tell us what to do next. It should tell us what to ask."

"Sure," Dreher said.

Barney looked lost and spoke in a whisper: "I don't know how."

"You will, though," Tagaki said. Barney shook his head.

It was quiet for a minute, and then Dreher said, "I think that's good for today." Barney nodded and handed him the papers. When they left I followed them outside and asked how they thought he was doing.

"Better," Tagaki said. "The recoveries on these take a long time."

"I know there's no magic wand," I said.

"No," Dreher said. "That's what we're working on."

I went back inside. Barney had fallen asleep, but when I came in he opened his eyes and said, "Henry. Hi."

"Hi," I said. "Do you want to take a nap?"

"No, that's okay. How are you doing? Are you okay?"

"I'm fine," I said.

"That's good," he said, and closed his eyes again. "I think we should cheer up, though. They have that available. I saw it."

17

none of this goes," Gerald said, pointing to the lizard enclosures and basking rocks. "Some people who care deeply about animals are coming by to get those later."

He and Chloe and I were carrying boxes from their Mill Valley Victorian to a moving van. There were movers, but Gerald had paid them a little extra to let us help.

"Can you and Patti use this table?" Chloe said. "I can't see it in New York." She was a head shorter than Gerald, beautiful in a moving-day sweatshirt. I said yes to the table and we wedged it into my Echo.

"Do you know what you'll be doing there?" I said.

Gerald shook his head. "Nothing with animals. The people at the Customs Service have gotten very worked up about how some of the animals are coming in. It's a good time for us to relocate."

"There's always something," Chloe said.

When the house was empty we sat on the front porch with beers while the movers closed up the truck. One of them, a guy the same age Gerald and I were when we met, brought his clipboard over for Gerald to sign.

"Okay, sir. We'll see you in New York," the mover said.

"You taking Eighty?" Gerald said.

He nodded. "We should be there in four days."

"No need to drive recklessly," Gerald said. "We're visiting in Wisconsin on the way."

"Okay," the guy said. "Thanks."

He turned to go. "I know a place in Nebraska," I said, "for Indian tacos."

"Oh, okay," the mover said. "Let me write it down."

I told him how to find the place near *Country Ways*. Then I gave him Danish pastries in Utah, a lady selling old shirts in Colorado, and a friendly bar with pool tables in Illinois.

"I would take note of these recommendations," Gerald said. "They're not available to the general public."

The guy put a fresh piece of paper in his clipboard. I gave him hamburgers in Iowa, a lake in Ohio, funnel cake in Pennsylvania, comic books in New Jersey, and a Chinese musician playing the *erhu* by the fountain of an outlet mall in Nevada. I kept going, surprising myself, drawing freely from the list of places I'd thought I never wanted to see again. He filled four pages on both sides. When I finally stopped, he said, "Wow. Okay. Thanks. We'll try and hit some of these."

"Yeah," I said. "Actually, it's kind of a great drive."

18

first geese," Deirdre said, spotting them in the rushes just before they took off in a loud *V* over the lake in Lawrence. It was afternoon and the kids were in school. Barney was walking on his own, although he sometimes had to put a hand on someone's shoulder.

"Do you remember the place in Houston?" I said.

"A little," he said. "The food." His real voice was almost back. "First rabbit."

It stared at us for a second and then ran into the high grass. Barney looked at his watch, stopped walking, and said, "I have to go to the lab now. We're having a meeting."

He was right this time. Deirdre dropped us off on campus, and Ralph Dreher and I helped Barney climb the stairs. "We're doing vascular endothelial for the HSCs," Dreher said. Barney nodded. He had to put both feet on each step and rest a minute before going up the next one. "The incubation's with mouse monoclonal nestin and then sheep anti-mouse."

It took us ten minutes to get to the second floor, where Dick Tagaki and four other people were waiting in a conference room. Barney took the latest edition of Dad's datebook from his backpack, put it on the table, and sat down.

"We brain-injured the rats on Tuesday," a young woman said. "We'll be injecting them tomorrow."

Barney read a printout and spoke slowly. "We should look at which ones express O4 and which ones express GFAP. That's something . . ."

He looked at the young guy sitting across from him. A minute went by in silence, and then Barney looked down, saw the datebook, and opened it to two pages of taped-in Polaroids of people with their names written underneath. "That's something Lucas should look at," he said. The guy nodded and made a note.

After an hour Barney got a headache, but Dreher told me that two months ago it had been twenty minutes. They were learning to catch the headaches faster, before they led to blackouts or throwing up.

We went downstairs, where Deirdre picked us up and took us to the house for dinner. Barney was back to cooking and Deirdre was weighing the portions again. After dinner, when I was about to go to the airport, Deirdre said, "Can you guys go get those presents?"

The kids ran out of the room and came back with two big packages they'd wrapped themselves, taping pieces of black-and-yellow paper together. "Like Aunt Patti's shirts," Pearl said.

The presents were two emergency backpacks, like theirs,

with flashlights, meal bars, tick spray, and first aid kits. "These are wonderful," I said. "Patti will love this."

I got full waist-up off Deirdre and a ten-second hug from Barney that came close to spraining my shoulder. At the airport I stuffed Patti's backpack into my suitcase and carried mine on, thinking about how people kept giving me backpacks, a conspiracy to get me walking. It was a great gift idea, and I was moved, but the airlines were going through cutbacks, and I ate my emergency meal an hour out of Kansas City.

19

Yesterday at breakfast Patti told me that her brother-in-law, Stewart, had decided to quit being a lawyer and become a smokejumper. "He's looking for a fire department that tracks into it," she said.

"Stewart?" I said. "Has he ever done anything like that?"

"No. It just came to him. He says he wants to make a difference. His parents are flying in. My mom's losing her mind. Stephanie won't stop crying."

"Stewart," I said.

"I know," she said. "Go, Stewart."

After breakfast I walked her to the corner. It's been a year since I helped Gerald move, and eight months since Patti and I moved ourselves. Our house is on Duquesne, six blocks from downtown Clayton, ten blocks from Riddenhauer's, and across town from the Tradewinds Apartments, which were torn down for condos six years ago.

There was a stiff breeze at the cross street, a preview of autumn. I kissed Patti, walked home, and went up to the room where I put out *Clayton*.

It's not one of those one-city lifestyle magazines, although that would be fine, putting headlines like UNREAL ESTATE and IF YOU KNEW SUSHI into type all the time. But *Clayton* is for people who collect Claytons, or live in them. We salute the repurposed department store of the month, and give directions to walks in the margins. Our readers compare notes on how to fend off the big-box and the high-end, an area in which they've had some success.

It's not all small towns, though. Our New York correspondent keeps the reader informed about bakery guys and urban songbirds. The veteran Washington reporter James Rensselaer vents under a pen name in a column called "You and Your Government." A caveman in Missouri writes about relationships. A Hudson River Valley composer of song cycles contributes a page called "Subliminal Hymnal." Like every title I've worked at, *Clayton* covers an enthusiasm. In this case the enthusiasm has no name, but it's there.

We're too small for Jillian to distribute yet, but she put us with her printer in St. Louis, and our order is a little bigger every month. So far the office staff is just me and the Silex, a one-pot unit I bought a month ago. I try not to let the last half inch of coffee get crisp, but sometimes there's the press of business.

I spent the morning on reader mail and ad sales, walked to Lofton Street for a sandwich, came home, and called Barney to plan my next visit. The headaches are easing and he's up to three hours a day at the lab now. Pearl is helping out there this summer.

When I hung up I went outside, picked up the hose, and hung beads of water in the flower bed. The enthusiasm is for what happens every day, always the same and different.

I worked all afternoon and then went back outside for a few minutes. There's a time of day when every house on the street is split by the same diagonal into sun and shade, and I try not to miss that.

I went back in, and then I heard my friends outside. Steve is still in Chicago, but everyone else is around. Scott and his wife, Melanie, came first, and then Jeff, who sank into the living room couch and said, "It's my ankles, hon. I don't know how I go on."

"You're a martyr, hon," Scott said. "I swear to God you are."

This is a thing called Tired Ladies on the Bus. No one remembers how it started. "At the end of the day, you can say you moved things along," I said.

"That's all you can ask for, hon," Melanie said.

We walked to the Cuban place on Stovall, which used to be the Thai place, and for a while a Mongolian barbecue. Dina and her husband were holding the table. Jillian and Jack wanted to come but couldn't get a sitter for Emmylou.

It was strange at first, seeing everyone's grownup faces, but I'm used to it now, and it's the old photo collages at Jillian and Jack's house that stop me. I didn't expect to live here again. The enthusiasm is for switchbacks as a means of transportation.

Patti and Megan got there last, and said they were paying because they'd gotten an order. They make a line of ladies' activewear, with passivewear on the way. The clothes are sold in more than four stores nationwide. The T-shirts are blank.

After dinner we all walked together as far as Lofton, where Patti and I split off to go home, stopping on Meader to buy the paper. These days I follow the news. There are days when the days seem numbered. The enthusiasm is for what we can do with what's left. Meet me under the big clock.

acknowledgments

Thanks to my spectacular editors, Peggy Hageman and Marjorie Braman, along with Amy Baker, Erica Barmash, Kolt Beringer, Robin Bilardello, Jenna Dolan, Jennifer Hart, Carrie Kania, Cal Morgan, and everyone at HarperCollins.

And to my cool, crusading agent, Chris Calhoun, plus Dong-Won Song and everyone at Sterling Lord.

Sam Douglas made great editorial contributions, for which I'm forever indebted. Bob Roe was unstinting with both literary insight and moral example. Nancy Hass, Jon Carroll, Tracy Johnston, Tom Moran, Denny Abrams, Joshua Baer, and B. K. Moran gave and gave.

And: Jim Barringer and Noël Lawrence, Lisa Brenneis and Jim Churchill, Sam Brown and Alison Teal, Greg Calegari, Kent Carroll, the Honorable Dean H. Chamberlain, Stuart Cornfeld,

Joe Dante, De Lauer's Super Newsstand, Christine Doudna and Rick Grand-Jean, Sean Elder, John Field, Mike Finnell, Mel Fiske, Danny and Hilary Goldstine, all of life's Haases and Joneses, William Hood, James D. Houston, Tim Hunter, Issues, Jonathan Kaplan, Bob and Maggie Klein, Wendy Lesser and Richard Rizzo, Peter Lynn and everyone at Spring Break Buggy Blast, Anwyl McDonald and Meredith Tromble, Marlene and Rick Millikan, Marcia Millman, the Nits, David and Janet Peoples, Luigi Pinotti, Colin Portnuff, A. Roger Pothus, Frank Ratliff, Frank and Mary Robertson, Andy Romanoff and Darcy Vebber, Jane Sindell, Martin Spencer, Michael Tashker, Richie White, Carter Wilson, Renee Witt, and Alison Yerxa.

My brother, Ken Haas, inspired me all his life and still does.

About the author

About the book

Read on

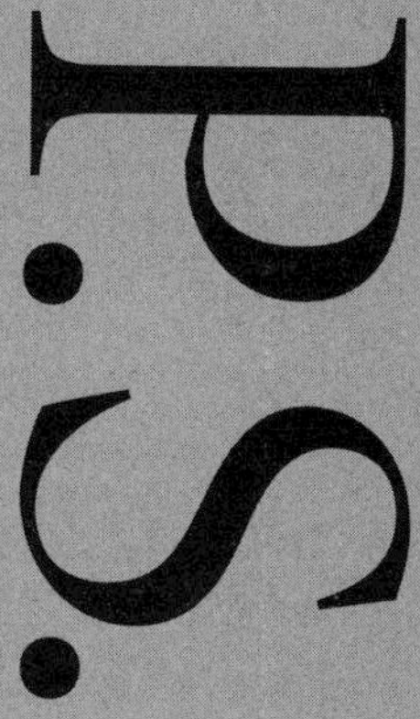

Insights, Interviews & More . . .

A Conversation with Charlie Haas

Tracy Johnston

***Why did you choose San Bernardino County as the birthplace of Henry Bay, the narrator of* The Enthusiast?**

I wanted him to be from a new suburb, a place where it would look to him as if the world came into being the same week he did. I wanted him to leave home without too many clues. When he takes that first job he kind of runs away with the circus, the circus being America the way it is now, this bazaar of fierce separate passions. He may find his own way of understanding the country and he may find his own enthusiasm, but he's not really looking for those things. He's just trying to find something he can do, make a living, and meet women. But looking and finding are different stories.

Henry doesn't have a great time at college. Were you drawing on your own experience?

No, I loved college. I may be one of those Peaked in Colleges who are mentioned in the book. I went to UC Santa Cruz, where I was surrounded by beautiful redwood forests, surfing beaches, hip people from Berkeley High School, and sincere people from Modesto. Raymond Carver was teaching there and I got to hear him read "Will You Please Be Quiet, Please?" at a party just after he'd written it. You'd go down to the piers and the seals would be right up on the pilings.

Is the Tom Patrick character based on a real person?

Yes, but the real person based himself on a character in a nineteenth-century novel that's in the public domain now, so I think we're okay.

You and your wife both write fiction at home. What's that like?

It's touching. These two pale ghosts passing in the hall, eyes fixed on the unseen, lips mouthing prospective lines of dialogue until they lose all meaning . . . the key thing is to maintain certain civilized standards so the entropy is tamped down. At lunch, for instance, we have a rule that anything with three or more ingredients is a recipe. A Weetabix with peanut butter on it, submerged in cottage cheese—all right! ▶

“Raymond Carver was teaching there [UC Santa Cruz] and I got to hear him read 'Will You Please Be Quiet, Please?' at a party just after he'd written it.”

A Conversation with Charlie Haas

(continued)

You've cooked lunch! Civilization is preserved. If it's fewer than three ingredients we've given in.

Given in to—?

Being writers. We're trying to stay as far up the evolutionary ladder as graduate students.

What was your strangest job?

Writing this book, without question. The job description could be as simple as "Share your truth and try not to bore the nice people," but doing that turns out to be very complicated. There's a lot of deliberate design but there's also a lot of séance. Some days I'd walk down to the BART station, choose a town at random, take the train there, wander around all day writing in a French schoolchildren's notebook, turn up miles from where I started like a missing French schoolchild, and start looking for a station where I could get a train home. The only normal thing about that job is the commuting.

***What books or writers influenced* The Enthusiast?**

I like to think I've learned something from the serious humorists, or the funny dramatists. Stanley Elkin obviously had a big impact, especially *The Franchiser*, *The Dick Gibson Show*, and *Searches and Seizures*. I love Anthony Powell for lots of reasons, but particularly for the poignant comedy of running into the same people at very different stages in their lives. Charles Portis, Walker Percy, Julie Hecht, and Nicholson Baker have all built great monuments out of idiosyncrasy. I'm a fan of the New York School poets—Kenneth Koch, Alice Notley, Ron Padgett, Ted Berrigan, and company—and I think they're in there too, a little. And Philip Whalen. Lawrence Shainberg wrote a novel called *One on One* that I think influenced how Henry thinks to himself. *Balloons are Available*, by Jordan Crittenden, is another one that got to me at an impressionable age.

On the other hand, parts of my book are influenced by a thousand nearly anonymous stylists at magazines such as *Mother Earth News*, *Airstream Life*, and *Transworld Skateboarding*. In a way this book is the literary heir of DeLauer's Super Newsstand in downtown Oakland. The people who write and edit those magazines are Henry's colleagues over in the real-life office. We may not know their names but they write a lot. Maybe they have to walk around all day with notebooks too. It can't be easy.

"On the other hand, parts of my book are influenced by a thousand nearly anonymous stylists at magazines such as *Mother Earth News*, *Airstream Life*, and *Transworld Skateboarding*."

Do you spend much time at those newsstands?

Yes, and money. Supposedly all these hobbies and interests are moving to the Internet but I don't see it. The trucks keep coming to these places to deliver magazines, and people keep showing up to flip through them. The Internet doesn't have guys coming in to buy the *Daily Racing Form* and some Swisher Sweets and chat up the bleary cashier.

Is writing an enthusiasm?

I think so. I think magazines such as *Poets & Writers* and *The Writer's Chronicle* function in the same way as *Mini Truckin'* or *Catfish* ▸

A Conversation with Charlie Haas

(continued)

Now—as a fire to gather around. I think the writing magazines under-emphasize gear, though. They should have some new-product roundups. "Ten Erasers You've GOT To Try!" "The New Spiral Notebooks—Sweater-Safe at Last?" That could bring some new people in.

Actually I think it's an enthusiasm because you're doing it just to do it. There are far saner ways to make a living, and in fact you may go crazy doing it. What I found, though, was that people kept encouraging me and helping me in various ways, so that I went a lot less crazy than I could have. It's like when a guy decides to Rollerblade across Texas and people show up along the route with Clif Bars. I've often wondered how the acknowledgements in some books get so long. Now I know.

Does This Novel Make Me Look Fat?

I HAVE A WONDERFUL AGENT, who's shepherded *The Enthusiast* through more than the standard calamities, but I'd never met him in person till the book was well underway at the publisher. He's in New York, I'm in Oakland; we phone and e-mail.

Finally I got to New York and we had lunch. A few minutes in he said, "I have to tell you something: I thought you'd be a fat guy. I think of Henry as being heavy."

I argued the minor premise that I always pictured Henry as unathletic but not fat, and the major premise that I'm not Henry, but of course that second one is slippery. There's a great thing Robert Louis Stevenson wrote: "The novel . . . exists, not by its resemblances to life, which are forced and material, as a shoe must consist of leather, but by its immeasurable difference from life, which is both designed and significant, and is both the method and the meaning of the work."

I love the part about the shoe (of course you use life to make a novel; are you going to make shoes out of tungsten?), but especially the use of "immeasurable," by which I think he means not "big" but just impossible to measure, because one minute the novel is a mile from life and the next minute it's a few millimeters. "Yeah, *you* measure it. Knock yourself out. I'll be over here writing *Treasure Island*."

> "A few minutes into the lunch my agent said, 'I have to tell you something: I thought you'd be a fat guy. I think of Henry as being heavy.'"

Everyone should have at least one job that's like a clubhouse, where your colleagues are your friends and you hang out when you don't have to. Mine was at *New West*, a California magazine now gone. Clay Felker, the founder, bought the furniture from the set of *All the President's Men*, so that the ▸

Does This Novel Make Me Look Fat?
(continued)

employees walked off an elevator in Beverly Hills and into a Hollywood remake of the *Washington Post*'s city room.

Jon Carroll, the editor, was in the habit of assigning me subjects I knew little about. (He didn't have much choice: I was young.) *New West* sent me on sports, art, music, travel, the psychology of advertising, the subtext of tourism and, because dreams do come true, a statewide survey of inner-city barbeque places. I was assigned to get drunk in Ensenada and to attend the first-death-anniversary Elvis fan convention in Las Vegas; to see the Sex Pistols at Winterland and the Clash in Santa Monica, and Reggie Jackson's three home runs in game six of the 1977 World Series.

“I was assigned to get drunk in Ensenada and to attend the first-death-anniversary Elvis fan convention in Las Vegas; to see the Sex Pistols at Winterland and the Clash in Santa Monica.”

As a magazine writer you learn to partner with the bigness of the world and the strangeness of the country. You keep getting thrown in the deep end, frantic about the deadline but thrilled by the possibility of coming back with something new. When I did, it was always about my fellow citizens, the worlds they made for themselves, and the things they'd say to someone curious enough to ask.

An acidhead in L.A. said, “When I was real small, I used to watch *M Squad* on television, with Lee Marvin as this snarling cop, and I had a fascination for the heroin addicts. Everyone knew that what they were doing was the worst thing for them, and yet they did it. It was like they were martyrs or saints or, I don't know, really dedicated people. And in the real environment of people I ate dinner with and went to school with, I'd never seen a dedicated person in my *life*. So from that point of view, drugs seemed neat.” A Disney “imagineer” said, “Mickey Mouse is made up almost entirely of curves.

That's very reassuring. People have had millions of years' experience with curved objects and they've never been hurt by them. It's the pointy things that give you trouble." Jerry Garcia said, "My favorite story is the one about boron. The element, you know, in the periodic table?" A woman at the Elvis convention said, "I've got this one room where I've got his records and his pictures, and I go into that room in the morning and start going through the stuff in there, and before I know it it's six o'clock and the day is *gone*."

The editors of Trips, *"the Magazine of Authentic Travel," saw a news story that said the king of Tonga had slimmed down to 400 pounds by bicycling. My assignment was to fly there, talk my way into a bike ride with the king (and his bodyguards), and not come back without pictures. This one ran in the first issue of* Trips, *which was also the last. Magazines are a riot.*

New West had a trade arrangement with the Beverly Wilshire Hotel down the street—ad pages in exchange for rooms where we could put up out-of-towners. B. K. Moran, the San Francisco–based senior editor, stayed there when she came south to close her stories. It was a grand hotel. Warren Beatty lived upstairs, and B. K. once found herself on the elevator with the Dalai Lama.

Closing nights ran late, with everyone bent over the page boards on the layout table, reading their stories one last time before they went to press. There could be no coffee near the boards, so you'd go to your desk for life-giving sips between paragraphs. We'd finish at two or three a.m., and then a fair portion of the masthead would go over to the Beverly Wilshire, hang around in B. K.'s room, and go swimming in the hotel pool in our underwear.

My first movie job was on *Over the Edge*, directed by Jonathan Kaplan and written by Tim Hunter and me, about young teenagers trashing the master-planned ▶

Does This Novel Make Me Look Fat?
(continued)

suburb they lived in. There was no money for an ensemble casting director, so Tim and I drove back and forth between L.A. and the location in Denver, recruiting pissed-off fourteen-year-olds, ancestors of *The Enthusiast*'s Misty, to play themselves. The route was lined with collectible towns.

The studio hated the movie and barely released it, but through years of cable TV showings it developed a cult following. One day Jonathan's assistant told him that a company in Seattle had called up asking for copies of it.

"What company?" Jonathan said.

"It's called Nirvana," his assistant said. The movie was apparently a favorite of Kurt Cobain's. In his *Journals* he calls it "a story of troubled youth, vandalism, parental negligence, and most importantly real estate development"—nailing it, as he so often did. When he died, a lot of us knew how those people at the Elvis convention had felt.

The late Buck Owens plays a small but crucial offstage role in *The Enthusiast*. When I first got out of college I worked at a record company and spent a day with him in Bakersfield. We went to his office, his studio, and his house, talking about songs he was thinking of recording and radio stations he was considering buying. He appeared to get a terrific kick out of who he was. I was thinking, "Wow, I'm driving around with Buck Owens," but he seemed to be thinking, "Wow, I *am* Buck Owens." Not ego—on the contrary, long-running amazement.

He did the driving, in a new car he'd just bought. He wasn't sure he'd keep it. "This car's got no *git*," he said around 85 miles per hour. "No *passing* gear."

"My first movie job was on *Over the Edge*, directed by Jonathan Kaplan and written by Tim Hunter and me, about young teenagers trashing the master-planned suburb they live in."

We were walking from the car to his house when the two biggest and scariest dogs I'd ever seen came racing toward me to take my head off. I froze. Mr. Owens got the dogs calmed down when they were a six-inch lunge from my throat. "We had a few things happen," he said as my pulse came down from its peak, "and I said, 'Well, we'll just get something out here that knows old Buck.' "

I'm a big fan and a modest practitioner of indoor rowing, which started as training for crew but is now a sport in itself, one that gave me a useful inkling of what was up with the more athletic characters in the book. The world championships, held every winter in Boston, are called the CRASH-B Sprints after their founding organization, the Charles River Association of Sculling Has-Beens. A college gym is filled with scores of rowing machines hooked up to computers and video monitors that show the competitors as little racing boats.

Every February I go to the Northern California qualifying event. The 2000-meter heats go on all day, adolescents through masters. When a race is over the rowers collapse where they sit, gasping, cramping, and sometimes crying. If you're not watching the monitors you often can't tell who won, because the winner is in no condition to exult or even look up. Sometimes someone comes over to lift the victor's arm, and people cheer. The arm, once dropped, falls like a rag, and the crying continues. In Boston some racers throw up. Enthusiasm.

> "I'm a big fan and a modest practitioner of indoor rowing, which . . . gave me a useful inkling of what was up with the more athletic characters in the book."

The tea convention where I researched the *Cozy* chapter was at the Las Vegas Hilton, where the Elvis convention had been held ▸

Does This Novel Make Me Look Fat? *(continued)*

years earlier. It was nice to be back, holding a reporter's notebook left over from my magazine years. You couldn't throw a strainer in that expo hall without hitting a potential character—importers, growers, and tasters whose jargon made wine geeks sound like actuaries. I met a middle-aged man—stout, cheerful, English-accented—whose family had been growing rooibos in South Africa for generations. I asked if he'd always been in the business.

"Yes," he said, "except for some years in a Buddhist monastery." He asked what I was doing at the convention, and I told him. "I see," he said. "And have you written other novels, or is this the first one to tear your mind apart?"

From Vegas I drove down to Ivanpah Dry Lake, outside Primm, Nevada, for Spring Break Buggy Blast. The major American kite buggy events are held in deserts. Instead of business cards, the kite dealers hand out lip balm custom-printed with their logos.

I went there almost the way Henry does, but I ran into the desert instead of driving. I thought that might be a useful icebreaker, since I was showing up without a buggy. "You were the guy running," people said when I approached them, and I think it did help me get some interviews and a short, blissful kite buggy ride. I got the story, felt time stop as the desert sped past my buggy, and jogged back thinking that the trip had gone perfectly, which would have been true if I'd thought of sunblock for my ears. They looked like glowing red shrimp by the time I got back to the hotel. Which is pretty Henry.

“ 'And have you written other novels, or is this the first one to tear your mind apart?' ”

Reading Group Questions

Who brought this salad?

Is someone sitting here?

Did we talk about changing to Thursdays?

Is this the nonfat?

What does anyone think about painting this room orange?

Did you read the book? Will it ruin it for you if I talk about it?

The Enthusiast Mix Tape

A musical concordance.

1. Henry
   "Skin It Back" by Little Feat
   From *Feats Don't Fail Me Now*

Henry doesn't "race" from town to town so much as careen, but still. (I once interviewed Paul Barrère, who wrote this song, and asked him about the title. "I was never baptized in the Jewish manner," he clarified.)

2. Barney
   "Pi" by Kate Bush
   From *Aerial*

"Barney's stare looked around our bland landscape and saw number series and decaying waves of motion." See also "Running Up that Hill (A Deal with God)," when Barney's in recovery.

3. Mom and Dad
   "Summer Samba" by Walter Wanderley
   From *Rain Forest*

The vocal version ("So Nice"), recorded by Astrud Gilberto and again by Bebel Gilberto, is relevant here, but Wanderley's vreep-vreep is what Dad's stereo burns into Henry and Barney's growing cortices.

4. Gerald
   "Big-Eyed Beans from Venus"
   by Captain Beefheart
   From *Clear Spot*

Live from next year's Species Showcase. "Fire-Eye'd Boy," by Broken Social Scene, was a serious contender, but you need a stethoscope to hear those lyrics.

5. Jillian
   "Act Naturally"
   by Buck Owens and the Buckaroos
   From *The Buck Owens Collection*

" 'Most people would say San Francisco,' Gerald said. 'Or Hollywood. But Bakersfield, that's good.' " And most people know the Beatles' cover of this, or Ray Charles's great version of "Crying Time," but the you-know-what starts here.

6. Wendy Probst
   "Little Room" by the White Stripes
   From *White Blood Cells*

Artists only.

7. Deirdre
   "Compared to What"
   by Les McCann and Eddie Harris
   From *Swiss Movement*

"The President, he's got his war"—recorded in 1969.

8. Larry
   "Debra" by Beck
   From *Midnite Vultures*

" 'Tell me you never wanted kiosk,' Larry said." From Beck's brief but engaging leather-trench-coat phase.

9. Agnes and Richard
   "Teahouse on the Tracks" by Donald Fagen
   From *Kamakiriad*

"It's your last chance/To learn how to dance"—Henry, do you copy?

10. Misty
    "Tom Boy" by Bettie Serveert
    From *Palomine*

You're never too old to have an angry adolescence.

11. Patti
"Shang a Dang Dang" by Lambchop
From *No, You C'mon*
I can see her walk.

12. Patti and Henry
    "Runaway Wind" by Paul Westerberg
    From *14 Songs*

And their marriage.

The Enthusiast Mix Tape ***(continued)***

13. Brent Targill
    "John Saw That Number" by Neko Case
    From *Fox Confessor Brings the Flood*

From the Original Blind Boys to a New Pornographer, in one mighty leap of faith.

14. The Shawnee National Forest
    "Chained to the Moon"
    by the Folk Implosion
    From *One Part Lullaby*

"What can I see from here?" My wife and I hiked the Shawnee for research, and the answer is plenty—butterflies drinking at puddles full of tadpoles, the twice-annual snake migration, and the Mississippi River going around being all timeless.

15. Corinne and family
    "When I First Came to this Land"
    by Pete Seeger
    From *American Favorite Ballads, Vol. 3*

In college I managed to get lost for a couple of days in the Los Padres National Forest, Big Sur section. Some people I met on the way out sang this around their campfire. It left an impression.

16. Clayton
    "Egg Radio" by Bill Frisell
    From *Gone, Just Like a Train*

The five friends, Tired Ladies on the Bus, and a beer at Riddenhauer's for the road.